"So...you have a son."

Cody maintained eye contact as if he suspected she might deny it.

Becca forced a smile. "Surprise!"

She gave the floor another once-over, and her diligence paid off. Farther down, she spotted a few more shards of the broken pitcher. Cody trailed behind her.

"He's adorable. Looks exactly like his mom. How old is he?"

"Four," she lied with surprising ease. For the first time, she appreciated that Max was small for his age. Her guilt was now wide-awake and fully engaged.

Was a lie any worse than an omission? How many times had she picked up the phone to tell Cody the truth? Fifty? Fifty thousand?

Fifty zillion, as Max would say?

Cody had made it clear he wanted to be a full-time dad when the time came. But his star was on the rise. He'd worked so hard to make sure it did. Furthermore, he'd seemed happy in a way he hadn't been in their marriage.

So she'd made the decision for both of them...

Dear Reader,

I've always loved a good "coming home" story. But I enjoy a "finding home" one even more. That's why I am so excited to share Becca and Cody's journey with you.

Becca spent her childhood moving from state to state. For Becca as an adult, finding home means creating one for herself. Cody had the opposite experience. He lived in the same house throughout his youth. As a professional bull rider, Cody now finds home in the next hotel room in the next city. They were briefly married when their paths first crossed. However, Cody wanted a rodeo career. Becca wanted to plant roots and have a child. Their dreams came true, just not while together.

Their paths cross once again in the fictional town of Destiny Springs, Wyoming, where the son Cody didn't know he had inadvertently brings them together. Now they must figure out what their hearts truly desire.

My heart's desire is simple. I hope that you will find a family among these characters and a home within these pages.

Warmest wishes,

Susan Breeden

HEARTWARMING

The Bull Rider's Secret Son

———

Susan Breeden

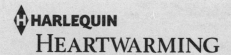

HARLEQUIN
HEARTWARMING

HARLEQUIN®
HEARTWARMING™

ISBN-13: 978-1-335-58460-1

The Bull Rider's Secret Son

Harlequin Enterprises ULC
22 Adelaide St. West, 41st Floor
Toronto, Ontario M5H 4E3, Canada
www.Harlequin.com

Printed in U.S.A.

Susan Breeden is a native Texan who currently lives in Houston, where she works as a technical writer/editor for the aerospace industry. In the wee hours of morning and again at night you will find her playing matchmaker for the heroes and heroines in her novels. She also enjoys walks with her bossy German shepherd, decluttering and organizing her closet, and trying out new chili con queso recipes. For information on Susan's upcoming books, visit susanbreeden.com.

Visit the Author Profile page at Harlequin.com.

For my baby girl, Frida.

CHAPTER ONE

"MOMMY! MOMMY! GUESS who I am!"

Becca gave Max a quick side glance while whisking the precious last batch of eggs. Her son loved dressing up as superheroes, real-life heroes or the occasional villain. Most of the time, she couldn't venture a guess. Last week it was someone called the Flash. The week before, Wolverine.

This week, however, the answer was easy. And a bit uncomfortable.

Still, Becca had to bite her lip to keep from laughing. The cowboy hat practically swallowed the five-year-old boy. Hopefully, his height and weight would eventually catch up to his age, which would increase by one digit in a couple of weeks.

"Wow, that's a tough one," she lied. "Give me a minute."

In reality, one minute would buy her about fifteen seconds to not only formulate a response but to finish her task at hand. The melted butter now covered the bottom of the skillet. The requisite bubbles would appear at any moment.

Three-plus years into owning and managing the Hideaway Bed and Breakfast, she'd perfected a solid, traditional feast. Even though she could make scrambled eggs in her sleep, Fraser Ranch had yet to make its delivery, which meant no room for error this morning.

Not that she was about to complain. The eggs were free. As were the sage proverbs with a quirky twist that old man Fraser imparted. The latest one being *Every path has a few puddles. That's why your emotions should always wear muck boots.*

Boy, was that an understatement. On the other hand, real puddles were a great source of fun for a single mom and her rambunctious little boy. Second only to their weekly guessing game.

Max's costume choice couldn't have been timelier since today was the day she'd vowed to shut down the rodeo topic once and for all. He'd gone on and on about bull riding for months. And one didn't hear about bull riding without hearing about Cody Sayers—the so-called Rodeo Rascal.

Ugh.

She still couldn't stomach that nickname, but at least she'd gotten used to seeing cowboy hats. Wyoming rivaled Texas in that respect. After years of associating them with her famous ex-husband, she'd finally reached a point where seeing one didn't make her ache from the inside out.

Trent, her neighbor's eighteen-year-old son and the Hideaway's part-time handyman, must have taken off his hat while mowing and grooming the grounds. Considering her own son's proclivity to ask forgiveness rather than permission when it came to borrowing other people's things, Becca had suspected he would eventually show up wearing Trent's cowboy hat.

"You *said* a minute. That was fifty million zillion minutes ago," Max prompted.

"Hold your horses. I want to get my guess right."

But first, the eggs. They sizzled like a beautiful culinary symphony as she poured them into the oversize cast-iron skillet. Using a spatula, she began folding and fluffing them to perfection.

"I'll give you a hint," he said.

Max retrieved the broom from its designated spot between the fridge and counter. He rode it like a stick bull around the kitchen, with their three-legged rescue labradoodle, Penny, hot on the little cowboy's heels. The stomping and bucking against the hardwood and counters caused the bowls of hash browns and sausage links and seasonal fruit to wobble in his wake.

That was her cue to answer. Now.

"I've got it! You're the Headless Horseman. Tonight, I'll tell you some secrets about him that no one else knows." If her embellished version of "The Legend of Sleepy Hollow" didn't steer Max's attention in a different direction, nothing would.

Max pouted over her answer. "You're not even looking good," he huffed.

Becca blinked. Boy, did he ever hit the nail on the head. She must have looked pretty haggard at the moment, even though she knew that wasn't what he meant.

If the eggs weren't taking longer than usual, she'd have time to change out of her yoga pants and tank top and into something nicer before setting up the buffet and greeting guests. Never knew when a handsome out-of-towner might decide to stay there. Or, better yet, a local enjoying a staycation.

Right now, however, she needed to take an extra minute for something even more important. Make that some*one*. She stopped fluffing even though the eggs weren't quite done, slid the skillet off the heat and gave Max her undivided attention.

"I'm sorry, sweetie," she said while studying his costume with the focus it deserved.

Authentic cowboy boots? Check.

Fringe vest he'd borrowed from her closet? Check.

Cowboy hat? Check.

Except…it wasn't just any hat. It looked exactly like Cody's old Stetson.

Nooo!

"Where did you get—?"

"Whatever you're talking about, I plead the Fifth," Hailey said as she brushed by, defending herself against a question Becca had yet to finish asking.

Which meant her best friend and assistant property manager knew it was forthcoming.

Which means she's guilty.

The woman had been trying to influence Becca to give Cody another chance, even though he definitely wasn't begging for one. In fact, they hadn't spoken since the divorce was finalized nearly six years ago. If that wasn't bad enough, Hailey entertained Max's questions about rodeos—and about Cody. Fortunately, her friend hadn't revealed anything of significance. Not that she would. Only two people knew that Cody was Max's biological father: Becca and Hailey.

And that's the way it was going to stay.

Becca certainly wasn't blameless in all of this. She'd unwittingly left photos that glamorized bull riding, along with newspaper clippings with Cody's name and photo, in places where Max could come across them with minimal effort. But not the cowboy hat that Cody had left behind. Until now, it had remained tucked away on a top shelf of the utility closet, behind a large box. Max couldn't have known about it, much less reached it, without someone's help.

The Fifth wasn't going to save her friend this time. *Mental note: get rid of everything. Including Hailey.*

Okay, perhaps not Hailey.

Becca drew in a deep breath and willed her heart to stop kickboxing her rib cage. Last thing she needed was for Max to ask why she was upset. With any luck, this cowboy phase would pass by as swiftly as her friend-slash-assistant, who selected a red Delicious from the fruit bowl then speed-walked through the shotgun kitchen and out the other side before she could be interrogated. At this rate, Hailey would burn off the calories faster than she could consume them.

Meanwhile, Max was burning some serious calories of his own. After taking a few yank-and-jerk laps through the kitchen and around the parlor on his imaginary bull, he was now pretending to be bucked off, à la Cody Sayers, no doubt. When he finally hit the ground, the hat tumbled across the floor.

Becca swiftly confiscated it, then hefted Max to his feet. That was when she noticed how the Stetson had silver-star embellishments rather than round medallions. A small-but-sanity-saving detail. She exhaled all the tension from her body.

It wasn't Cody's old hat. Must be Trent's after all.

Oh, the glorious relief. Like settling in front of a roaring fireplace after being out in the Wyoming snow for hours.

"Go change for breakfast, cowboy. I want to show you off to our guests," she said.

"Can I pour the orange juice?"

"Hmm. I don't know. That's the best part. I may want to do that myself," she said, channeling her inner Tom Sawyer.

Truth be told, she could use the help. Not only with breakfast but with other things around the B and B. The rooms were always in need of minor repairs. Trent could only do so much, given his other job as a wrangler for old man Fraser down the road.

"Pleeease?" Max cried.

"You'll have to put on your nice jeans and

the purple sweater that Grammy Haring got you last Christmas."

"Okey dokey." Max turned and ran to his room.

That was easy. If only certain other people in her life were so cooperative.

Becca collected the abandoned stick bull, returned it to its imaginary chute next to the refrigerator and placed the Stetson on the counter where Trent would see it. She transferred the skillet back to the stovetop. Several more seconds of low-and-slow heat—along with a cube of butter—and the scrambled eggs would be reheated and cooked to near perfection.

Somehow, she'd managed to not ruin them with all the on-and-off. What were the odds? Maybe this wouldn't be such a bad day after all. In fact, it might be a…"Lovely Day."

The thought alone awakened a serious earworm, as Bill Withers's voice filled her head. That tune always got her moving. First, the side-to-side neck slides, followed by some shoulder pumps. Finally, a few hip circles to bring it home—

"So, you're the one who stole my Stetson," someone said, bringing the whole private performance to a grinding halt.

When had Trent come in?

She reached for the pepper and gave the mill

a couple of twists for a dash of color and a subtle kick. Let the guests take it from there and season to their individual liking.

"Please tell me you didn't witness my awful dancing," she said without turning around.

"The truth?"

"Oh, I insist."

As soon as those words left her mouth, she braced herself for the kind of playful-yet-sarcastic punchline that only this particular teenager could deliver. Fortunately, she was pretty good about delivering back.

"I wouldn't call it *awful*," he said.

Definitely sarcasm. She was a lot of things, but a good dancer wasn't one of them. And she wasn't about to ask him what he *would* call it.

"Yeah. Right. Hey, you might want to check the floor. I think your voice dropped another octave. Going through puberty again?" she asked, as she gave the eggs one final plump.

"Why would you think something like that?"

Because his voice sounded way too deep and rich and a tad too gravelly. A premium espresso blend, one might say if comparing it to coffee grounds.

Premium. Like only one other man she had ever known.

Exactly like it, in fact.

A sudden sweat drenched her neck. Her

stomach seized, and her lungs refused to take in some much-needed air. She set the spatula aside and wiped her palms on her apron. The lump in her throat wouldn't allow another question to shimmy by and disprove her suspicion.

Instead, she turned around and had it confirmed the hard way.

Every path has a few puddles...

Except this wasn't any ordinary puddle.

This was a raging sea.

No way.

"Becca?"

As if he needed to ask. He'd long ago memorized every disobedient auburn strand of hair on his ex-wife's head. Yet, until she turned around, his unsuspecting thoughts were along the more generic lines of *If what I* can *see is any indication, that is one beautiful woman.*

His heart even confirmed it, fluttering at first and now pounding its verdict home. The old ticker had pretty much stopped working the day he signed the divorce papers and left behind the only woman he had ever loved. At her insistence. Now, his heart seemed to be back in business, despite his insistence that it stop this nonsense. Wrong place. Wrong time.

Wrong woman.

"It's you," she responded. Although her voice wavered, her deadpan expression gave nothing away. No surprise, no excitement. And, thankfully, no disgust. "What are you doing here?"

Of course, she wouldn't have known he was coming. The cook wouldn't have access to such information unless guest rosters were shared with the entire staff. His publicist had booked him under a different name, anyway. His whole reason for coming here was to surprise a certain person—his biggest fan. And possibly his smallest fan, judging by the loopy, childlike, first-name-only signature on the letter.

The adult who must have typed the contents remained anonymous. However, he or she had used the Hideaway letterhead and issued an invitation for Cody to call that number or write to that address anytime. Cody did one better. He showed up, unannounced.

The surprise, however, was clearly on him.

"My hat went missing. Someone suggested I check with the cook," he said, even though he knew that wasn't what she was asking.

"But what are you doing *here*? In Destiny Springs?"

She never did let anything slide. If she had, they'd probably still be together.

Cody straightened. Why did he all of a sudden feel defensive over a logical question? Except, yeah, he knew why. His first inclination was to be completely honest. But whoever came up with the notion that honesty was the best policy clearly hadn't met Becca.

Honesty had gotten him served with divorce papers. The kicker was, she'd known what she was getting into when she'd said *I do.* Knew he'd be away much of the time, working the rodeo circuit. She simply hadn't been prepared for the extent of it.

Neither had he. But Cody had been completely honest when he'd said that slowing down would be the worst thing for his career, next to quitting altogether.

She'd been honest, too. His extended career didn't fit into her time frame for settling down and starting a family. Still, he assumed she'd remain his biggest supporter—like his mother had done for his father—and trust that he'd make it up to her in the long run. *For better or for worse* was an all-encompassing clause in the Sayerses' book.

Not in Becca's, as it turned out. As he saw it now, she'd forfeited her right to know the gritty details about his life. Not that he intended to lie.

"I'm meeting up with a fan."

Becca snorted. "What's her name? I'll send some chocolate-dipped strawberries and champagne to the room."

Cody deployed his signature mischievous grin before remembering how much she used to distrust it. Judging from the eye roll, she still did. Then again, of course she'd reach that conclusion. The media made sure everyone did.

Come to think of it, the media was partly to blame for their divorce. The nickname they'd bestowed upon him had been the proverbial final straw.

Rodeo Rascal? What a joke. So he wore his Stetsons black and his T-shirts tight. Didn't mean he was up to something. And, sure, he could be a little devious at times. Having grown up with two older brothers, it was a survival tactic.

Then there was the harmless showtime banter with fans—mostly women. Couldn't exactly be rude, now, could he? It was showtime only, for goodness' sake. Never extended into his personal life. Of course, there were the fan letters from women and emails too, of which Becca was aware. He'd ignored them all, even though he didn't point that out to her.

Didn't think he had to.

Most didn't even request a response. They'd usually just rave about his *mischievous grin*.

Then it was his turn to snort. His right cheek had sustained permanent nerve damage early in his career. Landed on his face after being thrown from Major Disaster—three seconds into the ride—leaving him with not only a bruised ego but also a lopsided smile.

"Is something funny?" she asked.

He shook his head, never losing eye contact. "Believe it or not, I have male fans too," he said, neither confirming nor denying her assumption.

She nodded unconvincingly. Then she pinched her brows together and sniffed at the air. He smelled it too. *Smoke.* She swirled around, quickly removing the skillet from the stovetop.

"Oh, no! My eggs are ruined."

Because of me. "We can fix this." Cody took two long strides to the fridge and scoured its shelves.

She tossed the spatula onto the counter and dropped her hands to her side. "No, we can't. These were the last of them. And it's too late to go out and get more."

Just as well. Since physical preparation for the next two upcoming rodeo events wasn't an option, he needed to get back to the privacy of his room where he could do his visualization exercises, which always began the same way.

Set the rope, handle in deep.
Hips and legs, at one with the beast.
Free hand up, leave nothing to chance.
Follow his lead for an eight-second dance.

The visualization was one thing. He wasn't original in that respect. But if the media ever found out about his little mantra, they'd denounce it as some sort of hocus-pocus. But his life was literally at stake. He might be matched with Equal Opportunity Killer at the Houston Livestock Show and Rodeo three weeks from now. That one had a ninety-six-percent buck-off rate, which was wild.

That was, if he survived Scottsdale in two weeks.

Becca untied her apron, discarded it next to the spatula and began placing large bowls filled with sausage, fruit and potatoes onto a cart. He almost jumped right in but thought better of it. This was her territory, and he wasn't exactly welcome here.

"Can I do anything to help?" he asked.

"Not unless you can unburn those eggs. I need to get the rest of this stuff over to the buffet. Will you be there?"

Not a chance. He'd barely unpacked when he realized his Stetson had gone missing. Figured that was what he got for requesting an early check-in and hanging the hat on a post outside while he hauled luggage to his room. Besides, that particular hat was only for show—pre– and post–rodeo events.

This trip, however, it would be a show for one.

"Not today. Just looking for my missing property," he said.

"Well, you found it. Good luck with your… fan."

He reached across the counter and reclaimed the hat. A quick glance confirmed its structure hadn't been violated. At least, not beyond the abuse it had already been dealt. Good thing, since it was his lucky charm.

His father had had a lucky Stetson too, back in the day. At least it would've been, if he hadn't been widowed and forced to abandon his dream of a world championship in bull riding to raise Cody and his two older brothers—both of whom preferred unforgiving concrete and narrow skyscrapers to sandy clay and sprawling arenas. Someone had to make sure the Sayers name earned its rightful place in history. Cody intended to be that someone. In fact, he'd visualized the ultimate win at least a thousand times.

At that moment, however, he was visualizing something forbidden and entirely unlikely:

embracing Becca again. All the conjuring in the world couldn't make that happen.

He positioned his hat securely on his head, which was where it would stay until he got back to his room. Once his visualization exercises were out of the way, he'd track down his biggest little fan. Thankfully, the letter had offered some breadcrumbs.

Becca grabbed a white puffer jacket from a hook on the back wall and excused herself without making further eye contact. Through the kitchen window, he watched her enter a barn across the way, struggling to keep the cart from tipping over while crossing an uneven threshold.

Yep, she could have used some help.

"I should have insisted," he muttered.

But she didn't want it. Just like she hadn't wanted a therapist's or clergyperson's help in sorting through their marital issues.

I should have insisted...

He removed his hat and tossed it back on the counter. Maybe he'd never win her back. Not that he could if he tried. If anything, their lifestyles were more incompatible than ever. But this was an opportunity to prove he wasn't the self-centered man that she thought him to be. Prove he was good for more than bull riding.

Most of all, prove he didn't take advantage of every opportunity to steal the limelight.

He studied the overcooked eggs as he tied her apron around his waist, the pink floral terry-cloth still warm from her body. The unexpected connection and memories it evoked made his breath hitch.

Focus.

He analyzed the skillet in greater detail. Some of the eggs were salvageable, if a bit dry. A thorough spelunking of the refrigerator didn't unearth any chorizo. But he did find an unopened package of andouille sausage. Didn't come across a fresh jalapeño either, but he managed to snag some pickled ones. His questionable luck continued at the spice rack. No ancho chili powder. Regular chili powder would work in a pinch. And this moment definitely qualified as one.

Several dashes of paprika, cumin and oregano later, Cody was the proud father of the best cooking-by-the-seat-of-one's-pants Tex-Mex scrambled eggs with I Can't Believe It's Not Chorizo extravaganza he could manage. He transferred everything to the prettiest bowl he could find and slipped his hat back on because he couldn't carry it. No way was he letting it out of his sight again.

Which begged the question: Who took it in the first place?

No matter.

He hoofed it down to the barn but stopped at the entrance. The interior was both rustic and raw, yet warm and inviting. A long, community-style table stretched across much of its length. Several folks were already seated. Others waited in the buffet line along the side wall.

He watched and waited as Becca finished transferring food from bowls to warming trays then double-checked the coffee station, where she straightened the cups and saucers and condiments.

Eventually she'd look up and notice him, and he could motion her over. He'd hand off the dish and insist she take the credit. He couldn't risk being recognized, thus possibly making it all about him. Nope. No limelight on this trip. Only a single spotlight on the person he came here to impress most.

Speaking of which, a young boy was busy filling guests' glasses with orange juice from a dangerously large glass pitcher.

Could that be…*Max*?

The fan letter specifically mentioned that, as the owner's son, he often lent a helping hand around the place while dreaming of riding bulls someday. Anxiety whisked at Cody's insides until they weren't only scrambled, they were mush. Would he live up to his biggest little fan's expectations?

An undeniable yearning coursed its way through his already-tortured belly He wanted children someday. But only if—make that *when*—he could pass on the family name with a championship title attached.

As he tried to decide whether to approach the boy or hand the egg dish to Becca and wait for a more private setting in which to meet his fan, fate made the decision for him.

The boy caught sight of Cody. His little jaw practically hit the ground. A millisecond later, the gigantic pitcher he was holding slipped from his hands.

The crash-and-splash startled the guests, but not nearly as much as the little boy screaming at the top of his lungs, "Mommy! Mommy! Look who's here!"

Only one woman answered the call.

"Max, you know the rules. No yelling. Stay right where you are, sweetie," she admonished before looking Cody's way.

That's when the proverbial frying pan smacked him upside the head. Becca wasn't only the cook. She was the owner.

And Max was her son.

Becca sure hadn't wasted any time moving on after their divorce, had she? The implication kicked his gut with full, pointy-toed force. Obviously, he hadn't taken her urgent desire for starting a family literally enough. He'd let her down.

Or rather, we let each other down.

He gripped the bowl as tight as he would a braided bull rope, even though his grip on this situation was slipping. There wasn't enough rosin in the world to prevent it. His plan to impress her was backfiring. He could read it in her expression, even from where he stood.

The guests' attention quickly narrowed in on him. One woman said to another, loudly enough for everyone to hear, "Isn't that the Rodeo Rascal?"

Oblivious to the orange juice—which kept breaching borders on the ground beneath everyone's feet—all the guests turned still and quiet. They seemed to be anticipating what would happen next.

Will Cody Sayers last the full eight seconds? Or will he be thrown to the ground?

He couldn't begin to venture an answer. Didn't have a read on this particular beast. Too late to visualize his options. The chute had been opened, and the buzzer had yet to sound. The only thing he could think to do was what came naturally under pressure and what his fans seemed to enjoy most. Unfortunately, it was what his ex-wife appreciated least.

Cody straightened his posture, tipped his head to the group and put on his best mischievous grin.

Showtime.

CHAPTER TWO

"NOBODY MOVE!"

Becca jutted her arms in front of her, flashed her palms to the full-stop position and made eye contact with each person in the room. On top of everything else, she didn't need a lawsuit, should someone cut his or her foot on a piece of glass or slip on the orange juice.

Once she'd secured everyone's unspoken compliance, she pointed to Cody.

"You. Set the dish over there." She swung her arm around with focused precision and pointed to the far end of the serving table.

And then leave.

At least that aggravating smirk of his had made a quick exit. No doubt the guests had noticed too. She didn't have to look at them to know they were watching his every move. In fact, if she accomplished anything this morning, it would be to stay ignorant when it came to Cody and the fan he'd traveled so far to see.

It wouldn't do her any good to know whether that tall, leggy brunette was the one. No wonder she was so thin, the way she picked at the fruit on her otherwise bare plate. Or perhaps Cody came here to meet the perky, petite blonde with the Texas twang. Probably a Dallas Cowboys Cheerleader or some such. She must owe all that perk to the coffee she was guzzling since she seemed to be forgoing breakfast altogether.

Becca grabbed a handful of napkins, retrieved the industrial-size garbage can from the corner of the room and headed for ground zero. Max's lip quivered as she approached.

"I'm sorry, Mommy." A fat tear streamed down his cheek.

Her heart shattered as easily as that pitcher. "Aww, it's okay, sweetie. Accidents happen to everyone." But her adamant assurances and swift hug couldn't stop the waterworks.

That was one thing about Max. She never had to reprimand him for anything. He was a self-punisher. Even when he didn't deserve it.

"I don't want him to see me cry," he managed to say.

Becca scanned the room until she located the only *him* Max would be referring to.

No danger of that. Cody had transferred the contents of his bowl into a warming tray and was entertaining the women who'd previously shunned breakfast. They'd ignored Becca's directive to stay put until she could clear the floor. Instead, they congregated around him, full-size breakfast plates in hand, eagerly taking whatever it was he was dishing. Including that aggravating grin of his.

It felt as though everything had changed in the past six-plus years, yet some things never would.

Flirt.

Becca rolled her eyes and forced her attention back to Max, who was wiping his tears on the cuff of his sweater.

"How about you go to the house and get Miss Hailey. Have her bring paper towels and a mop and broom. You can get the carton of orange juice from the fridge and pick up where you left off."

"Really? You'll let me?"

"Absolutely! No one is a better orange-juice pourer than you. Maybe you can even offer Cody a glass."

At that, his damp eyes glistened in a good way, and that sweet smile of his blossomed.

Becca dared to glance at Cody again. The brunette was in the lead for his attention, it appeared, although the blonde had positioned herself within kissing distance.

Don't go there...

Too late. As annoying as those thoughts

were, it was a blessing he was otherwise occupied. Max would be back in a few minutes. The last thing she wanted was for Cody to spend time with her son.

Our son.

As if she needed to be reminded. She'd been in a long-term relationship with guilt for more than six years. She could come up with plenty of things to keep Max busy so that the two of them didn't cross paths.

Becca bent over, picked up the largest shards and tossed them in the trash. Fortunately, the glass didn't splinter. The floor would need a thorough sweeping and mopping, nonetheless. A large piece had hydroplaned all the way down to one of the thick oak legs at the end of the community dining table.

As she reached for it, someone snatched it away. She looked the snatcher in those ethereal blue eyes.

Cody resumed picking up a few smaller pieces in the vicinity. His hands had aged and roughened over the years. Gosh, they were just kids in their twenties back then. How many injuries had he sustained since she last saw him? She remembered one quite vividly. He'd gotten hung up during a competition. It did quite a number on his wrist. The surgery and recovery were almost worse than the injury. Her own wrist ached at the thought.

"You don't have to do that," she said.

She almost added a quip about deserting his fans. But that would have come across as jealousy. Her comment from earlier about the chocolate-covered strawberries still haunted her. Old feelings were rising to the surface, and she felt powerless to stop them.

"You're welcome," Cody said.

Then again, she didn't want to sound un-grateful either. "I'm sorry. Thank you."

"So you have a son." He maintained eye con-tact as if he suspected she might deny it.

Becca forced a smile. "Surprise!"

She looked down and gave the floor an-other once-over. Her diligence paid off. Far-ther down, she spotted a few more shards and resumed following the trail.

Cody followed behind her.

"He's adorable. Looks exactly like his mom. How old is he?"

"Four," she lied with surprising ease. For the first time, she appreciated that he was small for his age. Her guilt was now wide-awake and fully engaged.

Was a lie any worse than an omission? How many times had she picked up the phone to tell Cody the truth? Fifty? Fifty thousand?

Fifty zillion, as Max would say?

So many questions had gotten in the way. Would he have thought she'd gotten pregnant on purpose to trap him? Would the media have dug into their personal lives? For Max's sake, she hoped to never find out.

Cody had made it clear he wanted to be a full-time dad when the time came. They'd been in agreement on that much. The time part had been the problem. His star was on the rise. He'd worked so hard to make sure it did. Furthermore, he'd seemed happy in a way he hadn't been in their marriage. So she made the decision for both of them.

Judging by his pinched brow, timeline calculations were underway. She even caught him glancing at her ring finger. How would she explain that? Once again, the truth wasn't an option because then she'd have to explain… everything.

If she were being completely honest, she'd blurt out that those eyes of his were triggering major somersaults in her stomach. There was something about the clear pure blue of them that gave buoyancy to the pain of the past and the sin of the present.

All the more reason to bring those thoughts to a full stop.

Fortunately, the pattering of Max's feet running in their direction snapped her out of it. And, thankfully, Hailey was close behind, disaster gear in hand.

The woman was quite petite. And agile, even for a twenty-eight-year-old. Hailey reminded her of a filly, especially the way she always wore her long brunette hair in a thick ponytail. Yet, she was the strongest workhorse Becca had ever met.

Max slammed into Cody and wrapped himself around the man's legs with full force.

"Be careful," Becca admonished.

Judging from the way Cody swayed from the impact, he'd been as ill-prepared as she'd been. Although hers had been more of an emotional slam rather than a physical one.

Instead of being shocked or offended, he smiled the widest grin she'd ever seen on him. So wide it made the outer corners of his eyes wrinkle, which both warmed and frightened her. Something equally unexpected happened: he seemed like a natural with Max, even though she'd witnessed him seeming awkward around children in the past. Was that a good thing or a bad thing?

"You got my letter?" Max asked.

"I sure did," Cody responded.

The somersaults that had been torturing her

stomach now vaulted into her head, making it spin. "What letter?" Becca asked.

"The one Miss Hailey and I wrote."

Becca looked to Hailey, whose deer-in-the-headlights-of-an-eighteen-wheeler look gave her away. "You invited him?" she asked.

"No," Cody interjected. "They didn't know I was coming."

It took a few moments for Becca to connect all the moving parts. Did this mean what she thought it meant?

"So…Max is the fan you came here to meet?"

As sick as it made her feel, she hoped that her brain had somehow misconnected the dots and that the brunette was the fan after all, because this…*this* would be way too close for comfort.

Instead, there it was. That infuriating grin. Chased by one word that confirmed it all.

"Surprise!"

CODY HAD ALWAYS been a big fan of surprises. Until now.

For rodeo, he'd studied each bull's dossier, but he was still in for a surprise each time. Otherwise, where was the challenge? How would he ever grow as a bull rider? This situation, however, was a whole 'nother animal.

He would have been fine if she'd kept thinking that he'd come here to meet an adult fan. And he'd be even finer if she'd been even a little jealous over the ladies in the room, who had been blatantly flirting. Not that he was intentionally encouraging it or even wanted Becca to see such a thing, but at least he'd know he wasn't the only one who still had feelings. Unwelcome ones.

It was all he could do to block out the image of Becca dating again. Much less getting married, even though she wasn't wearing a wedding ring. But having another man's child? That hit harder than the dirt ground against his back. And it knocked the wind out of him just the same.

The best thing for everyone now would be for him to wrap it up with Max, get back to his room and do those visualization exercises. The Scottsdale event was less than two weeks away, followed by Houston. Winning both would have him sitting pretty for a shot at a world championship.

Yet, even accomplishing his biggest dream was impossible to visualize when two huge copper-colored eyes were staring up at him. Melting him in a way that nothing ever had.

The whole thing made him feel much too soft on the inside. Didn't matter how physically prepared he was, bulls seemed to sense the smallest degree of mental or emotional weakness.

"I have a great idea," Hailey said as she gently pried Max's arms from around Cody's legs, then knelt to his level. "My horses are probably getting a little lonely. How about you and Cody go check on them?"

"Okey dokey!" Max shrieked.

No, definitely not *okey dokey.* Not with Becca either, considering the look of panic on her face. Max grabbed one of Cody's hands and started tugging, but Cody stood firm.

"Let's ask your mom first," he said, adding a wink for Becca. At that, the worried crease between her brows softened a little.

Maybe his grin always set her off for some reason, but his winks seemed to reverse the damage. He wasn't above using every tool in his arsenal to defuse this situation.

"Okay. But no riding," she said.

"But Mommy—"

"She's right, cowboy," Cody insisted.

"Tomorrow?" Max asked.

"We'll see," Becca said.

The look she gave Cody told a different story, however. One that read *No riding today, tomorrow or ever.* Obviously, she'd brought her fear of livestock and roughstock to Destiny Springs.

He totally got it. She didn't want Max to get hurt. Even more, she didn't want to be the bad guy in this scenario. Neither did he. But, come tomorrow, one of them would obviously have to be. Today, however, he got to be the good guy.

Maybe a little too good for his own good, he decided, once he and Max started walking. The long trek to Hailey's stables could turn this little detour into an all-day event.

"Are you gonna move here?" Max asked.

It was question number fifty-one and counting. Not that Cody was complaining. In fact, he was amused by Max's inquisitive nature. But moving to Destiny Springs? He'd already been thinking that he'd shave off a week or more from his stay and go to Arizona early. He'd done what he came here to do: meet his biggest little fan. And way ahead of schedule to boot.

His publicist wanted a photo of the two of them, which would take all of two seconds and was intended to supposedly soften his rascal image. Problem was, he'd need Becca's permission to use the image. Considering her intense distaste for the media, that wasn't likely to happen. Unfortunately, his publicist wasn't likely to let it drop either, so he would have to ask at some point.

Truth be told, he hoped to spend a little time talking with Becca before boarding a plane out of here, especially since he'd previously assumed they'd never see each other again.

Either way, no good could come from getting too involved with Max. No telling what the relationship was like between the little boy and his dad. The thought of Becca moving on and having a child sank in deeper. The more he thought about it, the more it stung.

A cold wind whipped at their backs as they walked down the dirt road, but Max seemed impervious. Instead, he ran several steps ahead, then waited for Cody to catch up. All the while, turning his face upward to the crisp, blue sky and absorbing the unobstructed sun.

Max ran ahead again, then stopped, waved and yelled out, "Hi, Lilly!"

Cody looked around. No sign of anyone else. Only a lone heifer chomping away in a field. "One of your friends?" he asked.

"Uh-huh."

A quarter mile or so later, they reached Hailey's place. At least, he assumed it was. He'd relied on Max to get them there.

The property didn't have a sign marking the entrance, but the expansive grounds and stables suggested there was more to it than the modest log cabin sitting off to the side. Looked like old money had been spent at one time, but not much lately. The whole place begged for a cash infusion for some much-needed repairs and updates.

The rail fencing was in good shape. Cedar logs. The property accommodated a separate tack room and food storage, turnouts and a few round pens, from what he could tell. Not a person in sight tending to any of it.

Max picked up his pace and ran toward the stables.

Like I used to do.

Like all kids do, he quickly amended.

Max turned to see if Cody was following, then reversed course and ran back again. He took Cody's hand in his, as he'd done before, and pulled even harder.

He didn't know much about children Max's age. In fact, he didn't know diddly about kids in general. But he knew that this four-year-old packed a lot of strength for his size.

"C'mon. I want you to meet everyone."

Cody assumed Max meant the horses. The little boy obviously loved animals as much, if not more, than Cody had as a child.

"This is Courtney. She's my favorite, but

don't tell the others," Max whispered as they approached the bay-colored Arabian's stall.

Cody reached out, rubbed the horse's neck and was rewarded with a neigh. She looked plenty healthy but could use a little more grooming.

"How often do you ride?" Cody asked.

Max held up one finger.

"Once a day?"

Max shook his head.

"Once a week?" Cody asked.

Max shook his head even harder.

"Just once. Mommy says no a lot."

"She probably worries you'll get hurt."

Cody thought about his own mom and how she'd encouraged him to ride at a young age. That's because she understood animals. Believed that the benefits outweighed the risks.

Becca was always anxious around horses, and the bulls totally freaked her out. In fact, she'd once admitted that she covered her eyes whenever he competed. Not that she attended all his rodeos. Plenty in the beginning, but none toward the end.

"My mom didn't put me on a horse until I turned five. Maybe that will be your lucky number, too."

"I am five. One, two, three, four, five," Max said making a fist, then producing each finger as he counted, as if that were indisputable proof.

What?

"That means I can ride."

Max's follow-up argument offered Cody some relief. The little boy was padding his age in an attempt to trick him. He gave Max his best sideways look, but the little boy didn't blink. Still, nothing to get upset about here. He'd done a similar thing to one of their ranch hands when he was four. The man hadn't fallen for it. Neither would Cody.

"Nice try, cowboy. But whether you're five or ninety-five, I'm leaving that decision up to your mom."

Max simply shrugged and proceeded to introduce Cody to the rest of the horses: Bernice, Tom, Peter, Gabby.

"Wait till you see this," Max said, leading Cody to the tack room.

More like a tack palace. Everything a horse lover could want. Plenty of saddles, bridles and other equipment catering to the Western discipline.

His biggest little fan tried to heft a saddle from one of the racks.

"This one is gonna be mine," Max said.

Cody intercepted it and held the saddle low enough for Max to touch and admire. He didn't need for Becca's son to get injured on his watch.

"We should get back before your mom comes looking for us," he said as he replaced the saddle in its designated spot.

Max reluctantly agreed, but his enthusiasm picked up once again on the way home. He ran ahead, then backtracked and ran circles around Cody like a quarter horse at a barrel race, repeating the sequence with impressive focus and energy. For the first time ever, Cody wished he knew more about children, because those three words—*I am five*—continued to niggle. Max was smarter than Cody ever thought a four-year-old would be.

Someone either couldn't count or was lying. Or, in Max's case, embellishing.

The sun was almost at its apex, and Cody hadn't accomplished anything he'd planned for his morning. So much for staying the course.

"Will you talk to Mommy about letting me ride tomorrow?"

"Oh, I plan on talking to your mom." Otherwise, his focus was sure to be wrecked.

When his focus was wrecked, so was his bull riding.

If his bull riding was wrecked, so were his

chances for achieving what he'd given up everything else in life to achieve.

And he couldn't let anything stand in the way of that.

CHAPTER THREE

"I SWEAR, BECS, I didn't know Cody was going to show up here."

Although Becca heard the pleading in Hailey's voice, she was otherwise having an out-of-body experience. When Becca couldn't manage a response, Hailey confiscated the mop and placed it by the door, alongside the broom. At least they'd cleaned up all the broken glass and orange juice.

What a mess. But nothing compared to what might be happening down the road. What if Max talked Cody into letting him ride? The little boy had a knack for charming people into doing things they wouldn't ordinarily do. As far as the horses went, Max's charms had worked on her once, and only once. Hopefully, they wouldn't work on Cody at all.

Unfortunately, there wasn't anything she could do about it at that moment. The most she could hope for was that Cody picked up on her not-so-subtle stare that insisted Max wasn't to ride.

At least, not today.

Ugh. Had she really said, *We'll see*? Where had that come from?

In the meantime, she needed to clear all the plates and trays and prepare the area for afternoon tea and cheesecake. Hailey returned to help and to resume her defense.

"It was a fan letter. I swear I didn't mention you at all. You believe me, don't you?"

Becca paused from collecting dishes long enough to make eye contact. The young woman always looked away when telling anything short of the truth. This time, Hailey's gaze didn't waver.

Still, Becca wasn't about to let her off the hook so easily. At the very least, her assistant should help prevent further damage.

"Can you do me a favor?" Becca asked.

"Anything."

"Help me keep them apart. Spend the rest of the day with Max. At your stables. I'll pick up the slack here."

"Wow. You *are* serious."

"As a heart attack. Which is what I'll suffer if Cody finds out the truth."

Hailey pried the plates from Becca's grip, placed them on top of the stack she'd started and stilled Becca's fidgety hands in hers.

"Look at me. I will not breathe a word about

that. I'm sorry I helped Max with the fan letter, but you know how persuasive he can be."

"Like father, like son," Becca said.

"I hate to agree but, yeah, I can totally see it."

Becca pulled loose from Hailey's light grip and let out a long, pent-up breath before proceeding to lay out the ground rules.

"Start Max off with some grooming and equipment lessons or whatever you horse people do without actually getting on the thing."

Hailey saluted, then picked up a stack of trays.

The warmer that had held Cody's dish was the only one scraped clean. Whatever he'd cooked up, the guests had sure enjoyed it. Becca scanned the place. Empty. Everyone had finished eating and left during the blur of the last half hour.

"I think we're done here," she said after a final check of the floor.

"You are definitely done," Hailey said. "Get on back to the main house, take off those cute sneakers and relax. After I get these soaking, I'll take care of the trash. Then, as soon as Max returns, I'll kidnap him from evil Cody Sayers."

Becca was too emotionally drained to argue.

She grabbed the mop and broom as she exited the barn.

She'd no sooner put everything away at the main house and was headed to her room when Max bolted through the front door, nearly knocking down an elderly guest and toppling her walker in the process.

"Sorry, Mrs. Peters," Becca called out.

Having a covered ramp installed outside to the second level had been a good start, but she still needed to make a few accessibility modifications, including an indoor lift or stair assist. Oh, and training her rambunctious son to take it slower when guests were around.

She had the rest of her life to make her and Max's forever home safe and welcoming for everyone. Now that she had a B and B of her own, she was here to stay. No moving around, renovating properties and then flipping them, as her parents had done.

Becca shivered involuntarily. It had been so long since the media had spotlighted her parents' business as an American dream come true. And it had been, until one glossy publication flipped it by making Becca's personal life seem like collateral damage of her parents' accomplishment. The accompanying photo was an unflattering one of her eleventh birthday party. Just Becca, her mom and dad, and a few of their friends caught in an unsmiling moment.

Even though the implication couldn't have been further from the truth, Becca saw her life differently after that. She was left yearning for something more permanent and private, with lasting personal connections.

She'd vowed to never let the media into her personal life again. And she sure wasn't going to invite them into Max's.

"Mommy! Mommy! I saw the horses. Can I ride them? *Pleeease?*"

In her periphery, she noticed Cody helping Mrs. Peters dislodge the wheel of her walker from a split in the threshold. He held the door open until she was in the clear, then came in and closed it behind him.

In the meantime, Hailey had returned to Becca's side.

"Guess what, Max? I'm driving you back to the stables. We'll pretend they're your horses, and you'll get to learn how to care for them," Hailey said.

"Can Cody come with us?"

Not the request Becca had hoped for. "You both just got back. I'm sure Cody has other things to do," she said.

Not that she was aware of anything. They'd barely spoken. If he did go back to the stables, at least there would be two adults supervising Max's every move and keeping him safe. Hailey would be there to steer the conversations.

Becca tried to gauge Cody's thoughts about it. Clearly, he was doing the same of her.

"Actually, cowboy, I need to take care of a few things here, including having a talk with your mom. If there's time, I'll join you later."

Becca's breath hitched. *Talk? About what?*

Maybe she should have encouraged him to go to the stables. Whatever this was about, she had a bad feeling it wasn't going to be better than the alternative.

CODY LET THE question form in his mouth while waiting for Max and Hailey to leave. It was strange enough to have to ask for clarification, but that was no reason to put Becca on the spot in front of her son and her assistant.

Becca began her signature nervous tic of picking at her fingernails. It reminded him of the night he'd proposed. She'd seemed to know he was going to. Her answer had been an easy yes. This time, her answer should be equally straightforward.

"Is Max five? He seems to think he is," Cody said.

Becca stopped picking and looked up. "Five

is his favorite number. He also thinks he's six feet tall so…"

Cody exhaled. He'd suspected Max had been trying to trick him, but he had to be sure. Becca probably thought he was being paranoid.

"Is that what you wanted to speak with me about?" she asked.

Yes. "No. We just haven't talked in a long time."

She crossed her arms and rubbed them as if she were cold. "I suppose we've both been kind of busy."

He nodded. "I don't know that much about kids, but you've got an awfully cute one there."

"He can be a handful."

"The good kind, I suspect."

"Definitely." Becca tilted her head to the side and blinked, as if she didn't quite believe he thought any child was *the good kind.*

Sure, he'd never had anything glowing to say about children in general. At least, not until now. It wasn't because he didn't feel that way. He simply didn't know that many. In all fairness, he'd never said anything negative either. Only that there was something he wanted to accomplish before having little ones of their own.

Not to mention, riding bulls was the only thing he did well enough to make a living, which would be exceptional if he became a world champion. He'd be able to provide for all his family's needs and then some.

Even more important, he didn't want to start a family until he could be at home all the time, rather than on the road. He wouldn't want to miss out on all the firsts. First words. First steps. First day of school.

A rush of memories sideswiped him. The uncomfortable conversations that escalated into borderline arguments about the time-line for starting a family. Becca's sobs in the middle of the night when she thought he was asleep. The not-so-subtle hints about being left alone every weekend.

And the most heart-wrenching memory of all: the morning she'd said she didn't want to wait any longer for things to change.

Translation: for him to change.

His heart and mind had wrestled with it back then. Now, it had him pinned to the ground. It wouldn't do either of them any good to re-hash the past. Being under the same roof for two weeks wasn't going to help either. Which left the one option he'd already entertained.

"I'm afraid I made a promise I can't keep," he said.

She didn't say anything. Either she was wait-ing for him to finish or she was thinking the same thing he was thinking. He'd already broken a promise. To her. They'd talked about finding a house and making it a home. That was yet another dream she'd managed to fulfill without his help.

"To Max," he clarified. "I'm pretty sure I won't catch up with your son later at the stables."

"Oh, he'll track you down when he returns. He won't stop until he finds you. If not today, then tomorrow," she said.

"I'm planning on heading to Scottsdale tomorrow."

There. He'd said it, even though he hadn't set that plan in motion yet. Was that a look of relief on her face? Truth be told, he felt it too. He'd already started feeling something else, being around her again.

"I see. Well, Max may not understand, but I certainly do. Thanks for coming all this way to meet him. I know your time is valuable."

Ouch. Not the way he'd hoped the conversation would end. But they both knew it had to. Against his better judgment—but in sync with those old feelings—he leaned in and gave her a kiss on the cheek.

She swallowed so hard it was visible. So did he, although he tried to disguise it by clearing his throat.

Once in his room and safe from doing anything equally impulsive and downright stupid, he locked the door behind him and looked around for the first time. Without a doubt, Becca had decorated this room, right down to the flannel sheets.

She'd always talked about wanting them. Problem was, he ran as hot as Houston in August on most days. Seemed pointless to have sheets that would make it a hundred times worse.

He'd won the flannel-sheet argument but lost the one against having a mountain of throw pillows on the bed. Like this one appeared to have. Grabbing as many as he could, he piled them on a wicker rocking chair next to the window.

Matching flannel curtains?

He scratched his temple and laughed. It was as if the universe was punishing him for denying her the sheet set of her dreams to begin with. Before drawing the drapes, he looked out over the acres of bluegrass and spotted snowcaps in the far distance.

No wonder Becca had picked this place to be her forever home. Or, at least, he assumed that was her intent. Not that they would ever talk long enough for him to find out, especially when he hoped to book the earliest flight out tomorrow.

Even though he could take in the view all afternoon, he pulled the curtains shut. Before he could get the panels to meet, the rod jumped its tracks and the whole setup crashed to the ground.

"Awesome."

For all of two seconds, he considered calling in a maintenance request. Instead, he studied the bracket element. A screw was missing. Must have popped out when he tugged at the panels, yet he didn't see anything on the floor. He cleared the pillows off the wicker chair, and there it was.

Even without the proper tools, he was able to make the repair. A fallen curtain rod was a little thing to fix for Becca. Neglecting similar things had accumulated into a big heap of problems during his marriage. It took a single screw in a flannel-covered B and B room for him to realize how much he'd been responsible for that heap.

His diligence paid off in more ways than one. The curtains were thick enough to shut out the daylight.

If only he had that much luck shutting out the memories.

CHAPTER FOUR

ORGANIZED ON THE OUTSIDE. A total wreck on
the inside.

That's how Becca felt.

A good night's sleep would have helped
with the latter, but that hadn't happened.
She'd tossed and turned with images of Cody
showing up at breakfast and stealing the show
again. That didn't happen this morning, nor
had he checked out by the time it was over and
cleanup was completed.

Even after everything they'd gone through,
she hoped he wouldn't leave without saying
goodbye. After that, she could breathe a little
easier about Max and the horses. And a lot
easier knowing that the risk of Cody discover-
ing her secret would be reduced to near-zero.

For now, at least. After seeing Cody and
Max together, the guilt was on a rampage. She
could no longer envision taking this secret to
her grave. It wouldn't be fair to him or to Max.

If ever there was a wrong time to tell him,
this was it. Such news would be a dangerous

distraction. Eventually, however, she'd make it the right time. Even that much of a decision appeased her guilt a little. However, any feelings of relief proved to be short-lived. Three maintenance messages awaited her at the main house.

The requests were in Trent's wheelhouse. Unfortunately, he'd already returned to Fraser Ranch for the day. Good thing Becca had been too lazy to put on anything fancier than a fresh pair of yoga pants and a sweatshirt.

The first message was from Adrianna Hennessy in the Silk Room. The key had broken off in the door lock, so she couldn't secure her belongings and leave until it was fixed. Becca retrieved a duplicate room key, along with her handyman cheat sheet.

The second complaint was from Nathan Jones in the Denim Room. He'd noticed a strange hole drilled in the bathroom wall and was afraid someone might be watching him when he showered. *Seriously?* A little spackle and a putty knife should take care of that.

The final message was from the newlyweds in the Velvet Room, who were listed simply as the Vandercourts. Their toilet was broken. The one-star Yelp reviews were practically writing themselves.

She called each of the guests and assured

them that their concerns would be addressed ASAP, then retrieved a plunger and toolbox from the utility closet. As she started up the stairs, Cody was making his way down. Fully dressed but with hat in hand rather than on his head. Looked as though he'd showered, the way his dark hair appeared almost black when it was still damp.

Her hands were too full for them to easily pass each other, so she stopped on the landing and waited for him. Instead of squeezing by, he stopped as well.

"You're the handyman as well as the owner and cook? I'm impressed," he said.

"*Handywoman* to you. Not as handy as Trent, but he already left for the day. I'm glad you're still here, though. I was hoping we'd have a chance to say goodbye."

"So did I. But we don't have to do it now. Outbound flights are full. I'm on standby for tomorrow. Looks like you're stuck with me for one more day."

She tucked the plunger beneath her arm and switched the heavy toolbox from one hand to the other.

"You may be stuck in Destiny Springs, but you don't have to hang around here," she said. "Do some sightseeing. Hailey can give you some recommendations."

Anything to get him out of the house and away from Max. And from her, although for a different reason than she wanted to admit. Being this close to him was uncomfortable. Her breath kept hitching, her heart kept pounding, and her mind kept wandering back to how it felt to hold him.

A different kind of pounding—Max's eager footsteps against the wood floor, along with the pattering of their labradoodle—thankfully busted through those thoughts.

"Mommy! Cody! Can me and Penny go see the horses today?"

Why is he asking for Cody's permission? "You saw them yesterday, sweetie," she said. "Twice."

"But she didn't. Please?" Max asked.

"Hailey!" Becca called out, much louder and harsher than she'd intended.

Her assistant ran to the foyer. "Everything okay?"

"Max wants to see the horses again. Could you take him and Penny?"

She turned to Cody and whispered, "Sorry he put you on the spot again. If you want to go, you're welcome to do so. But as a guest. Not a babysitter." Not a bad coverup for her ulterior motive, if she did say so herself.

"Come with us!" Max pleaded.

Cody stared at her for what felt like the longest time with those calm ocean-blue eyes that she knew ran deep.

"Sorry, cowboy. I'll have to take another rain check. I need to help your mom for a while." He eased the plunger out from under her arm and tried to confiscate the toolbox.

She gripped it tighter. "No, sir. You're not going to do this," she said.

He persisted. "I want to. Ma'am."

As Becca relinquished, the tension drained from her body. "I insist on paying you."

"Not necessary."

Who are you? This wasn't the Cody she remembered.

"We'll see about that. The detailed list is taped on top of the toolbox. Start with the room at the end of the hall, on the right. They weren't specific, but something's wrong with the toilet."

"I gathered." He lifted the plunger as if he'd won a Nobel Prize for his powers of deduction.

"They're on their honeymoon."

"Then I'm surprised they even noticed."

"Not the type of thing one can ignore for long, if you catch my drift. Reality always finds you."

She hadn't meant to add the last part. The whole idea of newlyweds reminded her of their own honeymoon in Galveston. Close to home, but a world away from reality. She could've stayed in that place forever.

"Reality is fixable," he said.

She gulped. Part of her wanted to believe that, standing so close to him again.

The naive part.

Such naivety should be reserved for honeymooners. It was included in the package with all the other things that didn't exist in day-to-day life. Things like chocolate-covered strawberries and champagne for breakfast, or couples' massages overlooking the gulf. Or happily-ever-afters.

Cody turned and headed up the stairs. Max stood there with the saddest look on his face.

"C'mon, Max. Let's go to the stables," Hailey said, taking his hand.

With Cody going one direction and Hailey and Max going the opposite, Becca felt a tug-of-war ensuing.

"Thanks, Miss Hailey, but I wanna help Cody." Max broke free and ran up the stairs to his idol's side.

Hailey shrugged her shoulders. Becca looked to Cody, with Max practically glued to him.

Cody shrugged back.

Her shoulders, along with every other fiber

of her being, tensed at the reality that Cody had more gravitational pull than even the four-legged beasts that Max adored. Unfortunately, the beast that Max was gravitating to would do one worse than throw him to the ground and break his body. This one would also break his heart.

Cody would leave him behind tomorrow.

Cody would leave all of them.

THE UNEASY FEELING in Cody's stomach wasn't from anything he'd eaten because he hadn't consumed a morsel of food all day, having forgone breakfast altogether. No, it was from trying to digest all those mixed feelings.

First, about Becca. Seeing her again had done a number on him. He would have assumed that, after all this time, she would no longer wield such power. It was clear, however, that his power was lost on her. Strangely enough, that was the best he could hope for, because things would really get messy if her feelings were getting the best of her too.

Romance and bull riding didn't mix. At least, not for Becca and him. Their failed marriage was proof of that.

Second, and a bit trickier, were the feelings he was having about Max. How could he get so attached to a child he barely knew, and so quickly? That was insane. A little boy who would rather help him do handyman work than be around horses? When did that ever happen?

The honeymooners weren't in the room when he and Max arrived, so Cody used the master key that Becca had provided and let himself and his apprentice in.

Max didn't even blink when he discovered they'd be working on a broken toilet. In fact, he seemed more curious than anything as he watched Cody replace a piece that had cracked. He even begged to help, going so far as sticking his little hands into the tank to assist in positioning the new part and tightening it with a wrench.

"You wouldn't rather hang out with horses?" Cody asked.

Max shook his head.

He, for one, would rather be hanging out with Becca. He wasn't about to admit it, but he couldn't deny it either. He had a serious crush on her. Not that he'd ever stopped crushing on the most beautiful woman in the world. But that little dance he caught her doing in the kitchen yesterday? Logic and reason didn't stand a chance.

If they ever reached a place where he could joke with her again, he'd ask her what tune she'd been moving to. Cody shook his own head to try and dislodge the thought.

"Am I doing it wrong?" Max asked.

The question snapped Cody back to the task at hand. Sure enough, Max was turning the nylon nut in the wrong direction.

"You almost got it," Cody said instead of confirming the obvious. "Here, let me show you a little trick."

He placed his hand over Max's and eased his hand in the opposite direction to tighten the replacement piece that had broken off.

"Now, test the handle. Make sure it's on good and tight."

Max held the lever down while peeking inside the tank to watch the water drain and refill, then looked to Cody. When he gave him two thumbs-up, Max's smile spread from ear to ear.

Cody blinked. Like a camera shutter capturing a moment. In this case, a memory. For a split second, Max looked exactly like Cody had in childhood photos. Before being thrown off a bull and forced to dance cheek to cheek with the dirt, thus changing his smile forever.

Then again, all kids had that innocent, enthusiastic-looking grin when they were happy.

"Looks like we're all done here," Cody said.

He started placing the tools back in the toolbox. Max jumped in to help.

While his biggest little fan finished up, Cody studied the fix-it list and decided Miss Hennessy's broken-off key was more crucial than a mysterious hole in a bathroom wall.

"Okay, cowboy. Lead the way to the Silk Room."

Max hefted the toolbox even though the thing was probably half the little guy's weight. He insisted on carrying it as he led Cody down the hall and around the corner to the far end of the east wing.

"Mind if I ask you something?"

"You can axe me anything," Max answered.

"How tall are you?"

Max stopped and pushed his shoulders back. "Six feet!"

The little boy beamed at his self-description.

Cody beamed back. "I was gonna guess six foot two."

He knocked gently on the door as to not accidently push it open. A woman answered, wearing one of the Hideaway's oversize full-length guest bathrobes, with green goop slathered all over her face.

Even though Max thought it was hilarious and didn't even attempt to hide it, Cody found the goop endearing. Something similar had been part of Becca's morning beauty ritual, along with thick oil saturating the ends of her hair, and a layer of Vaseline or something equally sticky on her elbows. Although, in his opinion, Becca hadn't needed any help in the beauty department. Still didn't.

When the woman realized who they were, her jaw dropped. "I thought you were my friend from down the hall," she said as she unsuccessfully shielded her face with both hands.

"Sorry to disturb you, ma'am. We're here to fix your lock. How about we come back later?" Cody suggested. They could take care of the spackle job in the Denim Room in the meantime.

"No. Please, go ahead. I'll finish getting ready in the bathroom."

Cody nodded. "Okay, then. We'll need what's left of the key." The woman retrieved the remains from a dresser and handed him the piece. "Thank you. That'll do us. Won't take long," he said.

The woman grabbed her jeans and sweater, which had been laid out neatly on the bed, and closed the bathroom door behind her.

"Wow!" Max said.

"Wow what?" Cody asked, trying to act as if he hadn't noticed anything unusual.

Max giggled. "It's Shrek!"

Cody pressed his finger against his lips, then issued a quiet *Shhh*. "Silly. It's a nice lady who is pampering her skin," he whispered.

That made Max giggle even louder. Cody simply shook his head. The little guy would eventually get used to things like facial treatments, ginormous hair curlers and mani-pedis.

"So, we have a key that's broken in the lock. Ever had that happen to you?" Cody asked. Max shook his head. "Well, if it ever does, you'll know how to fix it."

Cody studied what was left of the key. None of the cuts survived, so most of it was still inside the lock.

"Hand me a screwdriver, cowboy." Max fished around and pulled out a Phillips head. "Nice catch. Now, can you find one that has a flat tip?"

It took Max a minute, but he made the right choice and proudly handed it over.

"We'll slip the tip into the lock, like this, and turn it back to the up-and-down position." Cody demonstrated, then turned it back to the incorrect position so that Max could take a run at it. "Your turn."

Max's little hands grappled with the tool as he tried to turn the thing. Made Cody think of Becca struggling with small tasks around their house during their marriage. Had she done so because she wanted to? Or had she been waiting for him to step up and do his share?

He knew the answer. His intentions had been good, but he'd never been quick enough on the draw. That applied to starting a family as much as it did to fixing a clogged pipe.

Specific examples of times she'd asked for his help with the little things jabbed at him like a dozen prickly needles, as did his typical response. *Don't worry. I'll take care of it later.* In most instances, *later* had never come.

Or, make that *came too late.* No matter what he did around the Hideaway, it wouldn't begin to make up for what he'd failed to do during their marriage. Then again, why was he even thinking it was a possibility? He'd be leaving tomorrow.

"What's next?" Max asked, having successfully finished the task.

"Now you get to go fishing." Cody grabbed the pair of needle-nose pliers. "Insert the tip of these into the keyhole. Try to find the broken part, then grab onto it and pull it out."

While Max was busy having a ball, the fully dressed but still-barefoot woman walked up to Cody's near side.

"How are you boys coming along with that?" she asked. The green mask had been replaced with fresh, glowing skin.

Max held up the pliers, complete with the key remnant. "I caught one!"

"Bravo!" Cody said. "One more step to—"

"Wait," she interrupted. "You're the Rodeo Rascal."

"Yes, ma'am. And this is Max, my corascal."

At that, Max proudly grinned.

"Is he yours? I definitely see a resemblance," she said.

"Must be the eyes and hair," Cody said, hoping she'd realize how ridiculous that comparison sounded. Max had Becca's red hair and copper eyes, which were on the far side of the color spectrum from his brown hair and blues.

"No, it's not that. I noticed you're both left-handed. And you have the same jaw and mouth shape."

Cody hadn't noticed either of those things before, but the stranger had a point. Still, two similarities out of dozens didn't make for a father and son. Besides, he hadn't been with Becca around *that* time.

"I'll take that as a compliment," he said, returning his focus to the task at hand, which included testing the other key before handing it over.

As soon as the woman walked away, Max said, "I think she likes you."

That's exactly what he was afraid of. In fact,

if there was one thing he hadn't wanted Max to witness, it was a scene like that, even though Cody hadn't picked up on anything more than a lukewarm fan vibe. Still, Max would probably tell Becca all about it. At which time her mind would contort it into something that didn't resemble the truth. Not that he had to answer to her for anything.

"Why do you think that, Max?"

Might be helpful to know what a four-year-old boy perceived as liking when it came to girls and boys. When Max shrugged, Cody figured the mystery of attraction was still a mystery and would unfold in due time. He wasn't about to make it happen any sooner. That was one good thing about not being a father: he wouldn't have to have the birds-and-the-bees talk.

"I think it's cuz her face turned pink," Max finally said.

She'd probably washed off the goop with hot water, so pink would be normal.

"Anything else?" Cody asked.

"She stares at you when you're not looking. She doesn't do that to anybody else."

Sure, the guest had looked at him once or twice before realizing he was the Rodeo Rascal. But a quick glance confirmed she wasn't looking at him now, much less staring. Besides, why would a young boy even notice such details, much less care? Except, Max obviously knew this guest, even though she didn't seem to remember him.

"How long have you known Miss Hennessy?"

Max scrunched his brows. "Who's Miss Tennessee?"

Now it was Cody's turn to be confused. Clearly, he didn't know how to communicate with children. And just when he thought he was doing so well.

"The pink-faced woman we were talking about." He nodded toward the guest who was now sitting on the edge of the bed, contemplating two different pairs of shoes.

Max huffed and rolled his eyes.

"Not *Shrek*. I'm talking 'bout Mommy."

CHAPTER FIVE

AUTUMN CHEESECAKE WASN'T just for autumn. Not in Becca's house.

Despite the fact that they were poised on the threshold of spring, she forged ahead with combining the graham cracker crumbs, sugar, cinnamon and butter, and pressing the mixture evenly onto the bottom of the springform pan. Her recipe was always a hit. The guests emptied the plate as fast, if not faster, than they had Cody's.

She paused long enough to look out the window and consume the view. Not a cloud in sight.

Sunny. *With a ninety-percent chance of drama.*

It occurred to her that autumn—like all the seasons, and like Cody—always came back around, and she had no control over it. Yet, certain aspects she could control. It was crucial that she avoid as much alone time with him as she could manage while he was there, to avoid a repeat of, or an even deeper dive into, any conversation involving the topic of Max.

Becca placed the pan in the preheated oven. She twisted the apple-shaped kitchen timer until it hit the ten-minute indicator. With portable mixer in hand, she combined the cream cheese and sugar, then added the eggs and vanilla and set it aside long enough to toss the apple slices with sugar and cinnamon. She practically felt her hips widening at the sight and smell alone. Forever resenting her curviest of curves, she envied women who had a more boyish, athletic figure. Women who weren't so soft and didn't have to buy a larger pair of jeans, only to have the waist taken in.

That was one thing she could say about Cody. He'd made her feel beautiful, always. And comfortable in her skin. Even though she was a good fifteen pounds heavier than when they last saw each other, he still had that effect.

The apple timer sounded its I-refuse-to-be-ignored *ringing*, jolting her from a place she'd had no business visiting: *there*.

She pulled the browned crust from the oven and shook her head at the absurdity of her thoughts. He'd hardly ever been there when they were married. He'd spent more nights in hotel rooms than he had in their own bed. And when he was there, it was all about the next event.

This afternoon, she wasn't going to let him distract her from her cooking. Wasn't going to burn the dish again, only to have him swoop in and save the day like he had at breakfast.

"Show off," she said out loud, by accident.

She swiveled to make sure he wasn't standing behind her like before, leaning against the doorway with that mischievous smirk. She inwardly cringed at the thought of him watching her so-called dance. This time, thankfully, she was alone.

Becca added the filling, then spooned the decadent sugar-and-cinnamon-coated apples over the mixture and sprinkled it with pecans. Ready for the homestretch. She popped the pan back in the oven and set the timer again. With that in the works, she moved on to the next to-do: get Max out of the house this evening and away from Cody. Then, do the same with herself.

She brushed her hands on the terry apron, picked up the landline and called Fraser Ranch. Max was good buddies with Vern Fraser's great-grandson, Perry.

"Hi, Vern. It's Becca."

"Yes, ma'am! I know. Your name and number pops up on the screen like magic."

Becca had to laugh. She often felt that way about technology. "Is Vanessa around, by chance?" she asked.

"I believe so. I'll holler at her."

Which reminded Becca, her mom was coming to Max's birthday party in a couple of weeks and staying at the B and B. Better follow up and make sure the woman wasn't planning to come early. She wasn't too fond of Cody anymore. That was one reunion Becca couldn't deal with right now.

In the background, Vern did indeed holler for his granddaughter. Moments later, Vanessa answered.

"Becca, what's going on?"

"A lot, but please don't ask. I was wondering if there's any chance Max could have a sleepover tonight with Perry." She held her breath while Vanessa contemplated the favor.

"Perry would love that. So would I."

Becca exhaled. "Thank you!"

"Bring him over as soon as you'd like. We'll be here all afternoon."

"I owe you one," Becca said.

"You owe me nothing. Except I'm glad you called. Vern will be delivering the eggs in the morning. He's got Trent busy on a project."

Without Trent, Becca would have to do any urgent handywork jobs herself. Or worse, Cody might offer to step in again. That was one person she'd rather not owe any more favors.

"Tell Vern to come around to the kitchen door. I'll be waiting."

Becca hung up the phone and looked around. Since she didn't want to leave the oven unattended, now would be a good time to tackle a colossal project: organizing her recipes. She could be productive while the cheesecake finished baking, rather than ruminate over the fact that her ex-husband and the son he didn't know he had were working together upstairs. Not to mention, it might be nice to add something new to the afternoon offering. Perhaps with chocolate. Or, better yet, caramel.

She retrieved the accordion file from the pantry. It was so heavy it was about to burst at the seams, so she grabbed a handful of clippings and began the triage process of keeping, tossing or putting them aside for further consideration.

By the time Cody and Max finished the maintenance tasks and headed downstairs and into the kitchen, she had whittled the file down to half its size.

"Mommy! Mommy! Guess who I got to meet?"

"Who?"

"Shrek!"

Becca looked to Cody for clarification.

"Miss Hennessey with the broken key. Seems she took a page out of your playbook. Had green stuff on her face when she answered the door."

Took Becca a minute, but she eventually got what he was saying. Once again, she was pulled all the way back *there*, when Cody had kissed her while she was wearing one of those avocado skin-conditioning masks. He was able to look right through it and into her soul, making her feel beautiful.

Comfortable.

Exactly the opposite of how this conversation was affecting her. She stiffened and looked for the nearest exit ramp. Fortunately, she found one.

"Guess what, Max!" she said.

"What?"

"The Frasers invited you for a sleepover with Perry tonight. How fun is that?"

Max's eyes brightened. "Can Cody spend the night too?"

There was only one answer to this request, and they both knew it. Cody seemed more amused than anything, the way he tried, but failed, to hold back a smile.

"I'm afraid not, sweetie." She stopped short of promising him that he'd see Cody tomorrow.

He might be on a plane before Max even got home. "Go pack a change of clothes and your toothbrush, and I'll take you over."

"How far away? I can walk him there," Cody offered. "I could use the exercise."

"About twice the distance as Hailey's. Too far."

"Then, I'll drive him. You look busier than I am."

She didn't like the idea of Cody spending more alone time with Max than was necessary, but it would give her time to execute her next task, which was to get herself out of the house and far away from another conversation.

"When I get back, I could rustle up some dinner for us," Cody said.

"Let's play it by ear," Becca said, sidestepping the proverbial wrench he'd thrown smackdab into the middle of her plan. The words tasted dishonest when spilling from her mouth. She hated that saying. It was one that Cody had used frequently in their marriage. The plans had rarely landed in her favor.

He pursed his lips as though he'd gotten a taste of his own medicine and didn't like it one bit. That hadn't been her intention. She was doing this for her own self-care. Not as payback of any kind.

As if on cue, the timer dinged. Becca swung

back around and retrieved the cheesecake from the oven.

Ahh, perfection!

Oh, yes. She was in total control today. In like Flynn with the powers that be. A winner, in sync with the universe.

Why, then, did it feel as though she was losing?

MAX BOUNCED UP and down in the borrowed booster seat, and against the belt restraints, all the way to Fraser Ranch as if he were riding a horse. Or maybe a bull. Cody would ask him as much if he wasn't busy fighting butterflies.

Specifically, the ones in his stomach that went into a frenzy every time he thought about Becca. Forget the fact that she was going to stand him up tonight for dinner. No doubt in his mind. That would be for the best because, once again, he'd been distracted from what he needed to do most.

"Déjà vu," he muttered.

Max stopped bouncing and looked at him. "What's that mean?"

"Means you feel like you've heard or seen or done something before. Ever had that happen to you?" Cody asked.

Max seemed to think about it all of five seconds and shook his head. "Can I carry the suitcase inside?"

"I see you inherited your mom's proclivity to dodge difficult questions."

Max cocked his head but thankfully didn't ask Cody to elaborate. He'd said too much already.

Once parked, Cody retrieved the suitcase from the bed of the truck. Max pried it from his hand and ran toward the house. It wasn't that heavy, but it made for an awkward canter.

"And her independence," Cody added under his breath.

Now this was a ranch, with what must be about twentysomething miles of fencing. Complete with roaming cattle. No telling what else was there that he couldn't see. It was the kind of spread a cowboy could really dig his bootheels into.

That was yet another way his and Becca's respective dreams hadn't aligned. He was surprised she even chose the Great American West, much less the Cowboy State. She'd talked about settling on the East Coast so many times during their marriage, he'd felt as though they were already there.

Max ran up the steps to the main house and let himself in the front door.

"Knock first," Cody called out belatedly. He

stuck his head inside the open door. "Hello? Anyone home? Max, where did you go?"

An elderly man emerged from one of the rooms, and a big smile blossomed.

"Well, I'll be. You're the Rodeo Rascal, aren't ya?"

This isn't happening. "That's what people keep telling me."

The man moved closer and extended his hand. "I heard you were in Destiny Springs. Thought it was a rumor. I'm Vernon Fraser, but you can call me Vern. Everyone else does."

The man's handshake was strong and confident and belied his otherwise-frail frame. His baggy jeans and oversize quarter-zip sweatshirt didn't do him any favors in that department.

"I drove Max over, but he let himself in and disappeared."

"That's what he usually does. Heard him run straight upstairs to Perry's room. Please come in. It's your lucky day. You caught me in the middle of squeezing oranges. Max insists on pouring everyone a glass whenever he comes over. For practice, he says. So I try to have it ready for him."

"Thank you, sir. I can only stay a few minutes, though."

Vern shuffled back in the direction he'd

come from, then looked over his shoulder and nodded for Cody to follow.

He heard plenty of stomping and shrieking and laughing of children overhead. Otherwise, the big house was quiet. Not to mention masculine, with a lot of tans and browns, suedes and leathers.

The old man set a glass in front of Cody, filled it with juice. "I'd leave room for champagne, but I know you drove here. I'm guessing you're stayin' at the Hideaway, since you had Max in tow."

"That's correct. I'll take you up on the offer another time."

Vern poured the rest into his own glass, which only filled it halfway.

"Well, would you look at that. Guess I'll have to add champagne to mine and squeeze more oranges later," Vern said, adding a wink as if that had been his plan all along. He pulled an aluminum can of bubbles from the fridge and topped off his own glass. "You here for the events in Sweetwater?"

"No, sir. On my way to Scottsdale."

Vern took a long swig. "You're a long way from Arizona, son."

And too close to the past, Cody wanted to add.

"That I am. You happen to have any bulls

on the property?" he asked, hoping to change the topic more than anything else.

"Yep, but none worth your time, if practicing is what you're thinking of asking. No bucks or kicks."

Cody took a draw from the glass of orange juice. Boy, did the fresh-squeezed stuff taste good. Reminded him of how Max had dropped the pitcher, and how he and Becca had worked together to pick up the pieces of glass. Too bad they couldn't have done the same with the broken pieces of their marriage.

"Becca, the owner, is a sweetheart, isn't she? Must think highly of you if she trusts you with Max."

Vern had no idea that he and Becca had been married. Not that she'd necessarily go around telling people, but it stung nonetheless. Still, he'd let her tell people on her own terms and timeline.

"She's single, you know," Vern continued. "And raising that adorable little boy all alone."

Cody could use a hit of that champagne about now. A shot of courage for what he was about to ask. "What about the dad? What's his story? Not that it's any of my business."

Vern looked distracted. He stood up, glass in hand, grabbed a Farmer's Co-op baseball cap and slipped it over his thick white hair.

"Let's take a walk. I just thought of something you might be interested in."

Right. None of my business. Cody grabbed his own glass, and they went outside to a massive structure, flush against the back of the house. Vern pulled a keychain from his pocket and popped the lock. Once inside, he led Cody to the back, to something large and covered.

Vern grabbed the edge of the blanket but paused. "Care to venture a guess?"

The silhouette all but gave it away. Anticipation swelled in Cody's chest at the possibility. "No way," he said.

As if Vern's conspiratorial smile didn't confirm it, he ripped off the blanket, revealing a mechanical bull. It took all Cody had to not scream and giggle and jump up and down, like the little boys were doing upstairs.

Vern brushed his hand across the contraption's back. "She's a bit dusty and long in the tooth. But last time I fired up old Sally, she worked just fine."

"She? Sally? You do realize…"

Vern nodded. "Only a woman could be this tough. They give birth, after all. I feel like I'm going to die when I get a splinter."

Cody had to chuckle. "Point taken."

"Sally isn't a substitute for the real thing—a bull, I mean—but maybe she could be a good supplement to those visualization exercises I hear you do."

"The media loves to talk about it, for some strange reason."

"Wanna give her a try? Like I always say, never put off until tomorrow what you can do today. Unless you get a better offer."

"That's very tempting, but I should probably head back."

Vern nodded slowly. "Uh-huh. Sounds like someone has a better offer. Probably for the best that we don't do it today, since I've had some bubbly and would be behind the wheel, so to speak." He pointed to a console in the corner. "You're welcome to Sally anytime. Knock on the door and fetch me. I'll drive."

"That's too generous."

"Not at all. I'm being totally selfish. It'll give me bragging rights to say the Rodeo Rascal himself practiced here."

Vern gave the contraption a slap on the backside before covering her back up. "Of course, I won't breathe a word about it until you're long gone."

"I appreciate that. Don't mention it to Max either. Otherwise, he'll be out here, wanting to ride. And he'll use his charms to rope you into it. Especially since his momma won't let him so much as sit on top of a horse."

Vern shook his head. "Riding horses would be good for the little fella. But I'm stayin' out of it."

Cody nodded. "Me too."

Vern led the way back to the front entrance of the house. Max and Perry had come outside and were kicking a ball back and forth in the open area.

Before he and Vern got any closer, Cody had to say it. "You never told me about Max's father."

Vern looked at him and squinted. "That's right."

Cody waited for him to elaborate. When Vern finally offered up a closed-lip smile instead, he knew that no information was forthcoming. At least Vern was the type who could keep a secret. The mechanical bull would be of concern to Becca.

"I guess I better get going," he said, although this visit had been an unexpected pleasure.

Max spotted the two of them and ran over.

"I'm heading out, cowboy. I'll catch up with you later," Cody said. He didn't want to get into the fact that he'd be leaving tomorrow. Max jutted his bottom lip, but the pouting ended the moment Perry came up to him.

"Okey dokey! Catch me later," Max said.

The boys turned around, ran up the porch stairs and disappeared inside.

Cody tipped his hat to Vern. "Thanks for the hospitality and for the offer. Greatly appreciated."

Vern returned the nod.

"By the way," Vern called out before Cody reached the truck. "I read that you recite some sort of fancy mantra when you visualize, but nobody knows what it is."

Cody turned on his heels. Now, where had Vern read that? Only a few people knew that he even had such a thing, and they'd been sworn to secrecy. Which only confirmed the obvious: a secret isn't a secret if more than one person knows. He wasn't about to add another person to the list, no matter how charming the man was. It was Cody's turn to dodge.

"That's right." He chased those two words with the closed-lip version of his signature grin and turned back around.

In the background, he heard Vern cackling.

In the foreground, nothing but a quiet dirt road. The perfect canvas to visualize against. Yet the only thing he could visualize was cooking dinner for Becca tonight. *Never put off until tomorrow what you can do today.*

Unless you have a better offer. Cody was hard-pressed to think of a better one, even though his common sense kept trying to buck the thought right off the top of his brain, admonishing him to focus on the prize he'd been chasing since he left Houston more than six years ago.

That issue would be resolved for him anyway. Every fiber of his being sensed that Becca wouldn't make herself available. Not after her five-word missive: *Let's play it by ear.*

He knew all too well what that meant.

In fact, he could have invented the phrase.

CHAPTER SIX

"You look stunning. Big date tonight?"

Becca stopped rummaging through her handbag long enough to acknowledge the compliment.

Hailey grabbed a diet soda from the fridge and settled on one of the barstools as if she didn't plan on going anywhere until Becca spilled the beans.

Yes, she'd put extra effort into her appearance. For the first time in months. She couldn't remember the last time she'd worn that emerald green dress. The wrap style was quite flattering. But *stunning*? That was an overreach.

"Oh, yes," she said. "A big date. With myself. I'm free for the evening, and I intend to go crazy. Single moms gone wild!"

Not even close.

Trent had shared some gossip that retired country-western music star Montgomery Legend was in town and might show up at Renegade. Possibly even do a cameo with the live band. Montgomery was her mom's favorite singer, and it would thrill the woman to no end to have his autograph. Maybe Becca could even snag a selfie with him. Hence the dress.

"Ah! There you are!" Becca held up the tube of lipstick that had been playing hide-and-seek at the bottom of her tote for the last three minutes.

Minutes that she couldn't spare. She wanted to get out of the house before Cody returned. Before he asked her again about having dinner together. The whole idea of sharing a meal and talking one-on-one for any length of time struck fear in her. Tonight, it would be all about her, sipping on a Virgin Mary, not watching the clock and listening to some music.

Although Fraser Ranch was a bit of a drive, Cody should have been back by now. Max could've easily talked him into meeting all the cattle and chickens and assorted critters. Her son made fast friends with all of them.

Maybe she should take a little detour and drive down that way. Make sure Cody wasn't stranded by the side of the road or involved in an accident.

She had to laugh at the notion. The man got thrown off and trampled by bulls for a living, and she was worried that he couldn't make it down a quiet dirt road without getting hurt? Why did she even care anymore?

Yep, she needed this night out more than she first thought.

"Mind if I ask where you're headed in case you go missing?" Hailey asked.

"Only if you don't send my ex-husband a letter with all the details."

The dig wasn't subtle, nor was it intended to be. Becca wouldn't even be in this predicament in the first place if Hailey hadn't helped Max.

"No more accidental shenanigans. I swear," Hailey said.

Becca cast her a sideways glance. Hailey was a pro at weaving loopholes into her promises. "No on-purpose ones either," Becca admonished.

Hailey pursed her lips and squinted, then looked down at Becca's boots. "You're going to Renegade, aren't you?"

"What gave it away?"

"Those are your dancing boots. The only other time I've known you to wear them is when you went dancing. At Renegade."

"Your powers of observation are uncanny."

Forget that Renegade was the only place to dance within a hundred miles. She'd much rather dance freestyle to some rock or hip-hop or pop.

"So I've been told."

"Then please use your powers for good and

watch for Cody while I finish getting ready. I don't want him to see me, if possible."

Hailey slid off the barstool and did as instructed.

Becca retrieved a compact mirror from her handbag, applied some lipstick and rubbed a finger across her front teeth. Despite adding a bit of bronzer, she still looked as pale and tired as she felt. Thankfully, the honky-tonk would be dark. Besides, she wasn't going there to meet anyone, so what did it really matter? Not that Montgomery Legend was a nobody. Far from it. It was more about escaping reality for a while rather than creating a whole new one.

"He seems nice, Becs. Just sayin'," Hailey called out.

Becca paused. "I never said he wasn't."

"I know. Otherwise, I never would've helped with the fan letter. I guess I thought he'd be more arrogant, considering he's rodeo-famous and all."

Becca still couldn't wrap her mind around the fame part. After they split, he'd become a household name in some circles, along with his Rodeo Rascal nickname. From what little news she'd been unable to avoid, he'd fully embraced it. Not that he'd ever shunned it.

Becca transferred a few items from her everyday tote to a dainty cross-body purse.

"Give it time. Cody has his fair share of self-confidence. It's bound to spill out."

"Which can be quite attractive," Hailey added.

No argument there, although she wasn't going to give her assistant the satisfaction of agreeing. Her heart still hadn't tamed since the moment she'd turned around and seen him leaning against the doorway. So self-assured.

He'd always been that way, so why was it getting under her skin now? No matter. He'd be out of sight and out of mind. At least for tonight. Max, on the other hand, would remain top of mind, although he was in excellent hands at Fraser Ranch and probably wasn't thinking about his mommy at all.

"I'll have my phone with me and turned on," she said. "If Max gets homesick, give me a call. I'll leave Renegade and swing by and get him."

"Don't keep the phone in your hand. Just pick it up every few songs. I'll go get him and will call you only if there's a real emergency. Go have some fun already. Then come home and sleep in."

Becca joined Hailey in the parlor and checked herself, one last time, from all angles in the full-length mirror near the front door. The cowgirl boots dressed her outfit down enough, but perhaps she should reconsider. It was more of a jeans kind of place.

"Hey, Becs. He's turning into the drive. Better scat."

Becca exited the kitchen door as Cody was coming through the front. Once in the clear, she breathed a sigh of relief, revved up the flatbed and headed toward a place that hadn't been tainted by her past.

Mercifully enough, it looked as though it was going to stay that way.

THE DRIVE BACK to the Hideaway had done Cody a world of good. Cleared his mind of this ridiculous desire to have dinner with Becca tonight. What had he been thinking? She'd clearly thought it was an awful idea as well.

An excellent idea, however, would have been to take Vern up on his offer. Cody could easily visualize incorporating his mantra with that mechanical bull. It would've taken his two-dimensional routine to full on 3D and allowed him to keep the most vital muscles activated and toned and on high alert. Unfortunately, his only opportunity had come and gone. He wouldn't have time in the morning.

He walked through the parlor, then the business office. No sign of Becca. No one except a couple sitting on the sofa, too wrapped up in one another to even notice him walk by. Must be the honeymooners.

Becca wasn't in the kitchen either. Only her assistant, sitting on a barstool, chomping on a large celery stick.

"Hi, stranger," she said, mouth half-full.

"Hailey, right? Is Becca around?"

She dipped the clean end of the stalk in a jar of peanut butter. "Just left. Anything I can help you with?" she asked before taking another big bite.

His stomach growled. "Any idea when she'll be back?"

Hailey shrugged. "Not anytime soon. She said she'd be gone a while. Did you guys have plans?"

"Apparently not. Mind if I have one?" Cody pointed to the bunch that had been disassembled and trimmed and washed.

"Knock yourself out. There's a leftover piece of cheesecake in the fridge. You're welcome to that instead."

"Thanks, but I'm actually a big celery fan."

"Seriously? That makes two of us. In fact, I don't know anyone else who would choose this over dessert," Hailey said. "We must be related."

Cody took a huge bite. Cool and crunchy. Hit the spot.

"Maybe I'm your brother from another mother," he said.

She laughed. "I always wanted one of those."

Cody finished off one stalk, grabbed another and pointed to the peanut butter. "May I?"

She nudged the jar toward him. "I didn't double-dip. I promise."

"Your parents taught you well."

"Thanks. I'm down to one now. Lost my dad five years ago."

"Lost my mom when I was six. My dad was on the hook to raise me and my two older brothers."

"Get out of here. I have two older sisters. Maybe we should set up our parents and become a modern-day Brady Bunch."

Funny, but there was a familiarity about Hailey he couldn't put his finger on. Maybe it was because she had written the fan letter on Max's behalf. Or maybe it was because he'd always wanted a little sister and was now projecting. Not that he needed to form ties to anyone else here. If anything, he needed to detach.

Yet, maybe Hailey could shed some light on Max's father. Even though Cody already didn't like the guy, he hoped Max wouldn't have to go through life without ever knowing him. No child should have to do that.

His stomach growled louder this time. The

celery-and-peanut-butter combo wasn't cutting it.

"Sounds like someone needs a proper meal," Hailey said. "I'd offer to make something for you here, but that's not my forte. In fact, I'm pretty much banned from using any of the appliances. Hence the celery and peanut butter."

"No worries. I'll figure out something fast and easy. It's been a long day."

"I imagine. I heard you took Max to Fraser Ranch. Did you meet Vern?"

Cody nodded. "Yes. We had a nice, long visit."

"With Vern, that's the only kind you can have. Super-sweet man, though. Drop-dead gorgeous grandson, too, if you're into the Breitling-and-Mercedes type. Pretty sure Parker has his sights set on Becca."

Hailey took another bite of celery and didn't blink. Was she trying to make Cody jealous? Because, if she was, it was working.

His stomach growled again. Louder this time.

Hailey giggled. "Eat something decent before the other guests complain about the noise. See a few sights while you're out. I can make some recommendations." She rummaged through a drawer next to her and produced a single sheet of paper. "This is the short list of establishments within reasonable driving distance. If you plan to have a beer or two, I recommend sticking close to home. I don't want to read about you in the papers for anything other than riding bulls."

The list was short, for sure. A steakhouse, a burger joint and a bar. "Which do you recommend?" he asked.

"Depends on what you're looking for."

"I like your idea about seeing a few sights."

Hailey pursed her lips. "Well, if sights are what you want to see, then I recommend you be a bit of a renegade."

He looked more closely at the list. *Renegade.* Brews 'n' Bites. Live music. Dancing. Pool. Exactly the kind of place he *didn't* want to go.

Then again, it might be perfect. He could eat without being watched, since patrons would be dancing and socializing with each other. In general, minding their own business. He always blended into a crowd when there was a band.

Best of all, it would take his mind off the crazy, whirlwind day.

And off Becca.

THE ONLY OTHER time Becca had been to Renegade, it was half empty. Not tonight. Must have something to do with the Montgomery

Legend rumor, which meant that perhaps it wasn't a rumor after all.

As soon as she checked her coat, she knew she'd made the right decision. The wrap dress was gifted with appreciative looks. No doubt, these cowboys were denim-weary. All the other women wore jeans.

She parked herself on the first available barstool but quickly reconsidered her attire. A wrap dress was the worst choice ever. The skirt parted and threatened to stay that way. She had to pin the ends together using her thighs and knees. So much for looking refined and elegant.

A quick glance around the horseshoe bar and beyond confirmed that she'd nabbed the last available seat in the joint, except for one at a six-top across the room. Not surprising. The parking lot was so full, she'd had to create a space on the side of the road.

"What can I get for you?" the bartender asked.

Either she was getting old or the folks they hired for such jobs were getting younger. Forget the fact that he didn't even bother asking for her ID. She, on the other hand, considered asking for his.

"Virgin Mary, please. Extra spicy."

"Yes, ma'am. Coming right up."

The live band started playing. The Emma-line Tucker Band, if the logo printed on the skin of the bass drum was any indication. Becca had never heard of her, but her voice was amazing. And the tune was catchy.

Made sense that they'd be good. If Montgomery Legend really was going to make an appearance, it would likely be when they had a decent band. Especially if he decided to jam with them for a while.

The bartender returned with her drink.

"How much?" Even though she planned to have more than one, it might be difficult to get the guy's attention if she decided to leave early.

"Actually, ma'am, it's been paid for. Enjoy."

"Wait! Who—?"

Too late. The youngster was already popping the cap off a beer and sliding it in front of another customer. She adjusted her skirt again, her knees doing a poor job of making the silky material behave.

"Bad decision," she muttered under her breath, then shook her head.

"Next time, have 'em put vodka in it," the man next to her said.

"Excellent advice," she said.

He smiled and resumed looking straight ahead. She halfway expected some sort of pickup line, but none was forthcoming. As soon as he finished his beer, he tabbed out, tipped his hat to Becca and left.

She scanned the bar for a familiar face. A few men kept staring, but no one came over to claim credit for the drink.

"Excuse me," she called out to the bartender, determined to get an answer. He leaned halfway in and continued to pop the cap on yet another beer. "Who paid for this?"

"The gentleman sitting next to you. The one who left. He bought a round for the bar. You got in on the tail end of the deal."

"Oh. I see. Thanks."

So much for someone being interested, even though that was the last thing she needed. On second thought, that was exactly what she needed. She simply wasn't in a place to return the sentiment.

She took in a long sip. The bartender did good. Super spicy. She needed another drink just to wash down her current one. Meanwhile, her knees were getting tired of holding her dress closed, so she stood and let the fabric do what it was supposed to do. Wrap and flow.

A stranger stopped in his tracks.

"Looks like you're either ready to leave or ready to dance. I'd ask you for the honor, but I'm the world's worst two-stepper."

He wasn't hard on the eyes by any stretch.

Age appropriate and charmingly self-depre-cating.

"Hate to break it to you, but I'm the worst," she said.

He put his hands on his hips. "Oh, yeah? Wanna bet?"

She set her drink on the bar. "You're on."

The man extended his arm, and she obliged.

"The one who breaks the most toes wins," he said.

They worked their way to the inside of the dance floor. The outside lane was reserved for better dancers. After a rough start, they fell into a not-too-embarrassing rhythm.

"What brings you here?" he asked.

"Montgomery Legend," she said. Might as well be honest. "How about you?"

"On-the-job training."

"You work here? Ouch! You got me," she said.

"Sorry! I was hoping that wasn't your foot. Guess that puts me in the lead."

"What kind of work do you do?" she asked.

"Dance instructor."

Becca burst out laughing. He looked so seri-ous. "Good one. What do you really do?" she managed to say.

"I teach ballroom dancing. Tango and salsa

too. I'm looking to expand my offerings to include the two-step. Ouch! That smarts."

"Guess that means we're even," she said.

"Not quite. You laughed at my reason for being here."

"Sorry. But it was rather funny."

He broke into a wide grin. "I agree. Just teasing ya."

They ambled along for a few more stanzas, managing to not collide with each other or anyone else.

"Oh, look! Isn't that Montgomery Legend?" he asked.

Becca glanced in the direction he was staring. "Where? I don't see him."

The moment she looked back at him, he spun her around in the most fluid motion and laughed.

"Gotcha! *Now* we're even," he said.

She had to smile. "You sure did, and we certainly are."

The song ended, and he escorted her back to her seat.

"Bartender, please get this lady whatever she was drinking. A Virgin Mary, right?" He plopped down a twenty.

"You don't have to do that. It was a tie, remember?"

"All I remember is dancing with a beautiful lady who made me laugh. Now I better get home and put some ice on this foot."

Becca snorted.

"Next time I run into you here, I'll be the best two-stepper on the floor," he said. "We'll put all those cowboys and cowgirls to shame. Deal?"

"Deal," she said.

He looked toward the entrance, then back at her. "Hey, I think Montgomery is here. Folks are getting all worked up about something."

Becca shook her head. "Not falling for it again. Not even going to look."

"Don't say I didn't warn you." He smiled, tipped his hat and left.

Only after she saw him fully exit did she look around, in case he hadn't been teasing. Sure enough, folks were congregating around someone. Too dark and crowded to see him, though. How would she ever get close enough for an autograph?

The band stopped playing, and Emmaline Tucker started talking.

"Hey, folks. Seems we have a special visitor tonight."

It was all Becca could do not to squeal.

"I hate to embarrass the fella," the singer continued. "Probably thought he could stay under the radar. But I'm afraid the rest of y'all would never let me live it down if I didn't point him out."

Becca continued to look in the direction of the gathering crowd.

Emmaline continued. "Tony, block the door in case our surprise guest tries to make a run for it."

Becca followed the spotlight, which landed on a black cowboy hat that looked like all the others. She had to get closer.

"Can I get a drumroll, Travis?" Emmaline said. "Ladies and gents, give a warm welcome to the Rodeo Rascal himself, Cody Sayers."

Becca nearly dropped her Virgin Mary.

Nooo...

The limelight had found him once again, confirming her greatest fear.

There was no safe place to hide from her past.

CODY SQUINTED INTO the crowd. The spotlight nearly blinded him.

This was even worse than the worst-case scenario he'd envisioned while driving over. Tonight was supposed to be downtime. Not showtime. At least Becca wasn't around to witness this embarrassing spectacle.

Cody deployed his trademark grin and waved. The guys shook his hand. The ladies insisted on giving him a hug as if he were public property and didn't have a say. He tried to dodge a few cell-phone cameras as he made his way to the bar. One of the patrons gave up his seat for Cody.

The bartender was Johnny-on-the-Spot. "Can I get you a beer, Mr. Sayers?"

"Zero-alcohol one, please. I'm my own designated driver tonight." Not to mention, his publicist had positioned him as being in Wyoming to meet a child fan. To clean up his rascal image and everything that implied.

The bartender set a cold one down, along with a couple of limes. Cody made a show of it for the phone cameras pointed his direction. Fortunately, the band launched into another song, and within minutes, the crowd dispersed and people got back to minding their own business. At least, most of them did. Besides, it wasn't as if he was a real celebrity. More like a compartmentalized one.

He texted his publicist. Told her not to panic if she saw any photos, because he'd hopefully dodged a bullet tonight. And, he would try to snap a picture with his young fan for her tomorrow. *Try* being the operative word.

"I heard you were in town," the man sitting next to him said. "I saw you ride in Colorado, some five years ago, and admired the way you covered. I said to my wife, 'You wait and see. That Cody Sayers is gonna be someone.'"

"I hope I won't make a liar out of you." Cody raised his bottle and clinked it against the guy's bourbon on the rocks.

The man let out a hearty laugh. "You're funny. I didn't know you had a sense of humor."

"Kinda have to, with what I do."

"I suppose you're right. Probably why the ladies love you. That pretty one across the bar hasn't so much as blinked since you sat down. Straight ahead at your eleven o'clock."

Oh boy. Only one way to handle this. A tip of the hat to be polite, a swig of nonbeer so the whole bottle wouldn't go to waste and out the door he'd go. Maybe the burger joint had a drive-through window, because he wasn't too keen on being filmed while he was trying to eat, and he could still feel a few cameras on him here.

"Eleven o'clock, huh?" Did he really want to entertain this?

"Yes, sir. Boy, is she a stunner."

"Lucky me." *Not.* Cody took a deep breath, looked across the bar with his trademark grin firmly in place.

She didn't smile back. Took him a full two seconds to figure out why.

Becca?

Instead, she looked away and struck up a conversation with the man sitting next to her. They both laughed about something.

He used to make her laugh. Couldn't remember the last time that had happened.

Perhaps it was the competitor in him—or the knucklehead in him who kept doing ill-thought-out, impulsive things—but all of a sudden, he was determined to at least make her smile. He summoned the bartender back over.

"Yes, sir?"

"See that lady across the bar, in the green dress?"

"Can't miss her."

"Ask her if she plans on eating that celery stalk that's in her Virgin Mary and, if not, would she mind sharing it with me. Tell her my dinner date stood me up, and I'm starving."

Bartenders probably heard every confession and secret under the sun and were asked to do all sorts of favors, but this had to be a first. It was private joke that the guy would never get. But if he played along, he would get a generous tip.

The young man did as Cody asked. Sure enough, she giggled, then looked at him again. He felt a giggle rise in his throat as well. Not because any of this was funny. He realized he'd done the exact opposite of what he'd come here to do tonight.

Someone tapped him on the shoulder. He turned to look.

"Can I take a picture with you?" the woman asked. The man with her nodded in approval.

"Sure. A quick one," he said.

The lady handed the phone to her partner and pressed her cheek against Cody's. The man backed up, then moved forward, then changed angles until he was satisfied he'd got two or three good ones.

The woman grabbed the phone and scanned through them while standing there.

"Thank you so much!" she said, apparently happy with the selection.

By the time Cody turned back around, the stalk of celery had been placed in front of him, and the seat at his eleven o'clock was empty. He scanned the bar, the dance floor and the pool tables. The vision in green was nowhere around.

Don't panic.

Too late. He could already feel it, the way his heart ticked up a few notches and every muscle tensed. Like when he knew he was about to get hung up during a ride.

Cody slapped a bill on the bar, grabbed the celery stick and headed for the door. He kept his chin down so that the brim of his hat obscured much of his face. He managed to weave through the crowd without being stopped again.

No sign of Becca outside.

Her truck was in its designated spot when he got back to the Hideaway.

The gas fireplace provided the only light downstairs. Becca must have gone straight to bed. He started to head upstairs to his room, but when he grabbed the banister, it jiggled. Some kids had been sliding down it earlier. Probably loosened a bolt or screw. Couldn't leave that unfixed.

He started opening doors and drawers in search of the toolbox he'd used for repairs earlier and located it in a kitchen pantry. After extracting the Phillips head, he knelt and tightened a loose screw at the base and tested it. That should work for a while, but the wood could use replacing soon.

Since no one was around, he plopped on the overstuffed sofa and soaked in the warmth of the fireplace.

In less than forty-eight hours, he'd managed to get too comfortable here. He'd reopened some wounds in the process and set the stage for new ones. The whole point of coming to Destiny Springs had been to surprise his biggest little fan. The biggest surprise was how much fun he'd had around the little cowboy. Felt as though he'd not only met a fan, he'd made a friend. No way he could simply disappear.

Nor did he want to leave on bad terms with Becca again, and something about what'd happened at Renegade felt that way. He certainly hadn't come here to entertain any feelings about her at all, but they were happening anyway.

That left two loose threads that his current flight out wouldn't allow him to repair. As soon as he could muster enough energy, he'd go to his room, fire up his laptop and cancel his standby.

His original reservation was still in place. He could spend part of his days practicing on the mechanical bull, some of his time visiting with his biggest fan and the rest proving he wasn't the mischievous rascal that the media made him out to be. Becca needed a helping hand around the B and B. More so than he'd originally thought.

And he happened to have two willing-and-able ones.

CHAPTER SEVEN

NOTHING WAS QUITE as unsettling as waking up from some crazy dream, only to discover it had really happened. Case in point: going to a club to meet Montgomery Legend and running into the ex-husband instead.

But waking up to find that ex-husband sleeping on the sofa in the community parlor? That was downright disturbing. Cody must have had quite a night at Renegade after Becca left, because he apparently couldn't even make it to his room.

She'd let her guard down last night. He'd made her laugh with the whole celery-stick request, only to turn on a dime and abandon her the minute a fan tapped him on the shoulder.

Why did she believe, even for a moment, that he had changed?

In many ways, however, she had not. She retrieved a blanket from a linen closet and draped it over his legs. Couldn't help herself. Cody didn't so much as stir. He'd always slept like a champ. By contrast, she could usually be found pacing the floors at night, worrying about whether he'd come home from an event unharmed. Or even alive, for that matter.

Oddly enough, insomnia became her best friend once she opened the Hideaway. It was the teammate she'd needed but didn't get in her spouse. She accomplished much of the initial renovation on this place during the predawn hours.

She padded quietly toward the kitchen but nearly tripped over something on the way.

Turned out to be the Phillips screwdriver. Cody had been the last to handle the toolbox. Had he left it lying around? It wasn't like him to be that careless.

The screwdriver wasn't the only thing on the floor. Something black and lifeless was hunched along the baseboard. A rat? Her lungs constricted.

No. Too big, judging by the silhouette. Whatever it was, it would have scampered away by now if it were alive. She watched it for a full minute, but it didn't move. Didn't appear to be breathing either.

With the toe of her house shoe, she nudged it. No response. Upon closer inspection, she noticed something shiny. Silver-star medallions.

Cody's Stetson. Or what was left of it.

Becca collected the limp, soggy remains. Penny must have used it as a bully stick, judging from the torn crown and puncture marks all over the brim. She was thankful Penny hadn't swallowed any of the metal bits.

Where was the puppy, anyway? Penny usually slept with Max in his room. Since he was at a sleepover, Hailey must have let her have free rein of the house.

She finally found the pup in the kitchen, asleep. Becca pulled the pocket door closed, turned on only the necessary lights and tossed the felt remains onto a chair in the breakfast nook. Vern would arrive any minute with the egg delivery. She'd wake up Cody after he left and before other guests started their day. The last thing she wanted people to see was Cody passed out on the sofa, mouth ajar and hair hopelessly tousled.

Like clockwork, Vern tapped at the door. Penny snapped awake but thankfully didn't bark.

It looked like a Christmas card, the way the frosty windowpane framed Vern's adorable, scruffy, gray-bearded face. She rushed to unlock it.

"Special delivery." He raised the crate. A bigger-than-usual one this time.

"Please, come in. May I help you with those?"

"A cup of coffee would help more. Haven't even had my first cup yet."

"Me neither. I'll join you."

Becca promptly set the coffee maker in motion while he positioned the crate securely on the kitchen counter. Vern removed his plaid wool scarf and draped it haphazardly on the edge of the bar, then took a seat at the breakfast table. Fortunately, he chose the hatless chair.

She emptied a carton of fresh strawberries into a strainer and rinsed them, then spread them out across some paper towels to dry while they talked. Penny was promptly at Vern's side for a petting session. He didn't disappoint.

"Max tells me he's getting to know Hailey's horses. Seems real excited about it too."

"She's been teaching him a few things about horsemanship."

"Good! I was hoping you'd let the little fella spend some time in the saddle. I'd have Perry on a horse in a jiffy if he showed any interest at all."

"Riding will come later. She's starting him off with the basics. Feeding and watering and whatnot." She privately hoped *later* never came, in this instance.

The coffee maker finished its task. Vern

got up and filled two mugs and returned to his seat. He placed her mug directly across from his and patted at the table for her to join. Looked like she was being set up for a heartfelt conversation. With Vern, the two went hand in hand, like newlyweds.

She recalled that the honeymooners staying at the B and B had left a message. They were pleased about the prompt repairs to their room. Two other guests left equally rave reviews about the new help around the place. As much as she wished Cody had never come back into her life, he'd certainly bailed her out yesterday.

Becca perched on the edge of the breakfast-table chair, careful not to further crush the hat. Not that it mattered. Penny had totaled it. She wrapped both hands around the warm mug and thought about how she could wrap up the conversation. This wasn't the best morning for a long chat. Not with her ex-husband passed out on a sofa in the other room.

"To what do I owe the honor of a personal delivery? Vanessa tells me you have Trent working on a special project this morning. Are you sure he's not trying to avoid me?" Becca asked.

Vern laughed. "Not a chance. He'd leave the ranch in a heartbeat to work for you full-time."

"Doubtful, although I could use the help. Not sure I could afford him, though. I hear you're very generous."

"I try to be. It's a good policy. Generosity always comes back around."

A heavy topic for this early in the morning. She nodded in agreement all the same.

"I worry about you sometimes, my dear," he continued. "You try to do too much."

And an even heavier one.

She took a sip of coffee. Sweetener. That's what was missing. She grabbed a packet from the sugar bowl sitting on the table between them. "I'm fine, Vern. I took on this project willingly. I knew what I was getting into. I'm not going to abandon it."

Speaking of coming back around, her own words did exactly that. She'd willingly entered into marriage with Cody. She'd known what she was getting into. Yet, she'd abandoned it when there wasn't enough sweetener.

Then again, so had he.

Vern let out an audible *Hmm*.

He always knew when she had something weighing on her, but she wasn't going to burden him with such problems. Not first thing in the morning. In fact, not ever. He knew she was divorced, but he didn't know the details or even the name. No doubt it wouldn't take long for him to put two and two together. Until then, she hoped to enjoy the anonymity she'd thought she would find here in Destiny Springs.

While they both sipped their coffee in silence, her long to-do list grew longer. At least she didn't have to worry about having enough eggs. Speaking of which...

"Coffee is a paltry payment for all of those," she said, nodding toward the crate. "Let me at least fix you something to eat. Biscuits and my secret sausage gravy, perhaps?"

"I guess I should confess something. Your food is why I wanted to deliver the eggs personally this morning."

"Really? You like them that much? Why didn't you say something sooner?" To think she rarely offered that option to her guests, and she'd only served them to Vern once. Perhaps she should branch out.

Vern shook his head. "Don't get me wrong, I love that dish. But I heard a rumor that you served something even better at breakfast the other day. Some kind of *migas*?"

Either the rumor mill had a loose screw or she was out of her mind, because she hadn't fixed any such thing two days ago. In fact, she'd burned the eggs. Cody, on the other hand...

"I'm not sure whether I have all the ingredients. Can I tempt you with something else?"

Vern polished off his coffee in record time, rinsed his mug out in the sink and looked around. "Didn't I leave my scarf right here?"

Becca remembered him putting it there, as well. Where it could easily slide off and end up in the wrong hands. Or the wrong mouth, in this case.

She stood. "Penny? Where are you?"

The sound of puppy nails on hardwood gave the culprit away. She had the scarf in her mouth, a fringed end trailing in her wake, and she was raring to play.

The chase was on. Fortunately, two legs proved faster than three in this scenario. Becca was able to reclaim the scarf. She slid the kitchen door open enough to nudge the pup back into the main part of the house. Upon close examination of the scarf, it appeared that no visible damage was done.

"I'll get this dry-cleaned," she said.

Vern eased it out of her grip. "Nonsense. I work on a ranch. This scarf has endured much worse than a little doggy spittle." He didn't take a seat again, which he'd usually have done. "I'm afraid my payment for the extra eggs this morning is a plate of those *migas*. No hurry, though. I'll be happy to swing back by around ten and crash your breakfast. Or even after your next grocery-store run. Just a few bites will do so I don't feel left out of the conversation."

"You're always welcome here, but rumors are tricky things. Trent shared one that Montgomery Legend was going to make an appearance at Renegade last night. He didn't."

"I heard that one too. Sorry you chased it. But I'll take my chances with the food. What have I got to lose?"

"I'll bring a plate to you when it's ready," she promised.

So much for not asking Cody for help.

SET THE ROPE, handle in deep…

The beast yanked and pulled, then yanked again.

Where was its head?

At least he could see its shoulders. That was the important thing.

But in that momentary lack of focus, he spilled off the bull and onto the soft, cushiony—cushiony?—ground, where the beast began to lick his ear…

Cody opened his eyes, thus putting a merciful end to the weirdest dream ever. Yet, that didn't explain why the inside of his ear was sopping wet. Still half-asleep, he tugged the corner of the blanket and swabbed his ear canal. A little better.

When he yawned and turned his head, he came face-to-face with a brown, shaggy-coated dog, inches away. Staring at him.

He shot up to a sitting position and scanned the room. Where was he, anyway? Still inside that weird dream?

Oh, yeah. The B and B.

Now he remembered. He'd sat down in front of the fireplace for a minute last night after tightening the banister. Must have fallen asleep.

He reached out and gave the dog a thorough petting. The furiously wagging tail told him that, although it had been several years since he'd owned a dog—make that *since a dog had owned him*—he hadn't lost his touch.

The sun was starting to rise, but thankfully no one else was around. Last night came barreling back to him like an angry bull with a personal vendetta. The look on Becca's face. The giggle. Her disappearance after he'd placated a fan. What little progress he'd made with Becca had been reversed in an instant.

Since he was going back to his original plan and would be hanging around Destiny Springs for a spell longer, he would have a little more time to hopefully undo this latest damage.

Then there was Sally. What an unexpected gift. The mechanical bull was going to be a game changer. Nothing like her that he knew of in Scottsdale. He'd go to Vern's this morning, fire her up and put in some practice time. It was exactly what he needed to reset his mind and emotions and postpone any discussion with Becca until they both were ready.

Judging by the way she'd bolted, she likely woke up feeling the same way.

Such conversations used to end up the same anyway. Like a dog chasing its tail and never catching it. Becca thought he cared more about his fans than he did her. He thought she should know that talking to fans was nothing more than part and parcel of his career. If he hadn't been able to convince her back then, he likely wouldn't be able to now. At least, not with words.

Cody made his way upstairs and located the room he'd barely used. He looked around for a one-cup coffee maker like so many hotels furnished, but no such luck. He brushed his teeth, took a quick shower and changed into a fresh T-shirt and jeans. His Stetson, however, wasn't anywhere in his room.

Must have left it downstairs.

Other than that, he felt like a new man. Ready to tackle the day and get his life back on track after the proverbial train wreck that was last night. Which begged the question: Had Hailey known what she was doing when she'd suggested Renegade, albeit in a round-about way? He might never know.

He opened his laptop and logged on to the airline website. His finger hovered over the Cancel Standby link for several seconds while he did a final gut check.

Yep, this felt right.

Once downstairs, Cody searched the parlor high and low for his Stetson. Even went back outside to his rental truck. Last thing he remembered was taking it off when he leaned back on the sofa for the minute that had turned into hours. It wasn't on the floor or coffee table or beneath the blanket that he had no recollection of crawling underneath.

He followed the scent of fresh-brewed coffee to the kitchen but paused before sliding the door open. Best to keep this as neutral as possible for now. He'd ask if she'd seen his hat, offer to pay for a cup of coffee and politely excuse himself.

As soon as he opened the door, however, his resolve was bucked to the ground. Although she wasn't dancing this time, she looked so warm and inviting in her oversize sweatshirt and leggings and fuzzy slippers.

He cleared his throat to let her know he was there. She stopped whatever she was doing and looked up. Before he had the chance to keep it simple and make a quick exit, Becca spoke.

"I'm glad you're awake. We need to talk."

"CAN I BOTHER you for a cup of coffee first?" Cody asked. "In a to-go cup if you have one. I'll pay you for it."

Ouch. That was quite the departure from his obvious flirtation last night. Not that Becca blamed him. If she didn't need a favor, she'd be grateful for the reprieve from having to explain why she'd disappeared so quickly.

Good thing she'd made a full pot. Everybody wanted a cup from her this morning, and she had a feeling she'd need more than a few herself.

She rummaged through the cabinet, located a thermal travel mug and filled it to the top. By the time she turned around, Cody had discovered what was left of his hat. She'd all but forgotten about it, with everything else on her mind. He held up the remains and raised a brow.

Becca eased the scrap from his hand and replaced it with the warm coffee mug. "Sorry about that. I'll reimburse you. Our pup usually stays in Max's room at night."

She wanted to add that the guests were usually tucked away in their own rooms overnight too, where something like this wouldn't have happened. But she bit the inside of her cheek instead. She still needed the *migas* recipe.

"My fault for sleeping on the sofa," he offered.

"I'm sorry for bolting out of Renegade last—"

"No apology or explanation necessary," he said, shutting her down.

They held each other's gaze for what felt like an eternity. "I just thought you should know that I went there hoping to meet someone else."

Both of his brows rose this time. "Sorry to disappoint you."

"No, I don't mean it that way. Montgomery Legend was supposed to make an appearance. He's my mom's favorite country-western singer. I was hoping to get an autograph for her. And maybe a selfie so she could brag about it to her friends."

As soon as the last part slipped out, she realized that was exactly what Cody's fan had been trying to do last night. Like any decent celebrity would, he had obliged. His slow nod indicated he was likely thinking the same thing.

Unfortunately, he had to abandon his flirtation with her to accommodate it. Therein lay the dilemma.

"I never knew that about Rose," Cody said.

She waited for him to ask how she was doing, but no such inquiry was forthcoming.

"Anyway, that wasn't why I wanted to talk to you," she continued.

"If it's about the hat, don't worry about it." He leaned against the edge of the counter as if settling in for a discussion. Wherever he was going that required a to-go cup could obviously wait.

"No. It's about the dish you made the other day."

"Oh, that. I guess it's my turn to apologize. My plan was to drop it off and hightail it back to my room. Try to locate my fan later—you know how that turned out."

True, he had simply been standing at the barn doorway instead of making a grand entrance. He'd gotten swept up in the circumstances. He'd also taken full advantage of it.

"No doubt you were popular, but your dish made the real news. Vern dropped off the eggs this morning, and he wants a sample. Won't take no for an answer. So I was thinking of asking you for the recipe."

"I can't."

Again, ouch.

"You wouldn't have to actually *make* it. I'll do the cooking."

"Maybe Hailey could try to whip up something similar for you," he offered. "Oh, except she's banned from the kitchen, right?"

How did he know that? Not that Hailey was literally banned. It was simply that the young woman couldn't boil water without it catching on fire.

"Is that what she told you?" *And did she also tell you I would be at Renegade?*

"We chatted a little."

Becca pinched the bridge of her nose to dissuade a headache that was coming on. She didn't need this today. "Forget I asked about the recipe. I'll come up with something for Vern. It's not like he'll know the difference."

Becca resumed slicing strawberries with more focus. Not that she should be surprised about Cody wanting to get to know Hailey a little better. She was an attractive young woman. What did surprise her was her own reaction.

Cody pushed off from the counter, placed both of his hands on her shoulders and gave them a gentle squeeze. The gesture felt familiar. He was trying to comfort her, but why? Her request seemed like a simple one. And, although she was a little miffed, it wasn't all that upsetting. Frustrating, definitely.

She straightened her shoulders, but he didn't remove his hands. Her feelings about it were ping-ponging. She wanted to feel his touch, she didn't want to feel his touch, she wanted...

"Does this mean you'll give me the recipe?" she asked.

He gave her shoulders a final squeeze, and her body relaxed at what felt to be an unspoken *yes*. Until his long exhale said otherwise, and his words confirmed it.

"I'm sorry, Becca. The answer is still no."

BECCA TENSED, THEN wiggled out from under his touch altogether and continued slicing and dicing strawberries within an inch of their lives. Probably not the best time to tease an ex-wife who, up until a couple of days ago, had disappeared from his life completely.

"The reason I can't give you the recipe is because I don't remember it," he said in the softest voice he could manage. "Honest."

She turned to face him. Gosh, he'd forgotten how stunning she was up close. He had mentally connected her faded freckles a million times. After all these years, he could still picture the map with his eyes closed.

"What kind of game are you playing?" she asked.

He stepped back. He knew her well enough to know when she needed space. "No game. You didn't have the ingredients I ordinarily use, so I had to improvise."

She shook her head. "That's convenient."

"I can re-create it though. I'm certain. Let me visualize for a minute."

She snorted, which was exactly what he hoped she'd do. She always did get a kick out of it whenever he mentioned his process. And it added a little levity to a discussion that had taken a wrong turn at his attempt to be clever.

He closed his eyes, shook his hands in a dramatic fashion, pressed his index and middle fingers to his temples and hummed.

"Yes, I see it now," he said. "A woman. Dancing."

"Very funny," she said.

"Wait… Something's on fire. Her auburn hair? No. It's something else. I see burned eggs and chorizo. No, andouille sausage."

He felt a playful swat on his arm and opened his eyes. That smirk of hers could possibly grow into a smile if he played his cards right. He stepped in and put his arms around her waist. She started to push away but didn't follow through.

"May I?" he asked.

She visibly gulped. In one swift move, he untied her apron and whisked it off, swooshed it in front of her like a matador, then tied it around his own waist.

"You're incorrigible," she said, shaking her head.

"If I'm going to re-create the dish, I'll need to actually walk through the process. Some visualizations benefit from hands-on application."

Like with bull riding. So much for getting in some practice on the mechanical bull this morning. This shouldn't take too long, however. Besides, there was something he wanted in return.

He culled through the spice rack in search of the familiar. Paprika, cumin and oregano. Definitely. From there, he scoured the fridge. Oh yeah, sliced, pickled jalapeños. And barely enough sausage to scrape by. It was coming back to him now.

"What do you hope to get out of this besides a new Stetson?" she asked.

"Nothing for me. It would be for Max."

It had been on his mind since meeting his biggest little fan. Besides, there wasn't anything he wanted personally. Except maybe a little more of what they were experiencing right now and for those few moments last night.

"Wait. Stop," she said.

He complied. He'd taken this game too far already. What he was about to ask wouldn't render an easy *yes*. Nor would it make a difference whether he helped with the dish.

She crossed those lovely arms of hers. "Why do I have the feeling you already know what my answer will be, even though I don't know the demand?"

"Because you're smart. And you're a good mom."

"I'm definitely not stupid. About most things, at least. How do you know I'm a good mom?"

"You'll go to any lengths to make sure the ones you love don't get hurt. I'm not sure I'm that noble."

He wanted to state the obvious, as well. There were different kinds of hurts. The physical kind, like she was afraid of and always focused on. And the emotional kind, like having to give up one's dream.

If Max were anything like Cody as a little boy—and from all indications, he was—a mother's love and support could make or break his dreams. Cody's own mother had encouraged him in that respect. He'd sustained injuries and never once questioned her love for him. As a matter of fact, he would have questioned it if she'd held him back.

Since Max's dad wasn't around, someone had to play devil's advocate.

"Not that noble, huh?" she said. "Care to elaborate?"

The answer would require more conversation than he was willing or had time to take on. He had a date at Fraser Ranch with a tougher gal than Becca, although that point could be debated.

"Not a chance," he said, adding that mischievous grin that she hated.

"Then, give me the basic ingredients."

"They're all right here," he said, blocking her view. "Lined up and ready to combine."

"What's your request for Max?"

"Let me teach him how to ride."

CHAPTER EIGHT

BECCA KNEW SHE'D been postponing the inevitable. In fact, that was what she did best.

"Horseback-riding lessons, huh?" she asked, even though it was rhetorical.

At least, she hoped it was. Max had been talking about riding bulls lately. But he'd been fascinated with horses all his life. Between the two evils, it sounded like Cody was encouraging the lesser one.

"Hailey has an older, seasoned quarter horse that would be a perfect starter. I figured that since you're encouraging him to be around them, and if he's eventually going to ride, maybe I could ease him into it. Safely. I won't leave his side."

"I thought you were leaving today. When is all this teaching supposed to happen?"

"Change of plans," he said but didn't elaborate.

Everything was getting even more twisted and confusing. "I need some time to think about it. When is your flight? I can barely keep up with my own schedule, much less anyone else's."

"In about a week and a half."

He might as well have said he was staying for good, because no telling what directions her emotions would go in that length of time. They were already scattered all over the place, wanting him to leave now, then hoping that he'd move closer in this moment and embrace her like he used to do. She thought she'd left those feelings behind when she moved to Destiny Springs. In fact, she'd made a point of it. Turned out, they'd been traitorous little stowaways all along.

Her heart wasn't the only thing she'd need to protect. Max's birthday was two weeks away. Ten more days was cutting it close. Cody could *not* be there, doing some math of his own. So she did something she'd never outwardly done before: encouraged him to ride bulls.

"Scottsdale, right? That's wonderful."

"I intend for it to be. I need the points. Then on to Houston. Can't miss that."

Becca bit her lip. She hadn't thought the mere mention of a certain town could still make made her stomach crumple up like tin foil. "Does your dad still live there?"

Cody nodded. "Alive and kicking."

"He must be very proud of you."

"I suppose. If he isn't now, he will be. I'll make sure of it. In the meantime, I'm gonna teach *you* how to cook a small batch of *migas*, and I'll take some to Vern." He pulled six eggs from the crate and turned on the front burner.

"You two really hit it off, huh?" Becca asked.

"Sure feels like it."

That was a good thing. She'd encourage that as well. More time at Vern's meant less time around Max. And her.

Cody proceeded to scramble the eggs, looking a little too at home in her terry-cloth apron. A little too mixed up with her already mixed-up world, like all the sausage and jalapeños and seasonings he was now combining. Unlike what life had dished out for her, the one he'd finished creating looked and smelled amazing.

"May I try it?" she asked.

He assembled a forkful of all the ingredients and raised it to her mouth. She eased the fork from his hand, unwilling to do that thing they used to do: feed each other.

It tasted even better than it smelled. "Okay, I get why my guests loved it," she said.

There it was. That confident smirk of his again.

"I hope you were paying attention to how I

pulled it all together because, as I mentioned, I don't have a recipe. I winged it. Again."

Honestly, she hadn't absorbed any of it. Her focus was wrecked on so many levels now. No matter what she was feeling, the outcome would be the same. He would leave again. Which reminded her of something else.

While Cody was busy searching the cabinets for a Tupperware container in which to take Vern's portion, she went to the closet and retrieved something she'd held on to for the past six years. She pulled it down from its hiding place on a shelf, then paused.

He needed it now more than ever, after Penny had used his other Stetson as a chew toy. More important, she owed it to herself to finally let go, and what better way to start?

But by the time she mustered up the courage and returned to the kitchen, Cody was gone. She clutched the hat to her chest, careful not to bend it. Rather than setting it on the counter, she would return it to the safety of the closet. Just until he was ready to leave. At least, that's what she told herself.

Her heart, however, wasn't buying it.

CODY CHUCKLED ALL the way to Fraser Ranch.

Giving Becca a taste of her own medicine and pulling a disappearing act when she wasn't looking? Priceless. Perhaps a bit juvenile too, he had to admit. Otherwise, his new plan was officially on track. A couple of lights were on downstairs when he arrived.

Cody gave the front door a two-knuckle knock.

Vern offered a full-bodied answer, throwing the door wide-open. "It's usually unlocked if someone's awake. Feel free to let yourself in next time," he said, then walked away.

The man took the concept of *open-door policy* to a whole 'nother level.

Cody closed the door behind him and followed Vern into the kitchen, where the man began fidgeting with a coffee grinder. The knob was seemingly stuck on the coarseness setting, so he unplugged it and began disassembling the thing.

"To what do I owe the pleasure of a visit?" Vern asked.

"I'm going to take you up on the offer to practice on Sally," Cody said. Might as well cut straight to the chase. "Think I should call her Sal instead?"

"Whatever works for you. She doesn't hear so good anyway, not having ears and all." Vern cackled at his own joke. All the while, he continued to fidget.

"You must be working up an appetite." Cody

tapped him on the arm with the Tupperware container.

That got his attention. "Is this what I think it is?" Vern pried it from his hands without waiting for an answer. "Did you bring enough for both of us?"

Cody shook his head. "Not this time. I know better than to ride on a full stomach."

"You're missing out. I hear this stuff is heaven."

Cody picked up a loose piece of metal from the grinder and examined it. He might as well have been looking at the inner workings of a rocket. "I guess we have different ideas on that topic, because I don't think of myself as that good of a cook."

"Wait. You made this? I thought it was Becca's dish," Vern said.

Oops. "The first batch was partially hers. I pitched in to help this morning."

Vern unpeeled the lid and inhaled. His eyes rolled back in his head. "I don't even have to taste this to know I like it. Thank you." He placed the container on the counter next to him and turned his attention back to the appliance.

"No, thank *you* for letting me take Sally for a spin. If you have some time after you finish that project, I'd love to get started. Then I'm going to stop by Hailey's."

"She's picking Max up in a while, if you wanna wait around. That little boy is raring to get back in time to fulfill his breakfast duties."

"I could always take him. Save Hailey a trip."

"Can't let you do that," Vern said.

"It's no trouble."

"You don't understand. My grandson Parker would be too disappointed."

Now that was a familiar name. The jealous pang felt familiar, as well.

Cody settled onto one of the dining chairs. "How so?"

"Don't tell him I told you this, but he fancies Hailey. He's just too hardheaded and bloated with pride to let her know. Ah! Found the culprit." Vern popped a piece back into place, reassembled the grinder and plugged it back in.

So Parker wasn't competition after all. Hailey *had* been trying to provoke the competitor in him.

"What does your grandson do?"

"Something with numbers and start-up companies. Says he wants to drum up some business in Destiny Springs, but I suspect his mom talked him into coming down from Chicago to help me. Can you imagine that? Me, needing help? I just fixed an appliance that was born before he was."

"Does Hailey know he's interested?"

"I suspect. Hailey's smart in the way women seem to be. Feminine intuition, or some such."

Becca came to mind. Did she know that his feelings for her had not only returned but had never completely gone away? Probably. Which was why she'd eased the fork out of his hand. Someone had to set the record straight. They weren't together that way anymore.

"Judging by how they look at each other, I suspect Hailey feels the same way," Vern added.

That was good information to tuck away in his pocket. "Eat those *migas* before they get cold. They dry out after reheating. I'll wait. I've got all day."

"Nonsense. I can multitask," Vern insisted. "Onward!"

With Tupperware bowl and fork in hand, he led them outside and around back. Once inside the separate structure, Vern removed Sally's blanket.

Cody did a few test jumps on the padded floor to test its resiliency. Not the most forgiving cushion, but anything was softer than what he was used to. The last thing he needed was to sustain an injury from being bucked off a machine and onto what amounted to a massive pillow. The media would never let him live it down if word got out.

And word always got out.

"What's this?" Cody pulled out something smallish and rectangular from under the rope.

Vern immediately confiscated it. "It's a remote. Configured the thing a while back for my kids and grandkids. It has one speed that makes a carnival ride seem like eight seconds on Bodacious. But it allowed me to stand beside them and still be in control."

While Vern warmed up the console, Cody climbed on Sally's back and jumped off again. That's when he noticed a toggle switch near the front, within easy reach.

"What does this do?" he asked.

Vern looked up from his task of limbering up the joystick. "That's in case the driver gets distracted and the rider needs to shut her down. Not foolproof, but any safety feature is a good safety feature. This older model didn't come with one, so I added it."

Cody put his hands on his hips and nodded. Impressive.

"Step back. I'm waking her up," Vern said.

Cody put a good six feet of distance between himself and the machine. She was slow to get going. Once Vern switched her to second mode, she started getting frisky.

Vern ran through the modes, increasing the speed and adding variety and complexity by manipulating the dials and joystick. He reminded Cody of a mad scientist. Especially when he progressed to the highest mode while yanking the joystick every which way and twisting the dial with wild abandon.

"Think you can handle her?" Vern asked.

"Safe to say I hope so."

Vern smiled, then flipped a switch on a separate but adjacent box. Sally went into overdrive, making a grinding shriek at every twist.

Cody took another step back. "Whoa! I've never—"

"And you never will again. I souped her up. Think of this gear as Sally on espresso. Not sure I feel comfortable taking you there, but if you can't handle her, no one can."

The adrenaline rush that coursed through Cody was a heady mix of terror and excitement. Whoever made fun of mechanical bulls clearly hadn't met this one.

Vern dialed her back down. Cody approached slowly. Cautiously. As if she was somehow capable of overriding the control box.

"Be gentle with me," he said as he hefted himself onto her back.

"We'll take it nice and slow," Vern said.

As if a rider ever had such a luxury. Even on the lowest setting, Cody discovered that he'd gotten a little soft over the last couple of days. Becca still had the power to do that to him. Getting out of that house as much as possible might be a good thing.

Vern shifted to second mode.

Hips and legs, at one with the beast.

That was a little more like it. Still not challenging enough, though. Time to get her moving. He nodded at Vern.

Free hand up, leave nothing to chance.

Sally bucked and twisted beneath him. His whole body itched to take it all the way to the top setting.

Follow her lead for an eight-second dance.

"I'll have the espresso, please," he called out.

Vern obliged.

Maybe he wasn't ready. He felt himself losing balance three seconds in. Vern read Cody's body language and pressed the emergency stop.

Cody jumped off as fast as he could, heart now pounding out of his chest. He hadn't expected that. Yeah, he wasn't leaving Destiny Springs until he lasted the full eight seconds on this one.

Unless it killed him first.

ROADKILL.

That's what Becca's *migas* looked like. And that was being kind. Clearly, she should have been paying closer attention when Cody was showing her how to make them. At least they passed the aroma test.

Besides, she didn't want the guests to get too spoiled. She had no intention of making this a regular event. A few of them had inquired about Cody and his *migas* yesterday, and she'd hinted that she would consider serving them today. Vern's request, however, had been nonnegotiable.

No use doing anything else to the dish at this juncture. Time to take all the food to the barn and get set up. She loaded the rolling cart, belatedly realizing the industrial coffee maker still needed to be set up. Hailey usually handled the heavy lifting in that department. Today, she was picking up Max from the Frasers. They were supposed to be back in time for the actual breakfast but not necessarily for the prep.

At least Trent had shown up after all. He was out trimming some bushes. She usually gave him a written to-do list in case he wanted to earn some extra cash. Today, she'd forgotten all about it.

All was not lost. She rolled the cart in his direction.

"Trent, if you have time today, will you fix the banister? It's loose at the bottom of the stairs. Kids like to slide down it, even though they're not supposed to. I don't want anyone getting hurt."

"Yes, ma'am. I'll take care of that after I finish up here."

"There are also some light bulbs that need replacing in the upstairs hallway. But if you could check the whole house, I'd appreciate it."

"I can do anything if the price is right," he teased.

"Good. In that case, I need you to make a Stetson."

He cast her a questioning look.

"Kidding," she continued. "But will you do me one more favor?"

He stopped trimming and rubbed a handkerchief across his brow. Even though it was a cold-to-the-bone morning, Trent never failed to work up a sweat.

"Mind if I hear the favor first?" he asked.

"Fair enough. It shouldn't be too unpleasant." She pulled out a fork, lifted the Saran Wrap covering the *migas*, composed a bite that included all the ingredients and handed it to him. "Let me know what you think. And be completely honest."

He seemed to truly savor it. At the same time, she'd set herself up for a playful insult.

"This is seriously delicious," he said.

"For real?"

"Oh, yeah. Can I have another bite?"

She dug out a clean fork and handed it to him. "Please. Help yourself."

Instead of digging in, he stared at the dish and shook his head.

"What? Too much oregano?" she asked.

"Not that. I just hope the mother of them eggs doesn't have to see what happened to her babies. But what it lacks in presentation, it makes up for in taste."

Becca bit her lip, but a laugh escaped anyway. She'd argue with him if she didn't agree completely. He proceeded to fit as much on his fork as it could hold.

"How about we leave some for the guests," she teased.

Mouth still full, Trent gave her a thumbs-up. She re-covered the dish and hurried to the barn, where she transferred the food to warming trays. Next, the coffee maker, and not a minute too soon. An early riser wandered in and examined the spread.

Becca was especially proud of the fruit plate.

Such juicy strawberries, neon kiwi slices and fat blueberries. Next to it, an assortment of muffins, biscuits and croissants. All made from scratch.

"Where are the *migas*?" the guest asked.

"Last warmer at the end of the table."

For the second time today, the dish got a serious stare-down.

Yep. Roadkill.

"They look different. Did Cody make these? Will he be here?"

"He helped. I don't expect him today, however."

Might as well disappoint her guests in advance. Although, the way things had been going, no telling where or when he might show up.

Once everything was in place and she got a breather, she checked her text messages. Only one. From Hailey. Confirming that she'd picked up Max and they were headed back but had to stop at her place for a minute. No mention of running into Cody.

Becca texted that she had everything under control and to keep Max at the stables. Show him more of those horse things. Before she could put her phone away, Hailey sent another message. This time, letting her know that the B and B was almost booked through the end of the month and the next two were filling up quickly. They'd been at only forty-percent average occupancy yesterday.

Strange.

Her assistant shot yet another text. This one felt like a full-body smackdown. Hailey was looking at the internet analytics. Overnight, their social-media platforms had more than doubled in the number of new visitors. The common denominator: three new search terms.

Cody Sayers.

Rodeo Rascal.

Migas.

This can't be happening.

CHAPTER NINE

THAT HAD TO be the cutest thing Cody had ever seen.

Even a litter of puppies or kittens couldn't compete with the sight of Max holding a curry comb, running clumsy circles over the near side of Hailey's quarter horse. She stood nearby, supervising, putting her hand over Max's to correct the pressure and motion.

Hailey was just the person he wanted to talk to. He was still itching to get to the bottom of whether she'd known Becca would be at Renegade, because he suspected they had a little matchmaker on their hands. When she noticed him standing there, she motioned him over.

"What are you doing here? You're quite the escape artist," she said.

"What do you mean? I'd argue that you're one. I searched the Hideaway top to bottom for you and Max. Took a chance y'all would be here."

Max looked up. "Cody! Watch me comb Bernice. She likes it."

Cody gave Max his undivided attention.

"Her name is really Charmed," Hailey clarified. "Max has his own idea as to what the horses should be called."

Cody smiled and nodded. Yep. Painfully cute.

"So why am I an escape artist?" he asked. "Did Becca tell you I hightailed it out of the house this morning when she went to the other room for something?"

Hailey squinted. "Uh, no. But it's interesting you would do such a thing. I saw your rental truck at the Frasers', but I didn't see you. By the time Max was ready to leave, your truck was gone and Vern was playing coy. He's a really bad fibber."

"Was he fibbing when he told me that the grandson you had mentioned—Parker, right?— wasn't interested in Becca after all? Were you trying to make me jealous?"

Hailey looked down at her field boots and jammed her toe against the dirt. "Maybe."

Meanwhile, Max was practically rubbing a hole in a very patient Bernice. Or Charmed. Or whatever. Cody had a whole new name in mind for her anyway: Max's First Schooling Horse. From what he could tell, most of Hailey's horses were exceptionally tame.

"Ever thought of putting your horses to work?" he asked.

"As in, what, offering horse-and-buggy rides around Destiny Springs?"

Cody shrugged. "Lots of things you could do."

"Sure. I'll work on some ideas in my spare time," she said jokingly.

It wasn't any of his business, but horses weren't born to stand around in stalls all day. Even in first-class digs like Hailey had going here.

"If you're planning to stay for a few minutes, I'll run inside and get all of us a drink. I'm sure Max is thirsty. He's been working so hard. What would everyone like?" she asked.

"Lemonade," Max blurted out.

"Water's fine for me," Cody said.

As Hailey disappeared inside the house, he contemplated his question about Renegade. Not a conversation he'd want to have in front of Max.

"Hey, cowboy. I bet Bernice would love for you to brush her up higher. I'll have to lift you. Is that okay?"

"Can I sit on top of her?"

"It's safer for both you and her if you're grounded. And safety is the most important thing when you're a cowboy."

Maybe he wasn't so bad with kids after all. Who knew? He hefted Max up a few feet, where it was comfortable for him to make circles and comfortable for Bernice to receive them.

"Is it safe to ride bulls?" Max asked.

Then again, maybe he wasn't so good with kids. He'd walked right into that one and had no clue how to back out of it. The truth was always a good start.

"Actually, no. It's not," he admitted. He wasn't about to lie about the most dangerous sport in rodeo. One of the most dangerous careers, period.

"Then, why do you do it?"

Oh, boy. How to even begin to answer that? Where was help when he needed it? Thankfully, Hailey was making her way back over, hands full with their beverages and gripping what appeared to be a bag of chips between her teeth.

"Look! Your lemonade is about to arrive."

He set Max on the ground and eased the curry comb from his hand. "How about you go help Miss Hailey carry those."

Max didn't budge. Instead, he dropped his chin to his chest.

Okay, so he wasn't bad with kids. He was the worst.

Cody knelt to his level. "Hey, what's the matter?" Hopefully it was as simple as changing his mind about the lemonade.

"I might drop it and upset Miss Hailey. I always drop things."

Cody had all but forgotten about the incident with the orange juice. "Well, then, we have something in common, because so do I. All the time."

As he said that, Hailey shrieked in the distance. Sure enough, one of the drinks had slipped from her grip.

"What do you know? Miss Hailey drops things too."

Max started giggling, which made Cody giggle. Once they started, they couldn't stop. Hailey finally made her way over with the two surviving beverages. She let the bag of chips fall to the ground.

"Glad I amuse you two. Good thing I decided to use the plastic glassware this time. By the way, that was *your* drink I dropped. Bro." She broke out into a huge, evil-looking grin.

If his own grin looked even half as menacing as Hailey's, no wonder Becca hated it.

"Before you start drinking that, Max, how about you go pick up the cup Miss Hailey dropped," Cody suggested. "A cowboy always pitches in to help."

Max ran in the general direction but missed the target area. Looked like he was on an Easter-egg hunt instead. That would buy Cody a few minutes alone with Hailey.

"That's quite all right about the drink. *Sis*. But I do have another question you probably won't answer."

"Then, why bother asking?"

"Because I want to see you squirm. Did you know Becca would be at Renegade last night, and if so, why did you hint that I should go there? Look me in the eye when you answer."

Hailey took a long sip of her soda. "Becca didn't have anything to do with it, if that's what you want to know. In fact, she'd probably fire me if she ever found out."

"Then, why did you do it?"

"What can I say? I'm a hopeless romantic. True love, second chances, happily-ever-afters."

"*Hopeless* is the key word. Becca and I tried once. Didn't work. In fact, it failed spectacularly."

"My intentions were good. But it won't happen again."

Max came running back with the cup in hand. "I found it!" he said.

"Here, I'll trade you." Hailey took the empty cup and handed him the lemonade, which he gripped with both hands and proceeded to guzzle.

"I need to head back to the Hideaway, where I plan to do a disappearing act of a different kind," Cody said. "If either of you need me, you can find me in my room. I'll see *you* later, cowboy."

"Wait!" Max set his cup on the ground, much too close to one of Bernice's hooves. Hailey promptly removed it from harm's way. "Pick me up again," he said.

Cody couldn't even venture a guess as to why, but he did as he was told, lifting him until they were face-to-face. Max raised one fist to the sky, pointed the other to the ground, bent one knee and had the most intense expression he'd ever seen on a child.

"Guess who I am," he said.

Cody studied the pose and looked to Hailey for pointers. She shrugged her shoulders. "I don't know. John Travolta? The Urban Cowboy?"

Max kept the stern expression but looked Cody in the eye and stayed in character. But which character? That was the question.

"Superman!" Max said.

"I was gonna say him, but I thought that was too obvious, since Superman wears a purple cowboy hat sometimes."

Max reached on top of his own head, removed the hat and placed it on top of Cody's head. "Now *you're* Superman," he said.

Cody's breath hitched. He stood corrected. Max combing the horse wasn't the cutest thing he'd ever seen. This was. He set Max back down on the ground.

"It's a good look for you," Hailey said.

He didn't have to see her face to know she was about to burst. No matter. He wasn't going to dignify it with a response.

"That's very kind of you to let me borrow this, Max. I'll take good care of it until you get home." Cody turned on his heels and headed to the truck.

"By the way," Hailey called out, "did Vern say who his grandson *is* interested in?"

Déjà vu.

If the situation wasn't so complicated and much too adult for Max, he'd be able to show the little cowboy a real-life example. Hadn't Vern called out a question when he was walking away? Didn't Vern also expect an answer when he hadn't bothered answering Cody's?

Conveniently enough, Vern hadn't been fibbing when he said that Parker fancied Hailey. Or that Hailey clearly fancied the grandson in return.

Cody looked back over his shoulder. "Maybe,"

he said, tipping the little purple hat at Hailey before climbing into his truck.

Paybacks. Gotta love 'em.

BECCA THOUGHT THE hardest part of a day without Hailey was over.

Wrong.

The phone kept ringing with people asking if the rumors were true about the Rodeo Rascal working there. The novelty of it had whipped rodeo fans into a frenzy. Those she could handle. It was her current guests' questions that were more difficult to dodge. They'd seen him around. Knew he was staying there. Were hoping to catch a glimpse of him again at breakfast.

The main ingredient missing from her *migas*, it seemed, was Cody.

Unfortunately, the thing she wanted to do least was the only thing that could appease her guests: ask Cody to help serve for a few days. Ease them out of the expectation by having him make it clear it was only temporary and that he'd be leaving soon.

As much as she didn't want to tangle with the social-media beast, it wouldn't do to have people book a room, only to find that their reason for coming had already left. Bad for business. If it were any other rodeo star, she wouldn't stress, because it wouldn't affect her personally. But this star was the secret father of her son. Didn't get much more personal than that.

The glossy image of her eleventh birthday party flashed to the forefront of her mind again. Her lack of childhood friends was nothing compared to the type of critique Max might be forced to endure. She put on her thinking cap, pulled out a pen and paper and began brainstorming.

First and most obvious: Comp Cody's stay.

Not great. The man had enough rodeo winnings to afford something even nicer than what she offered. While an admirable gesture, it wouldn't offer that much of an incentive.

Second: Make his dish part of her regular breakfast lineup and put his name on it. Or whatever name he wanted.

Not bad. That would appeal to his ego. To offset any attention it might get from media, she could rename all of her other dishes something fun or current, as well.

Third: Agree to his earlier request to teach Max how to ride horses.

Not a chance.

She set down the pen, dropped her forehead to the counter and squeezed her eyes shut. She'd have to come up with at least one appealing enticement, however. *Concentrate*.

A knock on the door frame assured that wasn't going to happen.

"Sorry to disturb your nap, ma'am." Trent snickered at his own joke. He had the same sense of humor as Cody. If she'd made that connection earlier, she probably wouldn't have allowed him to work there at all.

Now it was her turn to inwardly snicker. "No problem, but you better have a good reason for doing it," she said.

"Actually, I do. You mentioned the loose banister, but I can't find what you're talkin' about. Feels steady to me."

She headed to the staircase and motioned him to follow. Sure enough, the railing didn't budge this time. "If it had come loose, what would have caused it, and how would you have fixed it?"

He knelt at the base for a closer look. "Most likely, one of these screws would have loosened. Nothing a Phillips couldn't mend. Unless the wood underneath is rotting. But everything looks solid, and these screws are in tight."

That might explain the screwdriver she nearly tripped over earlier. All evidence pointed to the man who'd fallen asleep on the couch, even though he hadn't mentioned anything earlier about fixing the staircase. Back in the day, he'd have made a point of letting her know he'd taken care of even the smallest of tasks around the apartment.

No matter. The banister was no longer a danger. That was the most important thing.

"Any other imaginary tasks I can help with? I could use the extra money," Trent said.

"Your work ethic is admirable. Probably one of your best qualities," she countered.

Ruminate on that. She headed back to the kitchen, and Trent followed. He was making himself available on the right day, because she could use some help.

"If you ever get bored and need something to do, feel free to look here."

Becca walked to the far end of the counter, which was dotted with sheets of paper. She'd labeled each with its specific purpose: Maintenance Requests, Grocery List, Someday Tasks and Daily Chores. Most of which changed daily.

That area of the counter had become ground zero, although one of the items on her Someday Tasks list was to bring this system into the twenty-first century. Stop wasting so much paper, even though she'd shred a bundle every few months and drive it twenty miles to the animal shelter, which used it for bedding.

Daily Chores seemed to be the best match for Trent, although he wouldn't think so. That made it all the more fun.

"Ah! Here it is. My list of imaginary tasks." She picked up the piece of paper, waved it in front of him and proceeded to read. "Mop the barn floor and sanitize the dining table in preparation for afternoon tea and cheesecake. Make sure the guest bathroom downstairs is clean and stocked with toilet paper and hand soap, and refresh the potpourri dish. Go through the fridge and take any expired leftovers to the composting bin."

Trent seemed to deflate with each task she read off the list. Not his favorite things to do. Not anyone's favorites, but at least they were real. After going through a few more, she decided he'd been tortured enough. She set the list next to the one she'd started with negotiating points for the discussion with Cody.

"On second thought, if you don't mind feeding Penny and taking her for a walk instead, it would be a big help. After that, you could make a run to the store. You'll find the grocery list here as well."

She needed more sausage and jalapeños, for sure. Whether Cody agreed to help make and serve his dish or not, she would include it as part of the buffet until the novelty wore off and people stopped asking about it or planning their stay around it.

All of a sudden, the thought of him leaving again and the memories it evoked put a vise around her heart. Becca tried to speak but couldn't.

She didn't realize how obvious it was until Trent asked, "Are you okay?"

After a moment, she could breathe again. "Yes. Fine. Let's go find Penny."

She retrieved the leash, which she kept on a hook next to the refrigerator. Together, they scoured the place until they found the lovable labradoodle, schmoozing with the guests.

"We might have to kidnap her and take her back to South Carolina with us," one lady cooed.

"I wouldn't blame you. But before we pack her toy bag, she needs to go for her walk." Becca hooked the leash onto Penny's collar and handed control over to Trent.

"Once around the grounds," she instructed.

Penny pulled him toward the door, proving that she was planning to walk him instead of the other way around.

Becca turned to her guests. "Please let me

know if you need anything or have any questions. I'll be around."

"Will Cody be at breakfast tomorrow?" the woman asked.

"I hope so, but I can't promise," she said.

Her heart hadn't stopped pounding from a few moments ago, warning her that her plan to spotlight him over the next few days was a huge mistake. Perhaps it would be better to let the guests down immediately, rather than gradually. Not to mention, she could scratch point number three completely off her list. Keep Max safe and herself sane.

Reasonably sane, that was. She'd felt off ever since Cody had arrived. Even the thought of resolving this now relieved some of the tension. Yep. The list was about to meet its destiny: the shredder.

She hurried back to the kitchen only to find Cody, wearing Max's much-too-small, much-too-purple cowboy hat. That wasn't the most unsettling part. He was examining the lists.

"What are you doing?" she asked.

He took his sweet time in pivoting around to face her. That grin suggested he'd seen the list. The way he held it up in the air confirmed it. He gripped it with both hands. Like a sacred scroll.

"Let's see. What am I doing? Apparently,

I'm serving my *migas* at breakfast. That is, when I'm not busy teaching Max how to ride."

She rushed over to him. "That was a draft. You weren't supposed to see it. Didn't your dad teach you that it isn't nice to snoop?"

She grabbed at the list, but he held it high enough that she couldn't reach it. Trying to wrestle his arm didn't work either. Having to hold onto a rope for dear life had turned his muscles to steel. And keeping that hand in the air was partly how he made a living.

All she could focus on was that little cowboy hat, which didn't budge. Was it glued to his hair or something? Every time he'd jerk one way or the other, the thing stayed put. Soon enough, she was laughing so hard she was crying.

He'd gotten tickled as well and let his guard down long enough for her to snatch the piece of paper. She tried to hold it behind her back, but what was the point? He'd get it anyway.

"You might as well stop fighting and give in," he said.

He wrapped both arms around her waist so her arms and hands couldn't maneuver, all the while trying to pry the piece of paper from her grip. She let it slip to the ground as their fingers intertwined.

They looked at each other. Speechless. What could they say?

"What are we doing?" he finally asked.

Apparently, they were giving in.

THE FIRST THOUGHT Cody had was how soft her hands felt in his. The second one was that at least one of them had better come to their senses, because this could *not* go any further.

The landline rang. Their hands slipped apart. *Fate calling.*

While Becca took the call, Cody retrieved the list from the floor. By the time she hung up, his head had cleared a little. Until she gave him a certain look that had always melted him.

"So what do you say?" she asked.

It took him a moment, his head wanting to time-travel back to a few minutes ago. He glanced at the list again. She'd included a couple of appealing negotiating points, he had to give her that much.

"The second item. About naming the dish after me."

She shrugged. "You deserve the credit. Plus, I think it gives my guests something to brag about to their friends."

"I kinda doubt that." Although, yes, the guests were awfully attentive at the community table. Still, that would wear off quickly enough. Especially after he left for Scottsdale. "I'll agree to it under one condition."

Becca crossed her arms. "I'd meant to scratch through that third point before I was interrupted. I'm afraid if I agree to horses, he'll eventually want to ride bulls. I couldn't bear it with him, like I couldn't bear it with…" She didn't need to finish the sentence.

"I don't want him getting hurt either. Which is why you can trust me to be extra careful."

"I trust you. I just don't trust the horses."

"I'm not going to lie and say it isn't without risk. But that's true of most things in life."

Falling in love came to mind. He'd rather be thrown from a bull and stomped on anyday than go through the kind of pain he did when he and Becca had divorced. Yet his heart was setting him up for a stomping as they spoke.

"But that isn't my condition anyway," he continued.

"You're serious? Teaching Max isn't it?"

He shook his head.

"Go ahead, then." She started fidgeting with her nails again. What did she think he was going to demand?

"Max gets to pour the orange juice."

She visibly exhaled and laughed under her breath. "He already does that."

"From a glass pitcher."

"You saw what can happen," she said.

"And everyone survived. Maybe it's time to take a few chances. Live dangerously."

Not the best choice of words, but honest ones. He was living dangerously in the moment by imagining that the door wasn't completely closed on their relationship. That, after he won Scottsdale and Houston, then maybe…

Stop it.

Who was he kidding? If he qualified for a championship title, he'd still have to compete in Vegas. If he didn't win or even qualify to begin with, then the journey would start over again and again until he did.

He slipped the little purple hat off his head and looked at it. The thought of leaving all this behind sucker-punched him right in the heart.

"Wait here," she said.

No worries. He wasn't going anywhere this time. When she returned, she was carrying a hat. An age- and size-appropriate one.

She handed it to him. "You should have this back."

He swallowed. Hard.

Dad's hat. He recognized it immediately. For the past six-plus years, he'd concluded that he'd lost it somewhere. Turned out, he'd left it behind.

He was too choked up to ask her why she

hadn't picked up the phone to let him know. Or, for that matter, why she hadn't thrown it away. He was certain she'd felt he'd done that to their marriage and her chance for a family with him.

She'd not only kept it, however, she'd brought it with her to this place she now called home. That meant something, didn't it? But what? He could think of two possibilities.

In giving it back now, she was either opening that door a crack or closing it completely. Judging by the way she recrossed her arms, she was prepared to slam it shut, for good.

Problem was, he wasn't anywhere near ready.

CHAPTER TEN

No one could accuse the Rodeo Rascal of giving up when he should have.

Ironically, that was a good thing. Helping serve breakfast with Becca and Max for the past week was having the opposite effect he'd previously thought. It was honing his focus. The ability to tune out distractions was huge, and that muscle was being flexed. Nothing was more distracting—albeit in a good way—than being around Becca and Max.

The other challenge during the meals was to steer the conversation away from himself by asking questions of the guests. Where were they from? What had brought them here? How did they hear about the Hideaway?

He was beginning to sound as if he were on the payroll. That's why it didn't come as a surprise when they'd ask him vacation-related questions like, "What's the best dance hall around here?"

Renegade.

"How do I get to Yellowstone?"

Too far to walk, that's all I know. Ask Hailey for options.

"Anyone offer trail rides?"

Not that I'm aware of, but that's a good idea.

That's where Max kept stepping in, and not only with filling the juice glasses. He loved telling guests about Hailey's horses as much as they enjoyed listening.

Same drill every day.

Once Cody got his negotiated duties out of the way, he'd sneak in an extra task or two from a list of maintenance items on Becca's kitchen counter. She must have figured out by now that he was the one taking care of the little things, although she'd yet to thank him. However, she seemed more relaxed, which was thanks enough.

From there, he and old Sally did their thing at Fraser Ranch. Best decision ever to stay the extra week and a half. Sally kept him sane. Although she bucked and complained like all get-out, she'd yet to throw him.

Cody hoped he would continue the momentum today, but as soon as Vern unlocked the building, the key jammed.

"The thing sticks sometimes," he said.

"I know someone who can fix it." Max immediately came to mind.

Vern waved it off. "It needs replacing. I've

tinkered with it enough times to know when it's time to say goodbye. Not that we necessarily need to. I'm the only one who comes back here anyway. Besides you."

Once inside, Vern showed him something new about Sally: the tangled, spaghetti mess of wiring on her underbelly. The man hadn't been kidding about souping her up.

"Your handywork?" Cody asked.

Vern nodded. "Think of those as her blood vessels. Her lifeline."

"Funny. She's my lifeline these days," Cody said.

At that, the older man straightened. "I got some bad news, Rascal."

If anyone else kept calling him that, as Vern had taken to doing over the past few days, he'd demand they stop. Something about the way an octogenarian said it was endearing.

"You okay?" he asked.

"Yes. Nothing like that. Trent and I have to run to the Farmer's Co-op. Do you mind comin' back this afternoon?"

"Can't today, but I'll be back in the morning, if that works for you."

"Better offer?" Vern asked.

"You could say that. Max's first riding lesson. Becca agreed to let me show him the ropes."

"Well, good for her! And for the boy."

Becca got to decide the *if*, and Cody left it up to Hailey to decide the *when*. Max had done enough of the nonriding basics. Today, he graduated to getting in the saddle.

The way his biggest little fan had carried on, telling all the guests about it, Cody would have thought some major superhero was making a personal appearance. There'd even been a few moments when Max got so animated he almost dropped the pitcher.

"You're welcome to practice alone with the remote. Maybe your visualization can turn this carnival bull into a contender, if only in your imagination. Just don't let me come back and find you out cold on the mat. Or worse. Wouldn't reflect well on the ranch." Vern winked.

"Don't worry. If that happens, feel free to dispose of my body and any evidence."

"Plus, who would bring me *migas*?" Vern cackled.

Cody had made it a habit of bringing over a plate every day. It was the least he could do for being able to practice here. Not to mention, the eggs were from Vern's ranch to begin with.

"*Migas* notwithstanding, I wouldn't want you to crush that nice Stetson if old Sally threw you. Make that, *when* she throws you."

"I hate to break it to you, but that isn't going to happen. Not even with you in control." Cody reached up and adjusted his hat. Still couldn't believe he was wearing it again. "My dad wouldn't want anything to happen to it either. This was his. Won quite a few events while wearing this crown. That was back before we started wearing helmets."

"That's because your dad's generation of cowboys—and mine—was more hardheaded. Our thick noggins could take it. What's your father's name, by the way? Was he famous, like you?"

"Almost famous. Albert Sayers. But everyone called him—"

"Eight-Second Al. By golly, you're his son?"

"In the flesh."

Vern tilted his head back and looked up to the sky as if looking for confirmation from the heavens. Cody welled with pride, thinking about everything his dad had accomplished. Or rather, everything he could have but hadn't.

"What happened to him, anyway? Oh, wait, I remember reading something about your mom. May she rest in peace."

For a full fifteen minutes, Cody's family was more famous that he'd ever be on his own. At least when folks had found out his dad was exiting the rodeo altogether to see his wife through her terminal illness and raise their children, the media covered it with compassion.

"Life happens to all of us, I suppose. We have about as much control over it as a cowboy has over the bull beneath him. I've tried to finish what my dad started."

All of a sudden, he wanted to defy Vern, go solo and switch Sally to the espresso setting. Show the world what the remaining Sayers cowboy was made of. Except, how silly was that? He wouldn't even be able to get on top, once she got going. Besides, he wouldn't put that kind of liability on Vern's shoulders.

"And your dad's health?" Vern asked.

"Fine. Haven't seen him in a few years, which I'm not proud of. My brothers visit him even less. Busy with their big-city suit-and-tie careers. He's planning to come watch me compete in Houston. I'll go to his place and visit afterward."

Vern patted him on the back. "No doubt he's over-the-moon proud to have you as a son. Nothing more special than that bond."

Cody thought about Max, and the father who was missing out on such an incredible child. If he ever had a son, he'd want him to be exactly like his biggest little fan. Which reminded him of the question that kept coming up at breakfast.

"Has anyone ever offered trail rides around here?" Cody asked. "Rumor has it there used to be."

"I'd heard that one too, several years ago. Even got in my truck and drove around, looking for some sort of sign but never found one. Wouldn't have gone on one, anyway. Group adventures were never my thing. I've done plenty of solo rides in these parts, though."

Cody nodded. The rumor would have to remain that way for a while, because if this old-timer didn't have a clear answer, no one would.

Vern handed him the remote. "You let Parker or Vanessa know if you need anything while I'm gone."

After Vern left, Cody pressed the On button and watched Sally begin to sway. He powered her down again, secured his hat and hoisted himself on top.

Set the rope, handle in deep.

One quick kick and a press of a button, and Sally was in motion.

Hips and legs, at one with the beast.

He could take a nap and still stay on this dinky thing.

Free hand up, leave nothing to chance.

Sal would earn straight zeros for this

snoozer of a performance, and bulls always scored something.

Follow her lead for an eight-second dance. Five...four...three...two...

"Wow!" someone screamed.

What? Cody twisted to look, and he lost his balance in the process. He slow-rolled off Sally and landed on his feet.

"That did *not* just happen," he said under his breath.

Since it had, he saw an opportunity to teach the boys that this wasn't a toy, and that bull riding wasn't a game. He pretended to lose his balance again and allowed himself to fall backward on the cushioning, where he rested fully on his back. Eyes closed. Max and Perry ran over and started shaking him.

"Is he dead?" Perry asked.

Cody opened his eyes.

"Nope. He's alive," Max confirmed.

The boys each took an arm and helped raise him to a sitting position. In a real situation where he'd been thrown, he wouldn't have the luxury of being injured. No matter the pain— no matter how serious the injuries—he'd have to get up and out of the bull's way as soon as he could. Otherwise, he'd be inviting a wreck.

"That's so cool. I wanna ride. Can I? Pleee- ase?" Max asked.

So much for that bright idea.

Perry walked over to Sally and stood a little too close. She was still doing her carnival dance. Remote in hand, Cody turned it off, and they watched her ease to a full stop. Too bad the fall didn't kill him, because if this ever got back to Becca, she'd finish the job.

Max joined Perry, and they couldn't keep their little hands off Sally.

"This isn't a toy," Cody tried to explain to no avail.

Perry attempted to climb on top of her. While Cody tried to peel him off, Max took his turn at trying the same thing on the other side. It was like herding kittens. As soon as he'd managed to lift Max off the thing, Perry reached for the toggle switch on the side, and Sally was back in motion. He whisked them both out of harm's way.

"Again, boys, this isn't a toy. Understood?" Even though they were giggling and wiggling, he wasn't going to release them until they agreed. "Understood?"

He tried not to sound too harsh, because he wasn't angry. He was worried. But he found himself using the same tone his own father had used on him, for his own safety, when he pushed the boundaries.

Max stopped wiggling first. "Yes, sir."

Perry followed. "Yes, Mr. Cody."

He set them down and flipped the toggle to the Off position.

"Can we at least sit on it?" Max asked.

"Perry, I'll leave that up to your mom as far as what you can do, okay?"

Perry nodded. Cody was going to say that Becca would have to decide as well, but he didn't want her to know anything about this.

"Max, as far as you go   "

"Don't make me ask Mommy. She'll say no anyway. Let me sit for a second?"

Fortunately, Cody got a reprieve, because those big copper eyes were wearing down his defenses.

"There y'all are. I've made some strawberry punch and brownies," said a woman he didn't recognize. She rushed in and stopped short. She looked at Cody, then the mechanical bull. "I was afraid this might happen as soon as Vern told me you'd be practicing out here. You're Cody, right? I'm Vanessa. Perry's mom."

He'd gathered that much. He also gathered that his whole plan to keep this a secret from Becca would last about as long as those refreshments she'd mentioned.

Vanessa put her hands on each of the boys' backs and steered them toward the exit. "Let's go inside," she said.

"Vanessa? Please don't say anything to Becca."

"Don't worry. I'd be in as much trouble as you, if not more. I was supposed to be watching these little angels. But you look away for two seconds, they go looking for trouble." She shrugged and smiled.

After they left, Cody examined the broken lock. The key was still in it, and he couldn't figure out how to fix it to save his life. Then again, if Vern thought it was hopeless, then it probably was. That left him no way to secure the place and keep the little angels out.

He took a deep breath, exhaled and returned to old Sally's side.

Trouble. That's what she looked like now. All steel and leather, motors and wires.

Still, he'd gotten rather attached, which was why it pained him to do what he knew he had to. Couldn't risk having the boys come back out when no one was around. The way they got so worked up about Sally, it was just a matter of time.

Minutes, in his estimation. Vanessa stood little chance.

He located a pair of rusty old scissors, then dropped to his knees and looked at the mass of wires beneath her undercarriage. Couldn't bring himself to do it. Might not keep her completely still, anyway.

Cody located the primary cord and studied it. He found where it was plugged in and yanked the cord out of the socket. Unplugging it wouldn't be enough, however. The boys would figure that out in no time. After looking at every possible option, he concluded that there was no way to disconnect her without causing some type of damage.

Even though he didn't have Vern's parental consent, he assumed he'd approve, considering what was at stake. Besides, the damage he was about to inflict could be reversed.

"Sorry to do this to you," he said as he positioned the blades around the cord.

With one quick snip, he cut the connection with the best training partner he'd ever had.

BECCA WAS DETERMINED to perfect the *migas* dish, which she'd nicknamed Rascal's Rodeo Scramble. Not sure whether Cody would agree to it, but he hadn't offered anything better.

The way they seemed to be getting so close again haunted her, although the two of them were now managing to keep their distance while doing what she coined as their *breakfast dance*: crossing paths but staying at a safe distance. Going through the motions while side-stepping all emotions.

Fortunately, Cody would be leaving for Scottsdale in a few days. Otherwise, the surprise birthday party she was planning for Max would include an even bigger surprise. No way she'd be able to keep his real age from Cody at that point. The thought tied her stomach in knots.

Becca continued combining the ingredients for a new afternoon treat: chewy cinnamon caramel squares. Since it was an untried recipe, she needed a guinea pig. Fortunately, her trusty assistant property manager was in the next room.

"Taste test," she called out.

Hailey came running faster than Penny did when Becca would shake the Milk-Bone box. Becca trimmed a sliver from the edge and offered it up. Her assistant savored it and nodded in approval. With that, Becca removed the gooey block from the pan and began cutting it into bite-size squares. Two bites per guest. If the plate was empty when she returned, she'd know it was a hit.

"I needed to talk to you, anyway," Hailey said. "Guess what?"

"Do I have to?"

"No. You can be completely surprised. But

I wouldn't recommend it. And time is of the essence."

"Then, I suppose I'm as ready as I'll ever be."

"Your mother booked the Spandex Room."

Becca felt her face contorting. "She hates that room. Everyone hates it. I thought you put her in the Lace Room."

"I did. But that's when she was planning to fly in the morning of Max's birthday and surprise him."

"No. Please don't tell me—"

"I'm pretty sure I just did."

"Does she know?"

"I thought it would be better coming from you."

Becca grabbed a treat that had been earmarked for her guests and wolfed it down. "When will she be here?"

Hailey looked at her watch. "My guess would be any minute now. All the other rooms were booked. She'll have to be okay with it."

Becca popped a second treat in her mouth and scrambled to clear the baking mess she'd created. The other mess wouldn't be so easy to manage.

"Maybe so, but she won't be okay with Cody being here."

How would she ever explain? Her mother

disliked him more than she did the Spandex Room, and that was saying a lot.

"He isn't even around. He's probably at Vern's or at my place. Max's first riding lesson is today. Which reminds me, Max and I should get going soon."

The issues Becca had to worry about kept multiplying. She untied her apron, placed it on the counter and handed the plate to Hailey.

"Max and Penny are taking a nap. Do you mind putting this in the barn before you wake him up? I'd appreciate it."

Hailey took the plate. "Will do, boss."

Becca ran out the front door in time to greet her mother, who gave her the warmest, longest hug in return. Her mom always smelled like her name, Rose. With a hint of sandalwood.

What Becca wouldn't give to hug her dad again too. He'd always smelled like the fresh outdoors. Probably because he'd done all the landscaping when renovating the B and Bs, while her mom was in charge of the interiors.

"What a surprise," Becca said, pulling away from her mom. Something was different. "You've let your hair grow longer. And it's all one length."

Rose touched the silky ends, which grazed her clavicle. Becca had inherited her mom's color and her dad's waves. Her hair could only look that straight and sleek if she put an iron to it.

"I wanted to try something different. It's called a lob. I was starting to feel so old with the shorter cut. This makes me feel young again."

The woman had never looked her age, but now Becca was thinking they could be mistaken for sisters.

"I thought you might be able to use some help in pulling together the party," Rose said. "I knew if I offered you'd say no. Now that I'm here, you have to let me help."

"That is very sweet of you. But I'm afraid I have to warn you about something."

A look of concern splashed across her mom's face. "Is everything okay with Max?"

"Yes. Better than ever."

Rose put her hand over her heart. "Good! You gave me a scare."

"You might not want to remove your hand yet. Cody is here."

"Your Cody?"

Becca nodded.

"But why?"

"I'll fill you in on the way to your room," she said as she picked up her mom's suitcase. "Hailey said she didn't tell you about the other bad news."

"There's more?"

"This may actually be worse than the news about Cody," Becca teased as she led her mom up the stairs.

To the room where even more secrets would have to be revealed.

HAILEY AND MAX had finished tacking up her quarter horse by the time Cody arrived.

"Good timing. We're ready. You're on!" Hailey said.

Cody accepted the challenge and jumped right in. "How about we start with leading your horse to the corral. Stand on his left side and hold the reins like this. With your right hand, grab the reins here, closer to his mouth. Your left hand will manage the slack."

He demonstrated a couple of times, then handed them over. Max seemed a little hesitant about the right-hand duties.

"Don't be afraid," Cody said. "As long as you don't hold too tight, he'll be happy to let you lead." Max moved his hand up. Cody checked the placement and tension. "Perfect. Now, let's go have some fun."

Max did a good job of leading, but Cody was positioned to step in, if necessary. Hailey retrieved a mounting block and caught up with them in the corral.

"I know you've done this once, but let's go through it again," Cody said.

"Actually, we skipped this part the first and only time. I put him directly on top. Becs was afraid for him to try," Hailey said. "She thought the horse would spook and bolt right out from under him."

Max waited patiently for instruction. His level of attentiveness and maturity was impressive. Looked like Cody had a genuine cowboy on his hands.

He went through the steps of mounting, and Max seemed confident enough, aside from being afraid of hurting the horse by holding on to its withers. Together, the three of them took a couple of spins around the smaller corral. All the while, Max educated Cody on all the points of interest around them.

"That's where the horses get to run around and play," he said, pointing to a larger corral. "And that's where they take a shower." He waved toward a grooming station next to the stables.

"Looks like you were born to be a tour guide. Ever thought about leading trail rides someday? I hear the area needs it," Cody asked.

Max nodded enthusiastically. Becca would be pleased to hear it, under the circumstances.

No doubt, she was imagining Cody preparing him for bronc riding. Thing was, the closer he got to Max, the less he wanted the boy to idealize the rodeo life.

After they had circled the corral a few more times, Hailey and Cody took Max through the steps of dismounting and removing the tack. They were almost done when Hailey suggested they take a break and go inside.

"Who wants hot chocolate?" she asked.

Max waved both of his hands in the air. Cody raised one of this.

"Got it. Two for Max, one for Cody."

She went inside while Cody returned the saddle to its appropriate place. He wasn't about to leave the chores for her to deal with. Max, the human sponge, remained at his side, absorbing it all and wanting to do more. But their hostess was waiting at the doorway, waving them inside.

Hailey's home was larger than it appeared on the outside, but still rustic and cozy. Max claimed the overstuffed recliner and immediately began playing with the levers. Hailey made a beeline to the open kitchen area.

"May I help with anything?" Cody asked.

"Nope. Inside these walls, y'all are my guests. The only help allowed is helping yourself to anything in the fridge."

Having been duly put in his place, he changed the topic. He leaned against the kitchen counter and watched her pour hot boiling water into three separate mugs and add powdered cocoa mix.

"Marshmallows, please." She pointed behind him. He reached for the bag and handed it over. "Any for you, and if so, how many?" she asked.

"Surprise me," he said.

She proceeded to put a solid layer on top of one, then handed it to Cody. "Take this one to Max."

Good. Too many marshmallows for his taste. By the time he returned, she'd assembled his. The cup was overflowing with them. Looked like a blizzard in a mug.

"Perfect," he said. Taking a sip required some maneuvering, but he wasn't going to give her the reaction she was angling for.

She leaned against the counter, next to him. Together, they watched Max. The little boy was now walking around the living area, giving imaginary tours of the bookcase and sofa.

"How long have you known Vern?" Cody asked.

She blew out a breath. "Gosh. For pretty much all my life."

"Is he always generous with his time and resources?"

"You'd think so, but the truth is he's very careful about who he trusts and who he lets into his life."

That didn't parse with the Vern he knew. "He trusts me. And he barely knows me."

"He knows *of* you, though. Plus, you're a cowboy, like him. Y'all might as well share the same blood."

"If that's true, then we all might as well be related, since you're a real-life cowgirl." Not to mention, they'd become fast friends, but even faster supposed siblings since he'd arrived.

He was going for a laugh, or at least a smile. Instead, she raised her brows and fixated on whatever Max was doing.

"Some of us are more related than you can imagine," she said. At that, she looked down and studied her hot chocolate as if it were the first time she'd ever seen it.

"I don't understand," he said.

She shrugged. "It's a feeling you get about someone. Like with us, for instance. Doesn't have anything to do with DNA."

"I guess I get it. Sort of."

"You must not have grown up in a small town," she said, looking at him now.

"Spent most of my life in Houston. Never

lived in anything much smaller, but I passed through plenty."

"It's a different way of life. You gotta be built for it and want an extended family. That means embracing the bad in folks as well as the good."

He'd never thought about small towns that way. Becca had always been such a private person, yet she ended up choosing a place where everyone knew her business?

Give him a big city any day of the week. In that environment, he was either Cody Sayers, the Rodeo Rascal or just another face in the crowd. Usually the latter. Even when he was recognized, it was no big deal. There was a bigger big shot or celebrity around the corner.

"Not sure that's for me."

Although, once the words escaped his mouth, he wanted to take them back. Strange, but this had felt like home the minute he stepped foot on the dirt.

"Not a family man, huh?" she said. It was clearly an assumption rather than a question.

She knew the basics about his and Becca's history. Perhaps more.

"I could be one if I put my mind to it," he said.

"I have no doubt. You're a natural with Max. More marshmallows?"

"Don't mind if I do," he said, reaching into the bag, then popping several in his mouth.

Max's imaginary trail ride had progressed to sitting around a campfire, roasting the marshmallows he'd picked off the top of his drink.

Cody had to say it. Couldn't resist. "You really think I'm a natural?"

"Absolutely." Hailey offered a swift smile of affirmation.

Did his grin look as big and silly as it felt? Just as quickly, it slipped away. There was something else he wanted—no, needed—to find out.

"What do you know about Max's dad?" he asked. Now that he was emotionally invested in the kid, he wanted to find some sort of footing around the issue.

"I'm pretty sure he's a decent guy. Possibly a great guy," Hailey said.

"I'm almost sorry I asked. Didn't he bail? Is he in the picture at all?"

She shrugged. "He's met Max. They hit it off. Do you want my honest opinion?"

"Probably not."

"Well, I'm gonna tell you, anyway. I wish Max's father were in the picture full-time."

"Now you're just trying to hurt me."

She pushed off from the counter, swung around and faced him, and slammed the mug down. The liquid chocolate spouted in all directions. Cody's entire body tensed. What did he say wrong?

"That's *exactly* the confession I was going for. You're still in love with Becca," she said with controlled force.

They both looked to Max, but he was busy making imaginary s'mores and pretending to eat them.

"I didn't use those words," Cody said.

"Didn't have to."

That Hailey was a tricky one. He'd always wanted a little sister who would challenge him. Looked like he'd found one.

"You aren't going to repeat our conversation, are you?" he asked.

"No more than I'm repeating anything about hers and mine to you."

"Fair enough."

"Whatever you do, don't ask me to reveal the identity of the father. It's not my place."

"I'd never put anyone on the spot like that."

Not to mention, he really didn't want to know. Hailey liked Max's dad, and that was good enough for Cody. Even though the jealousy pained him, the knowledge that Max's father wasn't entirely unlikable was somewhat reassuring, in case he ever did come back into the picture.

Hailey's phone pinged. She checked her messages.

"Remember what I said about Destiny Springs being a small town?"

He nodded.

"It just got a lot smaller. At least, for you."

"How do you mean?"

"I probably should have warned you earlier, but better now than never. Becca's mom came to town and is officially settled in at the Hideaway. Becca's asking how much longer you and Max will be."

Rose Haring. Delicate, refined and as subtle as a Sherman tank when it came to protecting the ones she loved.

Hailey confiscated Cody's mug and put it in the sink. "I'd offer you another cup, but I think you better get back. I'll take Max back over in a while. Feel free to grab some marshmallows to go." She tossed the bag toward him.

"Why? We were just getting into some fascinating territory. An emotional trail ride, if you will."

Hailey laughed. "Oh, I suspect you're about to go for a ride, bro."

"Sounds like you know Rose."

"Met her once. She was very nice to me. But I didn't leave her daughter in the dust. Pardon my directness."

"Since you seem to be on her good side, do you have any advice?"

"Just a little ditty I got from the person who would know best. Vern. You ready?"

"Sure. How bad can it be?"

"Here goes. *Keep your friends close and your enemies closer. And never let family out of your sight.*"

Translating that into his situation with his ex-mother-in-law didn't equal *bad*.

It equaled *impossible*.

CHAPTER ELEVEN

"WHY DOES HAILEY hate me so much?" Rose asked.

Becca finished hanging her mom's clothes and tucked the suitcase in the corner of the closet. "She doesn't. You changed your plans. This was the only room available."

"You're the owner. Can't you pull some strings and let me switch with someone?"

Becca might have to consider it if her mom didn't stop complaining. What the woman *did* accomplish was to prompt Becca into moving her planned redesign of the room to the top of her Someday Tasks list.

Spandex had seemed like a fun idea at the time. Who wouldn't love an eighties fitness theme, complete with a mini home gym built right in? With props that included three-pound dumbbells, a jump rope, a portable stair-stepper and assorted accoutrements of that era?

Turned out, no one loved it. Worst idea ever.

"If you hate it that much, you can have my

room. I'll stay in here," Becca offered as a final attempt to put the discussion to bed.

"I wouldn't want you to do that. This room is actually rather interesting. Take this pillow, for example." Rose reached out and ran her hand across it.

The pillow jerked, uncurled and rose to its feet. Then it barked.

Rose recoiled and put her hand over her heart. "I think I had a mini heart attack. What is that?"

"Sorry. It's our labradoodle. Penny sleeps wherever she wants. I'll grab a fresh comforter."

"No need. As long as she doesn't bite. When did you get a dog?" Rose extended her hand, slowly this time, and Penny proceeded to lick it.

"When we saw her walking alone down a dirt road. It was love at first sight."

"She's a lucky girl."

"We're the lucky ones."

"I think she likes me. When will Max get home?" Rose asked.

"I'm not sure. Might be a while."

"Let's wait downstairs so I can surprise him. We'll have some of that cheesecake you've told me so much about."

Of course that would be the day Becca

had tried a new recipe instead. Otherwise, it would have been an excellent idea. Except, Hailey and Max might have some extra baggage in tow when they returned, in the form of Becca's ex-husband. She needed to make sure her mother didn't accidently spill the beans about Max's party. Especially his real age.

Becca took a seat on the edge of the bed, next to her mom. "I need to talk to you about something first."

A queasy feeling coursed through her at the thought of finally telling her mom the truth. She would have thrown up by now, except she hadn't eaten anything but a couple of cinnamon caramel squares.

"I'm going to come right out with it," Becca said.

"Cody is Max's father," Rose offered before Becca could blurt it out.

"You knew?"

"I've had plenty of time to figure it out. You kept saying you'd tell me when you were ready. Started looking as though you'd never be. Besides, you aren't the kind of girl to rebound after a breakup or to take risks. Is that why Cody is here? Did he find out?"

"No. And I'm trying to keep it that way. But with this party coming up, that might be impossible."

Rose gave Becca a reassuring pat on the hand. "I won't say anything, sweetheart. As far as I'm concerned, I don't remember how old Max is turning. Besides, I'm still hoping you'll find a real man to settle down with someday."

"I hope you'll play nice. And Cody *is* a real man."

Her mother tilted her head. "Are you falling back in love with him?"

"He'll be leaving for Scottsdale, then on to Houston. What would be the point?"

"Maybe if he knew about Max… Not that I'm hoping he'll stay. I still haven't forgiven him for leaving in the first place."

"Well, I have. Otherwise I couldn't forgive myself for not telling him."

"He chose the road over having a family, Rebecca. Don't forget that minor detail."

Having her mother on her side caused tears to well up. And just when she thought she'd spent her lifetime allotment.

"I was afraid he would think I was trying to trap him. If we'd gotten back together, I would have always wondered if he wanted to be there," she said.

Rose pulled her close. "I would wonder the exact same thing in your shoes."

Finally, a shoulder to cry on. Becca had kept this secret for so long, letting it slip out only once. To Hailey. Never imagining that her assistant and her ex would ever cross paths. Hailey's idea of support was to paint an idyllic picture of Becca and Cody getting back together someday and being a happy family. Becca dabbed the tears she couldn't seem to stop.

"What should I do now? He'll be leaving in less than a week," she said.

Rose squeezed her even tighter. "You let him go."

THANK GOODNESS BECCA didn't hear him kick the front door shut behind him or see the boot mark he left on the paint. Hopefully he'd get rid of it before she noticed. Right now, his hands were full with two grocery bags of ingredients for his *migas*.

Rascal's Rodeo Scramble. He had to laugh and shake his head at that one, although it was rather catchy. She'd come up with it before he'd had a chance to mull it over. As an option, he'd suggested I Can't Believe It's Not Chorizo. When she countered with I Can't Believe Cody Thinks That's a Good Name for It, he decided her original name wasn't so bad after all.

Penny hopped down the stairs and immediately got underfoot, almost tipping him over. Her enthusiasm matched Max's.

"I bet I know what you want," he said.

A package of andouille sausage had fallen out of one of the sacks. Except the pup showed no interest. Instead, she followed Cody into the kitchen, running in front of him and circling his legs. Max had done a similar move on their walk back from Hailey's.

After fixing his breakfast dish for nearly a week now, he finally had a grasp on how much food he'd need to get with each grocery-store run. Becca planned to keep serving it after he was gone, so those calculations would help her with future planning, as well.

He set the bags on the counter and promptly put the meat in the refrigerator. Before unpacking the rest, he decided to get a few housekeeping details out of the way. First, remove the boot scuff. He didn't want to see that added to one of her lists.

When he returned to the kitchen, he dried the serving platters that had been left in the drainer next to the sink, even though that wasn't on her list.

Much better.

He removed the other items from the bags, placing each one in its designated spot. As he did, an overwhelming sense of calm rushed over him. The only way he could describe it was that this place felt like home. His head insisted that was a bad thing. His heart disagreed.

Now that old Sally was incapacitated, he'd have to return to visualization only, which would best be done in his room with its soft mattress and complete silence. He could practically feel the flannel pillowcase against the back of his neck. Eyes closed, he imagined it now.

Until Penny started barking.

"Where's my little angel? Is he hiding?" someone called out from the other side of the kitchen door.

When the woman slid the door open, she was all smiles. Until it sunk in that Cody was standing there. His smile picked up where hers left off.

"I'm right here, Rose." He extended his arms for an embrace, even though he was under no illusion that it would happen. Back in the day, she would have given him a real hug. And he would have hugged her back even harder. Those days were long gone.

Her calm, unaffected reaction told him that she'd been warned of his presence.

"I was looking for Max. Have you seen him?" she asked.

Cody let his arms drop back to his side and resumed putting away the groceries. "No, ma'am. Just got back myself. I'm sure he's still with Hailey. They were lollygagging when I left."

"If you see him, don't mention I'm here. It would spoil the surprise."

He turned and looked at her. The woman somehow made athleisure look like cocktail attire. It came down to the way she carried herself, which time hadn't affected.

"I probably won't see him again tonight. And you won't see me. I'll be in my room."

Rose nodded politely and left as Becca entered. Penny stayed glued to him, and he was grateful. Nice to have someone on his side. Becca worked around them both and reached for the dish towel he'd been using.

"I'll be out of your way in a minute," he said. "I can't speak for Penny."

"You're not in my way," she said. "And I can't speak for Mom."

Becca looked at the dish drainer and cocked her head. Cody knew why, but there was no reason to take credit for it unless she brought it up.

"Everything okay?" he asked.

She blinked a few times. "Yeah. It's just that I thought... Never mind." She folded the dish towel, returned it to the counter and rubbed her eyes.

"Your mom doesn't think too highly of me. But I understand," he said.

If only he could say the same about his feelings toward his ex-mother-in-law. He missed her. In fact, he missed all the branches on Becca's family tree, but Rose had been his favorite. Now, she acted as though he was a casual acquaintance. Or a door-to-door salesman.

"I'll do my best to stay out of her way," he added. "Hopefully, her room isn't next to mine."

Becca looked out the window rather than at him. "It's a couple of doors down. She hates it, so I imagine she won't be in there much."

"Why? The rooms are nice. What little I've seen of mine."

"They're all different. Each has its own theme and fabric. Yours, as you can probably guess, is flannel."

"What's hers?"

Becca turned around and rested against the counter. "I'll tell you if you promise not to laugh."

She's opening up. He moved next to her under the guise of looking out the window.

"Faux fur?" he guessed.

Becca seemed to think about it. "Actually, that's not half-bad."

"Now you're scaring me."

"It's spandex," she said. "Boo!"

Yikes! She wasn't kidding. He bit his lip to keep from saying anything. No wonder Rose wasn't in the best of moods. That gave him an idea, though.

"I'll trade rooms with her," he said.

Becca squinted as if she didn't trust the offer. "What's the catch?"

"No catch."

Sleeping on spandex would be more comfortable than enduring Rose's wrath for the duration of his stay. Not that the offer would necessarily make a difference, but it was worth a try.

Rose returned to the kitchen, hands on her hips.

"I can't find him anywhere," she said.

"I've got some great news. Cody offered to switch rooms with you," Becca said.

"You're welcome to look at mine, if you want to check it out first," he added.

Rose toyed with her gold-chain necklace. "That's not necessary. Thanks, though, for the offer, Cody."

A forced smile crossed her lips. A hairline crack in her Sherman-tank veneer. It was a start. Sure, the offer was too little, too late in the grand scheme of things. But no one could say he didn't try.

Might as well leave on a high note. He nodded at the ladies and excused himself to his room. Without so much as taking off his boots, he plopped down on the flannel bed and closed his eyes. Finally, some alone time. Except Vern's words played around in his head about never letting family out of his sight.

Instead of visualizing Scottsdale, his thoughts turned to Renegade. How Becca had gone there to get Montgomery Legend's autograph for her mom. Maybe even take a selfie.

Her words.

He swallowed back a giggle at the thought. But the whole thing tickled so bad, his whole body trembled.

Ever since he was five, he'd competed in the Houston Livestock Show and Rodeo in one event or another. As many people went to see the headline musical entertainment as they did to watch the cowboys and cowgirls strut their stuff. In all those years, one name was always on the musical lineup. That same name always sold out.

Cody had gotten to rub elbows with the best of 'em. Even ended up on a first-name basis with some.

Becca wanted an autograph or selfie with Montgomery Legend?

Child's play.

He wanted nothing more than to turn that forced smile of Rose's into a fully blossomed one and make his ex-mother-in-law a fan of Cody Sayers, the man, once again.

Jackson Hole wasn't that far away. Time to catch up with a genuine rodeo legend.

And ask him for a very special favor.

ALL MORNING AT BREAKFAST, Cody seemed unusually content, and Becca knew why. Scottsdale.

His demeanor always changed when a competition drew near. This would be his calm-before-the-storm phase. At least Cody was keeping up with his end of the bargain to tell guests that his appearance here was temporary but that his legacy would live on through his signature dish.

According to Hailey's analytics, it was working. Bookings were holding steady. No uptick in reservations, but no cancelations either. Rascal's Rodeo Scramble was now trending as a search term. She'd noticed another surprising term that was piggybacking: *trail rides*. Someone in the area must be offering them. Or planning to.

Becca paused from refilling the condiments to watch Cody and Max in action. Cody was walking around the table with his tray, personally serving up second helpings. Max stayed on his heels, pouring orange-juice refills.

Cody looked up at Becca and smiled, as if he had sensed her watching. Amazing how he was still able to hook her with those eyes, then torture her with that wicked grin of his. But was something other than Scottsdale behind it today?

Rose came in and sat down, even though she'd originally planned to wait until Cody had left. Her presence should have wiped the smile off his face. Instead, it got bigger. The smile didn't so much as twitch when she curtly declined a first serving. Then she remembered her mom had gone to bed early and had yet to surprise Max.

Her son—being so focused on the task—realized she was there only after she accepted his offer for orange juice.

"Grammy! Grammy!" Max shrieked.

Cody set the serving dish on the table and took the pitcher from Max's hands before he had a chance to drop it out of sheer, unbridled excitement. Max threw his arms around his grammy's neck, and she embraced him with full force.

After finishing his rounds, Cody joined Becca on the sidelines.

"Good save on the pitcher," she said.

"Selfish move on my part. Didn't want to hear you say *I told you so*." He playfully nudged her shoulder with his.

"You're in an exceptionally good mood today," she said.

"I can't deny it."

"Scottsdale?"

He bit his lip. "I'm ready. After unexpectedly running into Rose, nothing can spook me."

Becca couldn't argue with that. Rose was being quite cool to Cody. Bad for him, but very good for Becca. She didn't need her mom to be nurturing any notions that he might stop chasing his dream, declare his undying love and move to Destiny Springs.

Let him go.

No, her mom would keep Becca grounded in reality, whether she wanted it or not.

"By the way, I'm taking you, Max and your lovely mother out to dinner tonight. Already made the reservation," Cody said.

She looked at him, but he continued looking straight ahead. "That's awfully presumptuous. Maybe we have other plans." Which they didn't. Monday night was their weekend leftover mash-up, as usual. Although that kind of qualified as a plan.

"Thought I'd take my chances."

"May I ask where you intend to take us?"

"You may. Ribeye Roy's."

Dollar signs popped up in her head. Lots of them, with an equal number of stars for excellent service. "I hope you're buying, because that's a little out of my budget."

"I do the paying whenever I do the inviting. Always have, always will."

His tone indicated that he'd taken offense at the suggestion. Justifiably so. He'd always had integrity in that way.

"I know you do," she said.

"Besides, a certain someone offered to comp my room for helping with breakfast. All that extra cash is burning a hole in my jeans."

He nudged her again as he said it. Always the charmer. Or the tease. The line got blurred at times.

"Okay. I know Max will say yes. I suppose I can be flexible. But I'll have to check with Mom."

"Have Max ask her. I bet she won't be able to tell her adorable grandson no, even when it comes to me."

True. Her mom would do anything for Max. But Cody was being a little too confident, in her opinion. Max and his grammy were having a grand time chatting away while the guests ate. Her son's boiling-over excitement finally reduced to a medium simmer.

"Mom isn't as easily influenced as you seem to think," Becca said.

"Then, let's see, shall we? Call Max over here."

"You're bossy today. Why?"

"I'm about to prove my point."

"Max," she called out, "come here a sec."

When Max ran over, Cody handed him the tray. "Offer your grammy some of my *migas*."

Max cocked his head. "She said she didn't want any."

"Maybe she changed her mind."

Tray in hand, Max returned to Rose. Becca watched in awe as her mom lifted the serving spoon and lobbed some *migas* onto her plate while Max did his best to hold the dish steady. Rose turned and looked straight down her nose and over the top of her reading glasses at Cody, as if she'd been placed in a very awkward position and did not appreciate it.

"Okay. You win," Becca said. "But judging by the look she gave you, she won't be any nicer to you in public. Not even with a fifty-dollar fillet placed in front of her."

"Again, I'll take my chances."

Becca sure wasn't looking forward to tonight. There would be plenty of topics to keep in check, including the biggest one of all: Max's upcoming birthday. Yet, her mom would be a dependable copilot should any turbulence occur. Meanwhile, the warmth from Cody's arm had worked its way through her sweater, and she realized he was still lightly pressed against her.

Cody straightened and took a step forward, putting an abrupt end to that.

"If you don't need me for anything, I'm going back to my room for a while. Offer still stands to trade with Rose," he said.

She was sure he meant it. He was clearly trying to get back on Rose's good side. It was rather sweet that her mom meant that much to him. Becca had always appreciated that they were so close.

"She doesn't hate you," Becca said, even though she wasn't so sure it was true.

Cody looked over his shoulder and smiled.

"I know. In fact, she adores me," he said. "She just doesn't realize it yet."

CHAPTER TWELVE

THE SKEPTICISM WAS as thick as sixteen-pound prime rib roast. At least, that's how Cody would describe Becca's and Rose's moods as they entered Ribeye Roy's.

Max was a different story. He started out happy and ended up downright ecstatic when he came face-to-throat with a life-size Black-Angus replica situated inside the entrance.

"Can I ride it? Pleeease?" he asked Cody.

The answer would always be the same. "Ask your mom, cowboy."

Hopefully, the steakhouse didn't have a mechanical bull, because that topic would surely ruin some appetites.

"You can stand beside it on the way out, and we'll take some pictures," Becca said.

Cody approached the hostess to provide his name and reservation information, but she'd already pulled five menus and was waiting to seat them.

"This way, Mr. Sayers."

She led them to a round table closest to the

roaring fireplace at the back of the restaurant. Best table in the house, as he'd requested.

Cody eased the menus from the hostess's hands. "I'll take it from here."

"As you wish. Your waiter will be with you shortly," she said to the group.

Cody placed the top menu in front of the seat nearest the fire and pulled out the chair. "Rose, why don't you sit here, where it's warm." He remembered how much she minded the cold. This place was a bit drafty, although the fire was strong enough to heat the entire table. "Max, you sit next to your grammy, and your mom can sit next to you."

He placed the menus down in that order. Max followed Cody's example and pulled out the chair for his mom. Neither Becca nor Rose balked at Cody taking charge, which was good. He wanted everything to be perfect.

He placed the fifth and final menu in front of the remaining chair that separated him and Rose.

"Who's sitting there?" Becca asked.

Max giggled. "It's the Invisible Hood!"

Cody shrugged and smiled. "That's one possibility. Superheroes get hungry too."

"You invited someone and didn't tell us?" Becca asked.

Cody neither denied nor confirmed. "Are

you warm enough, Rose? If not, I can run out to the truck and get my jacket. Or I'll ask them to add another log to the fire."

"I'm fine. Thank you." That sliver of a smile appeared again, although it visibly pained her to acknowledge his generosity.

Becca leaned in and whispered to Cody, "Aren't you overdoing it a little?"

"Oh, you haven't seen anything yet," he whispered back.

While the waiter went around the table taking everyone's drink orders, Becca practically bore a hole in him with her stare.

This was more fun than riding old Sally.

Rose picked up a menu and shared it with Max. He bounced in his chair when he found out they served Wagyu sliders and wedge french fries with the skins.

"These are some fancy prices, Cody. What's the occasion?" Rose asked. Her serious tone implied that she expected a serious answer.

"I wanted us all to have a special evening out. Becca works so hard, you've come all this way, and I'll be leaving soon."

"What about me?" Max asked.

"Well, you're the hardest worker of all. Not many people can pour the perfect amount of juice in those glasses," Cody said.

Max beamed. Rose's expression, on the

other hand, changed completely. The pressed smile blossomed into an O and her eyes widened.

Cody didn't have to turn around to know why. "Everything okay, Rose?" he asked.

Becca looked in the same direction. "Isn't that—?"

"Montgomery Legend," Rose managed to eke out before drawing in a sharp breath. "And he's headed this way. Oh, my! Do I look okay?"

Cody pushed his chair out, stood and turned around.

"Cody Sayers. You rascal, you! How long has it been?"

The two men traded a hearty handshake.

"If memory serves, it was three years ago in Houston," Cody said. "Your farewell performance, right?"

"I see all those concussions haven't damaged your memory. I was struggling with the date. But you're right. It's true what they say about retirement. The years start to run together."

Cody turned around, glancing first at Rose, who'd somehow touched up her lipstick since he'd turned his back. "Monty, I'd like for you to meet my ex-wife, Becca, and son Max."

Monty tipped his hat. "Pleasure."

"And this is Becca's mother, Rose."

Monty walked around the table, took her hand in his and placed a delicate kiss on the back of it. "I've heard wonderful things about you, Rose. But Cody failed to mention how absolutely stunning you are."

Cody felt like stealing Becca's line about laying it on too thick, but he refrained.

"Runs in their family, as you can see." He winked at Becca, who seemed equally star-struck and flustered. "Have a seat," Cody instructed. "They've taken our drink orders. I wasn't sure what you liked, so I didn't even attempt a guess. Back in the day, it was Woodford Reserve, neat."

"To be honest, I've been on a diet-soda kick lately. Watching my figure." Monty patted his belly as he took a seat next to Rose. Cody sat as well.

Monty hadn't taken any shortcuts in fulfilling Cody's request. He was all decked out in a black leather blazer and white button-down. His jeans were pressed, and his boots were polished to a blinding shine. When he removed his Stetson, his thick, longish, mostly-salt-with-a-touch-of-pepper hair fell perfectly into place.

If Cody wasn't mistaken, Rose was blushing.

He picked up his menu as if having dinner with a true country-music legend was an everyday occurrence. Couldn't have been further from the truth.

Rose nervously fidgeted with a lock of hair. She seemed to be struggling against a full-on smile. When Cody caught her eye, she ultimately surrendered.

They enjoyed a bit of silence while everyone studied the menu. Max already knew what he wanted and was becoming restless. Not the most kid-friendly restaurant. Hopefully they could find a few things to talk about that would interest a youngster.

The waiter placed a cutting board with a freshly baked-and-sliced loaf, along with a huge slab of salted butter, in the center of the table. Monty reached for the board and offered Rose the first choice.

"Best sourdough this side of Devil's Tower. I recommend the heel. Has a nice, crunchy-crumbly finish," he told her.

Rose used the tongs to take one of the ends, then fetched the opposite heel and put it on Monty's plate before anyone else could claim it. The two shared a conspiratorial smile.

Cody favored the heel as well, but he wasn't about to complain. The way his ex-mother-in-law and Monty were hitting it off was so much tastier.

The waiter placed a cloth napkin in each of

their laps, then took their orders and refreshed their water glasses.

"So you two know each other from rodeo?" Becca asked, filling the silence.

"Sure do," Monty chimed in. "I was there when Cody got bucked off Have Mercy at his first rodeo as a bull rider."

Cody scratched his temple. "I think I broke the record for shortest ride ever."

Monty laughed. "Yeah, I'm pretty sure you did. But you got right back on in the next event. The rest, as they say, is history."

"I had a good role model," Cody said. "Taught me to never give up."

Cody checked to see if Becca was even listening. She was. Her expression was part curiosity, part admiration, if he had to put a label on it.

"Cody's dad was a rising star, you know. I watched him go the full eight on Down-N-Dirty at *my* first rodeo performance," Monty said, directing his attention to Rose and Becca.

"I wanna ride bulls," Max said.

Cody looked down at his fingernails. He wasn't going to touch that topic. Apparently, neither was Becca.

"Funny you say that. I was thinking you look like a champion mutton buster," Monty said, as if he detected some tension.

"What's a button mustard?" Max asked.

The giggles trickled around the table.

"You have to stay on top of a crazy, wild-and-woolly sheep for six seconds. Now, *that's* fun," Cody explained.

"And prestigious. It takes a lot of moxie. I watched Cody compete in those events when he was about your size," Monty said.

"Not as easy as you might think," Cody added. "I managed to fall off a few of those too. The rodeo clowns would pick me up and brush me off, and I'd run to the sideline where my dad would be waiting. No matter how low I scored, he'd tell me I was a winner for trying."

That earned him a warm smile from Becca. When she reached over and squeezed his hand, he nearly lost it.

"Perry and me saw Cody fall off a bull at his house," Max blurted out.

Oh, boy. Just when he thought they'd steered the topic to a much warmer and fuzzier one.

Becca withdrew her hand and placed it back in her own lap. "Is that so?" she asked.

Max giggled. "It didn't have any legs or a head."

Cody figured he had less than eight seconds to come up with a good explanation, which left nothing but the truth as an option.

"Vern has a mechanical bull. He offered to

let me practice. The boys walked in on me. And, yes, I fell off."

"Did you get to ride it, sweetie?" Rose asked Max.

"No. Mommy wouldn't want me to."

Everyone looked to Becca.

"We don't know for sure, because we didn't ask," Cody said. "But I'm afraid I have some bad news for you, cowboy. Last time I tried to start the bull, it wouldn't budge."

Hopefully that would let Becca off the hook. At least, long enough for her to cool down, because things were starting to get heated. And it had nothing to do with the fireplace. Cody made a scissor-snipping gesture with his fingers, for her eyes only.

She cast him a puzzled look. "We'll talk about this later," she whispered.

"Mechanical bulls aren't toys," Monty interjected. "Got thrown from one myself in Texas. At Gilley's in Pasadena. First and only try. Decided I better stick to music."

"Well, I, for one, am glad you did," Rose said. "Stick to music, I mean. I'm certainly not glad you got thrown." She promptly picked up her water glass and took several gulps, as if she wished she wouldn't have piped in at all.

"I appreciate that, Rose. No wonder Cody thinks so highly of you," Monty said.

She demurred, then looked at Cody and offered up an effortless smile. The kind she used to gift him for no special reason at all.

That's what I'm talkin' about.

"I'm hoping Max will choose a career that doesn't include angry animals that weigh a gazillion pounds," Becca said.

"Don't worry, Mommy. Horses are nice and only weigh one zillion," Max said, holding up a single finger.

Monty laughed. "Close, Max. Most horses come in shy of a thousand pounds. In fact, my granddaddy rode 'em. He used to go on trail rides in Destiny Springs when he was a young man."

"I thought that was a rumor," Becca said.

"No, ma'am. According to him, they'd start at some magical place called Sunrise Stables. He'd tell me all about the fancy entrance sign with the big, smiling sun looking down on an even bigger smiling horse. I always loved that story."

"I've never noticed one like that. Maybe they're not around anymore," Becca said.

"Sounds almost too magical to be true," Cody said. "Any chance the story was just that? A story? And it ended up getting circulated?"

Monty seemed to think about it, then shook

his head and smiled. "You might be onto some-thing," he said. "Come to think of it, he used to tell me the place was owned by a family with an equally whimsical name. The Goodnights. Or maybe the Goodyears."

Or the Goodwins. Except Hailey's stables didn't have a sign at the entrance. Unless it had been taken down.

The waiter brought their entrées, each cooked to perfection. For the most part, they ate in silence, except for Rose and Monty.

Turned out, Monty had stayed at two of the bed and breakfasts that Rose and her late hus-band had renovated and flipped. Both times, he had arrived shortly after they'd sold the properties and moved on.

"Oh, I'm a big fan of B and Bs," Monty said.

And becoming a bigger fan of Rose, Cody suspected. The more she revealed her ex-ceptional business savvy, the more intrigued Monty seemed to be. Not that Cody could blame the guy. That was a side of his ex-mother-in-law that he admired and respected as well.

All the while, Max kept busy playing with his remaining oversize french fry, pretending it was a horse that was racing around salt-and-pepper-shaker barrels. Once through, he posi-tioned the tip of the fry over the ketchup cup as if it were taking a drink of water and dipped it halfway in before shoving the whole fry in his mouth.

Becca took advantage of the moment.

"I should be mad at you about letting Max see the mechanical bull. And letting you get your way about the horses. But I've never seen Mom so happy. Thank you for doing this."

That made two thank-yous so far tonight, and from the people who'd barely given him the time of day earlier. Then there was Monty, who seemed genuinely interested in Rose. If it was all an act, Rose would end up being heart-broken and would blame Cody, setting him back even further.

But it was good to take chances. Like the ones he took every time a chute opened.

He studied Becca while she wasn't looking. If all the stars aligned, would he be willing to take one more chance with her?

The real question was, how could he not?

The looks Rose gave Cody were sweeter than a triple-fudge brownie with milk chocolate icing, dark chocolate syrup on top and rocky road ice cream on the side. Sugar overload.

The whole thing was making Becca queasy. She reached for her water and downed it.

"I wrote a song about riding bulls, you

know," Monty said. "'I Need More Time' is the title. Folks think it's a love song. I suppose it is, in a way."

"I'd love to hear it," Rose said. "Are you familiar with the tune, Cody? Sounds like something you'd like."

Ugh. Did her mom even remember her own daughter was sitting at the table? She'd barely looked her way. At least the night should be wrapping up soon. They'd all managed to clean their plates. No need to order dessert.

Plus, the mere sight of the dessert cart—piled high with thick slices of cake, wedges of pies and an assortment of powdered sweet squares with honey—would trigger the topic she'd managed to avoid all night: Max's upcoming birthday.

She could picture it now. Max would see the cake and mention his special day. Monty would ask his age, and Max would tell him. Rose would be of no support to her now, having switched to Team Cody.

What Becca needed was a distraction. For once, she was happy to blend into the wallpaper. Cody, Rose and Monty were so busy talking among themselves they wouldn't even notice what she was about to do.

She slipped a pen and piece of notepaper out of her purse. On her lap, she jotted down the name of the song and a note to ask the band to please play it. She folded the piece of paper in half and waited until the waiter glanced her way.

Becca tilted her chin up, smiled and pointed at her empty water glass. She slipped him the piece of paper, put her finger to her lips and issued a quiet *shh*.

In her periphery, she noticed Cody watching.

He leaned in and whispered, "Passing notes in class again, Miss Haring?"

"None of your business, Mr. Sayers."

Thankfully, he let it drop. Several minutes later, the band started playing the tune.

"Hey! Isn't that Monty's song? The one you were just talking about?" she asked the table.

Rose, Cody and Monty stopped chatting and listened.

"What a coincidence," Cody said, giving Becca a knowing look.

It was her turn to deploy a mischievous smile, although her intentions weren't what he likely suspected.

"Maybe Monty could offer to step in and do the vocals," Becca said.

"That's awfully sweet of you, Becca, but I don't know. This guy sounds pretty good. Wouldn't want to steal his spotlight."

Not the answer she was going for, but she respected the not-wanting-to-steal-the-spotlight part.

"Maybe you two could dance?" Cody suggested.

Monty patted his stomach. "As soon as my dinner settles, I hope this lovely lady and I will dance. If she wants to, that is."

Rose tilted her head. Her smile screamed *Yes!*

"Well, we can't let this beautiful song go to waste." Becca stood and extended her hand to Max. "May I have this dance? I'll let you sit on the creature up front for as long as you want when we're done."

"Really? Okey dokey!"

As Max proceeded to tug her away from the table, she whispered to her mom, "He doesn't need any sugar this late. Please order dessert to-go while we're gone, if you don't mind."

"That's fine with me. I couldn't eat another thing," Rose said.

Before they so much as stepped on the dance floor, Becca and Max garnered the sweetest looks. The little boy didn't have the first clue how to do the two-step, but they managed a couple of rounds with her taking the lead.

The next song was a slow one. Becca took Max's hand, thanked her partner and led them to the side, nearly running into Cody in the process. How long had he been standing there?

"May I have this dance?" he asked.

"I promised Max he could sit on the bull or whatever that thing is."

"That's okay, Mommy. You can dance with Cody first."

She released Max's hand, and they watched to make sure he found his way back to the table before launching into that slow sway, like they used to do so perfectly. They never stepped on each other's toes on the dance floor.

Off the dance floor? That was a different story.

She often thought about how he'd suggested they talk to a counselor or therapist or clergyperson to try and work through their differences. Translation: have someone convince her that she needed to let Cody do what he needed to do and wait to start a family. Ultimately, she'd decided she couldn't sustain such a difficult dance with a semiabsent partner.

Turned out, she'd had to do the single-parent dance completely on her own.

He pulled her close, but far enough away for them to look at each other. His gaze ran over her hair, her eyes, her lips. It reminded her of their last-ditch effort to salvage the marriage. The eleventh-hour attempt to have the relationship not become completely unglued. The result was the most wonderful thing to have ever happened: Max.

She swallowed hard. She wanted to tell him everything in that moment, while he was in her arms and couldn't run away. Would he choose to leave again, if he knew? Or would he feel trapped, like a bull in a chute, right before the gate flew open?

Not one bull she'd ever heard of chose to stay confined once they had a choice. But Cody wasn't a bull, nor was he perfect. He was a good man, though. One with a passionate career goal.

He ran a hand through her hair, then touched his index finger to her lips. When she didn't flinch, he put his hand back on her waist and pulled her closer. They both knew what was going to happen next.

It was what would happen after this inevitable *next* that wasn't so clear.

KISSING BECCA WASN'T anything like Cody remembered.

It was infinitely better.

The soft, brief connection packed a punch that he hadn't seen coming. Hard to act cool and composed with his heart beating out of his chest and when it felt as though he was grinning from the inside out.

He still felt off balance, long after they walked off the dance floor and back to the table. That was why he suggested Becca be the one to hoist Max on top of the Black Angus on the way out while Rose snapped pictures with her cell phone. She even urged Cody to stand beside Max in a few.

"Send me copies of those, if you don't mind," he said to Rose.

"Absolutely!"

Cody couldn't help but think such an enthusiastic response wouldn't have happened a few hours ago. And that was okey dokey with him.

He took a moment to check his phone messages. Three from his publicist. Didn't have to read them to know she was hounding him about sending a photo. The more he thought about it, the less he liked the idea, Becca's approval notwithstanding.

But Pamela Stone refused to be ignored for long. Best to get this discussion over with. Or at least kick the can down the road. He stepped away far enough to be seen but not heard.

"I was about to send out a search party," she said in lieu of a greeting.

"Sorry. Been busy."

"Too busy to read my texts, I assume. Because otherwise you would have called immediately."

Cody's stomach cinched. "What did I do now?"

"Nothing that I'm aware of, but that's not why I was calling. *Rodeo's Brightest* wants to profile you for a book. We're talking high-end coffee-table fare. Perfect place to showcase you and your fan. Everyone will see the Rodeo Rascal in a new, softer light."

That cinch in Cody's stomach tightened to a marble-sized knot. "And if we leave the fan out of it?"

"I'm afraid that's the angle I pitched, and the one they're willing to pay top dollar for. Think it over, Cody, but I can save you the trouble. There's only one answer if you want to shed your rascal skin. Besides, what parent wouldn't want their child's picture alongside the brightest rodeo star of all?"

I can think of one.

Cody ended the call with nothing more than a thinly veiled sigh, then rejoined the group. He'd been a bit of a rascal tonight, that was for sure. Stealing a kiss without asking first, although it felt more like she was the one who'd kissed him.

After Monty finished posing for selfies with

a few of Ribeye Roy's customers, he pulled Cody aside.

"Cute kid y'all have there," he said.

"Actually, he's Becca's. Unless you know something I don't know," Cody joked.

Monty laughed. "Afraid I don't have any good news for you there. I just assumed."

He was the second person to reach that conclusion. The first had been Miss Hennessy, the guest with the broken lock.

"I should have clarified. But if I did have a son, I'd want him to be exactly like this kid." Max was now pretending to be bucked off the immobile beast, while Becca urged him to sit still.

"My guess is it's not a matter of *if* for you. It's a matter of *when*, considering how much you enjoy being around this one. Just a personal observation," Monty said.

"Monty? Do you mind? I'd like a picture of you with Max," Rose said.

The man didn't hesitate. If Rose asked him to jump, he wouldn't even bother to ask how high. He'd go out and buy the biggest trampoline he could find. That was Cody's personal observation. The man was such a gentleman. One who'd always conducted his personal life with the utmost integrity. Married his childhood sweetheart and, by all accounts, was faithful to her for forty plus years until she'd unexpectedly passed. All that traveling and all the tours and necessary miles couldn't tear them apart. Their love had been like Teflon.

Cody and Becca's marriage had been more like tissue paper.

After a few crazy photos, Monty rejoined him.

"I owe you a big one, Monty."

"How so?"

"For coming all this way and being such a sport. I've never seen Rose so happy. I mean, she was always the dream mother-in-law, but the divorce put an end to that. I finally scored some points back tonight, thanks to you."

"Cody, I should be thanking you. I haven't been on a date—arranged or otherwise—since Trudy passed. She insisted that I not be alone, but I was never inclined. Until now. I'm hoping Rose will agree to see me again."

Monty was either totally serious or he should win an Oscar. Cody crossed his arms, shook his head and let out a long, audible sigh.

"I'm not so sure if she'll be agreeable to that, Monty. But I'll try to influence her decision and will put in a good word for you."

Monty looked crestfallen. They looked to Rose, who couldn't stop smiling. At Monty.

Cody busted out laughing.

Monty shook his head. "You had me there for a minute. No wonder they call you the Rascal."

Monty had nailed it. That was exactly how Cody had gotten the nickname: for his wicked sense of humor. Becca had always assumed it was because he was a flirt. If he'd been such a thing at all, it certainly hadn't been intentional.

The bull-and-Max photo shoot finally ended. A cheerful Becca helped Max off the wooden beast.

The evening had succeeded in ways Cody hadn't even anticipated.

He wasn't sure where this would lead, but for the first time ever, Becca seemed to understand what bull riding meant to him. Possibly even accept it. Funny thing about that, however. He could see himself in her arms every night, rather than working the circuit. Riding hadn't crossed his mind even once on the dance floor. And those bulls not only crossed his mind on a regular basis, they pretty much owned it.

Unfortunately, ownership would have to be turned back over to them. At least temporarily. Scottsdale was less than a week away, then Houston. From there, Vegas.

Strange, but that didn't sound nearly as appealing as it had a week ago.

And not even remotely temporary.

CHAPTER THIRTEEN

CODY LOOKED SKYWARD for the answer to a question that had kept him awake half the night.

It was looking like he'd found it. Two empty hooks dangled from thick chains at the top of the horizontal metal bar that framed the entrance to Hailey's property. If his theory was correct, the hooks used to hold a sign that read *Sunrise Stables*.

Hailey was in the process of tidying up the stalls when Cody approached. Several yards away, Max was busy filling a bucket with water.

She glanced at Cody. "You look so serious. What gives?"

"You've been keeping a secret from me. I thought we'd become closer than that," he said with the most serious look he could muster.

She stopped tidying and struck a pose. More like struck an attitude as she folded her arms.

"What secret are you referring to?" she asked.

Why was she on the defensive? It was supposed to be a joke.

"You mean there's more than one?" he teased. Or tried to.

She glanced at Max, who'd finished transporting water to one of the stalls. "Just tell me."

"Sunrise Stables. The rumor about the trail rides. It's true, isn't it?"

She exhaled, unfolded her arms and tucked her hands in her back pocket. "Where'd you hear that?" she asked, squinting against the sun.

"My friend Montgomery Legend said his grandfather used to ride. Monty remembered him describing the sign. A smiling sun and horse? Claimed the owner's last name was something like Goodnight or Goodyear. I'm thinking those are good guesses, but not good enough. Get it?"

She half smiled, then looked away. "Got it. And, yeah, it's true. The trail rides started with my great-grandparents. Any hopes of reviving it officially died with me. You're looking at the final nail in the coffin."

She nodded in Max's direction and started walking. Cody followed.

"So you didn't want to continue the tradition. There's no shame in that," he said.

He thought about his own situation. How

bull riding was in his family's blood but his two older brothers wanted nothing to do with it. Fortunately, Cody did.

"It's not that I wouldn't have. It skipped a few generations. The tradition had already been reduced to a rumor by the time I inherited the place, and all those resources and the connection were no longer available."

Hailey stopped at a stretch of fence, closer to Max. She looked away while twisting her long ponytail around her hand and wrist like some sort of a lifeline.

"Yet, you have all these horses."

"I've had horses all my life. For my pleasure, not for others or for profit. I take older ones off people's hands when, for whatever reason, they can no longer take care of them."

Cody patted the quarter horse's neck. "They're lucky to have you."

"I'm the lucky one. They're all so gentle. Not a mean bone in any of these bodies. Unless you cross 'em."

"Looks like you have vacancies." Cody nodded toward three empty stalls. "What happens when you're at capacity? Do you have to turn horses away?"

"I suppose I'd have to. Unfortunately, I'm pretty much at capacity already. I don't have enough help, as you can probably tell."

"Come here, Max," Cody called out. Max set the bucket down and joined them. "Do you know of any cowboys who could pitch in and help Hailey at the stables every once in a while?"

He raised his hand and waved it. "I can help!"

Cody brushed his hands together. "Problem solved."

In hindsight, he probably shouldn't have put that idea in Max's head. It would be another thing Becca would have to say no to.

Hailey rolled her eyes but added a sweet grin. "Since all I can afford is child labor, I'd be willing to negotiate," she said. "In the meantime, Max, would you mind counting the feed supply bags for me?"

Max nodded and ran off again.

"Montgomery Legend, huh?" she said. "I knew you were a big shot yourself, but you certainly have some impressive friends."

He thought back to that look on Rose's face. He hadn't simply cracked the ice queen. He'd completely melted her.

Speaking of melting... That kiss from Becca on the dance floor... Cody rubbed the sides of his mouth to try to contain a grin.

Hailey nodded. "Uh-huh. Talk about secrets. You're obviously keeping one."

"Thinking about last night. I'd asked Monty for a favor. To come to Destiny Springs and charm my ex-mother-in-law on my behalf."

Hailey cocked her head. "To get on Becca's good side?"

"Why do you ask when you already know the answer?"

"Because it's fun to see you deny the obvious. What isn't as believable is your claim about Montgomery Legend being in town last night. I would have heard about it through the grapevine by now."

"It's true. Hey, Max. Who did you get to meet last night?"

Max ran back over. "I got to meet a bull. And I got to ride him for *hours*!"

"A Black Angus," Cody clarified to Hailey.

"Now you're both making up stories," she said.

Which reminded him, he had evidence. He'd asked Rose to send him copies of the pictures she took last night, which she promptly did but he'd yet to look at them. He retrieved his phone from his pocket.

Judging from the quantity, she'd been a little camera-happy. Must have taken dozens. He scrolled until he came across one of Max on the Angus and Monty standing beside him, smiling. He handed Hailey the phone.

"I stand corrected. Mind if I look at the others?" she asked.

"Not at all. But it might take a while."

"I didn't get thrown, but I wanted to." Max yanked and jerked, then fell to the ground, giggling the whole time.

Cody gave him a hand up. "No, you don't. It hurts. Real bad."

Hailey was too engrossed in the photos to back him up.

Although, for Cody there was always some satisfaction in being bucked off. When he was on top of a bull, he forgot his regrets and mistakes. When he was thrown, it was atonement for all of them. Except one: giving up on his marriage to Becca.

Hopefully, Max would never experience that kind of regret. Or the pain of being discarded to the ground and trampled like delicate grapes at a winery, except beneath the hooves of an angry, two-thousand-pound bull.

"This one is interesting." Hailey handed him the phone.

There, on the screen, was a photo of Becca and him. Slow dancing. Looking into each other's eyes. *About to kiss*.

The next pictures were of Monty and Max at the table. Thankfully, Rose had stopped short of capturing the most intimate moment. He breathed an internal sigh of relief as he tucked his phone back in his pocket.

"Well, you already confessed that you're still in love with her," Hailey said.

"Didn't say the words," he countered.

"We've been through this."

"I know."

Even if they hadn't, it was obvious from the photo. Couldn't deny that. Truth was he'd never stopped being in love with her. He was hoping Hailey would tell him that Becca was still in love with him too, because despite the kiss he wasn't at all sure.

"How many days before you leave?" she asked.

"You're coming to my surprise birthday party, aren't you?" Max interrupted.

"Max, you weren't supposed to know about that," Hailey said.

He giggled.

Cody, on the other hand, didn't find anything funny about it. "When's the big day, cowboy? I'll check my calendar."

Max counted to himself and held up seven fingers.

"Days?" he asked.

Max nodded.

In three days, he'd be leaving Destiny Springs for Arizona. In five, he'd be on the

back of a bull. And in seven, he'd be getting
ready to head to Houston. He couldn't have attended anyway, but still.

"Not sure I can wrangle that, but we'll find
another way to celebrate. Okay?"

"Okay," Max said.

What? No *okey dokey*? This *was* serious.

"To answer your question, Hailey," he said,
holding up three fingers where Max couldn't
see.

"C'mon, Max. Let's go check on the hay and
shavings supplies," Hailey said.

Max launched into a run, but Hailey didn't
budge.

"A lot can happen in three days," she said.

With that, she pushed off from the fence,
leaving Cody alone to ponder the possibilities.
It also left him with one unanswered question.

Why hadn't Becca told him?

BECCA PRESSED THE stack of still-warm towels against her chest and inhaled the clean,
fresh scent as she carried them upstairs. Her
thoughts were pulled back to last night on the
dance floor, Cody's body pressed against hers.
He was so warm, and he smelled so good. Like
spring, summer and fall, all in one.

It was a nice respite, but reality had given
her a wake-up call this morning. The heavi-

ness of even more guilt weighed her down, especially after seeing Cody and Max together for a longer stretch.

She knocked on the door of each room before entering to replace the towels, empty the trash and do some general tidying up.

The day was flawless. Cold, but with the clearest, bluest of skies. Seemed as though they hadn't had any rain, or so much as a cloud, since he'd arrived.

Most folks were either sitting outside near the gas heaters or had left the property and gone sightseeing, making it the perfect time for this chore. In fact, she might permanently take it off Hailey's to-do list and put it on hers.

Every time she walked into the rooms, she thought of ways to improve the decor. Although guests came and went, this was her and Max's forever home. The entire place was hers to do with as she wished.

Even if it involved spandex.

Funny how her mom had stopped complaining about being stuck in that room. Then again, the woman was too busy enjoying herself. Becca was kind of surprised that her mom could eat breakfast this morning with a grin that big. How did she manage to chew? Not to mention how she raved about the Rascal's Rodeo Scramble.

Becca reached the Spandex Room and knocked.

"Come in," Rose called out.

Becca opened the door to catch her mom in the process of returning the set of three-pound dumbbells to the rack.

"Were you...?"

Rose grinned. "Guilty."

"Does this have anything to do with a certain country-western singer?"

"He's staying in town. Offered to take me dancing, since we really didn't have a chance last night. Too busy talking and all."

Becca nodded. "I see. An official date."

"It's not like that," Rose insisted as she fluffed and arranged the spandex throw pillows on top of the bed.

"Right. Here are some fresh towels. You'll want to take a shower after working up such a sweat in preparation for your nondate."

Rose sat on the edge of the mattress and patted it as an invitation for Becca to sit. More like a command. That bed was turning out to be their version of a therapy couch.

Becca stopped short of following through when she realized the full extent of what her mom had been up to since breakfast.

"Are you wearing the leg warmers?" she asked.

Those were supposed to be a tongue-in-cheek prop. Seeing them on her own mom was going to make it difficult to take any heart-to-heart talk seriously.

Rose didn't pick up that conversational thread. She didn't answer at all. Becca recognized the look of concern, perfected after years of mothering and grandparenting.

Penny pushed the door open and joined them, reminding Becca that she didn't have time for some much-needed therapy. Too many things to do.

"Put on some walking shoes and meet me in the parlor," she instructed.

Becca headed for the door before Rose could refuse. Penny stayed behind. Her mom had even won over the labradoodle.

"Make sure she comes with you," Becca added, pointing to the pup.

"Okay, sweetheart. Whatever you say."

Becca hurried downstairs and retrieved the leash from the kitchen hook. By the time Rose caught up, the woman had added the terry-cloth headband—another intended prop—to her walking attire.

The labradoodle took the lead through the front door, down the steps and around the side of the house. A few guests still dotted the patio, sipping coffee or mimosas. They all stopped chatting and turned to stare at either the adorable three-legged labradoodle or the eighties poster child.

Or maybe they noticed the extra guilt Becca had packed on overnight.

Once she and her mom were alone, Becca asked, "Did you want to talk about something in particular?"

"I wanted to apologize," Rose said.

"For what?"

"For being so hard on Cody, then being so nice. I must seem like the flakiest mother a girl could ever have."

"He has that effect on people. You're only human."

"He had it on you last night, didn't he? Don't deny it. I have evidence."

"You have *what*?"

Rose stopped walking and fished her cell phone from her fanny pack, which made Becca snort out loud.

"What's so funny?" Rose paused and looked up.

Becca pointed to her belt bag. Yet another prop. She'd forgotten about it until now.

"Laugh if you will, but this little purse is coming in quite handy. And I must say, my legs and forehead are nice and warm. I may have to steal these nifty things when I leave."

Becca rolled her eyes. "I won't report you."

"Oh! Here they are." Rose turned the phone screen toward Becca, then scrolled through photos until she reached the next set, with Max and Monty, then backtracked to the last photo of Becca and Cody on the dance floor, looking at each other.

"How many did you take?"

Rose slipped the phone back into the fanny pack and zipped it shut. "Enough to get a clear picture."

Thankfully, her mother hadn't gotten the full picture. Not after Becca's confession about keeping Max a secret. To make matters even more complicated, she had to go and kiss Cody with those same lips that had remained silent for more than six years.

Oh, and he'd be leaving again soon. Otherwise, those lips would have to explain the unexplainable.

"I have to tell him, Mom. But I still don't know when. Or even if I can bring myself to do it."

"I was thinking that exact same thing, because it's pretty clear to me that you two are still in love."

"Why are you so convinced of that?"

Rose gave Becca that familiar, knowing

look. A combination of experience, intuition and hope.

"You can tell me anything, Rebecca. But you can't tell me anything about your feelings for Cody that I don't already know. And vice versa for him. Do you remember the last photo I took of the two of you? Or do I need to show you again?"

Becca remembered it well. They had pulled apart to look at each other.

A few moments before we kissed.

"We were dancing. You got all that from the last photo?"

"No, sweetheart. I 'got all that' from the next one. The one I purposely deleted."

LAST NIGHT HAD been all about Rose. Tonight, it would be all about Becca.

If anything could coax her out of her hiding place, it was Cody's five-alarm chicken enchilada casserole. Okay, so maybe his dish wasn't as fancy as the six-ounce peppercorn fillet Becca had polished off at Ribeye Roy's, but hopefully he'd get an equally good review.

Aside from breakfast, where they didn't so much as rub shoulders, he'd barely caught a glimpse of her all day. He suspected why: the kiss.

Or perhaps she was feeling guilty about

keeping a secret. Was she afraid he'd change his plans and stay for Max's party? Or did she simply not want him to feel guilty about not being able to attend? No matter. He'd let it go. Even though he felt at home here, this house belonged to her, as did Max.

Still, last night, when Monty reminisced about the rodeo and seeing him compete, Cody could have sworn Becca's interest had been piqued. Perhaps for the first time ever.

Cody grabbed a mitt and opened the oven door. The smell of melted cheese made his mouth water. When he turned around, he realized he had company.

"Aren't you adorable?" he said to his guest.

Penny wagged her tail and barked. No doubt, the pup was jonesing for some casserole.

"Where's your momma?" he asked, referring to Becca. The hot-and-cheesy aroma had to be making its way through the house by now.

"That smells amazing," someone said. "What time is dinner? Hint, hint."

Three guests stood at the doorway. He recognized one of them from earlier. Cody removed the oven mitt, set it on the counter and rested his hands on his hips.

"I tell you what, if my date stands me up tonight, I'll share this with y'all. How does that sound?"

"Then, I'm secretly hoping she's a no-show," one of the ladies said, then left him alone with a couple. More newlyweds, from the looks of it.

"We heard that someone was offering trail rides. How would we go about arranging that?" the man asked, as if Cody worked there.

"I heard that rumor too," he said. "In fact, I may have been responsible for spreading it. No one offers trail rides anywhere around here, but who knows what the future holds?"

The couple nodded in unison and left, holding hands the entire time.

He and Becca used to do that a lot.

"I'm certain your future doesn't hold any of this casserole," he said to Penny. "Much too spicy. But I'll sneak you an extra Milk-Bone."

As soon as he said that, it occurred to him that he'd left out a crucial ingredient in the casserole. Black beans.

All was not lost. He could serve those on the side, assuming he could find some in the pantry. No time left to make another run to the store. Too bad he hadn't thought of it when it mattered. His focus had been hijacked by Rose's photos from last night. Especially the one where Becca was facing the camera, eyes closed, chin resting on his shoulder. He'd never seen such a sweet smile. Pretty much matched the way he'd felt at the moment.

He checked the apple timer. With five minutes remaining, his mad search began.

Pantry first. Plenty of canned goods. Some garbanzo beans and black-eyed peas, neither of which would pair very well with his dish. He opened cabinet after cabinet until he found something else of interest.

Tucked far away—behind the oatmeal, cereal and Pop-Tarts—he spotted a chocolate-cake mix lying on its side. Looked like it had been forgotten. Not what he was looking for, but it might be a nice surprise dessert if he could pull it off in time.

When he retrieved the box, a baggie with some candles slipped off the top and onto the counter.

"I better ask permission on this one. Might be reserved for a special occasion."

Max's birthday?

He sat the box down and stared at the baggie. Six purple candles.

The timer buzzed, so he grabbed the oven mitt and retrieved his masterpiece. The cheese bubbled on the top.

Penny whimpered. A tiny bit of drool escaped her mouth.

"After this cools down, I'll spread some

cheese on your Milk-Bone. Just don't tell Becca."

"Don't tell Becca what?"

His evil plan to lure her to the kitchen had worked. She was barefoot and beautiful in an oversize, soft powder-blue sweater and jeans. He closed the space between them and gave her a sweet peck on her lips, which didn't seem quite as receptive as they were last night.

Sure, he and Becca would have a lot to work through if they wanted to move forward. But he felt as though they'd had a breakthrough last night.

"Before I answer, where's Max?" he asked.

"Playing in his room. Guess it's just the two of us at the moment."

He returned to the cabinet and located the Milk-Bones.

"I don't want to have any secrets between us, Becca. Truth is, I was going to put some cheese on Penny's treat, without your consent," he said, hoping for a smile.

Hers qualified as a tentative grin. He removed the apron and placed it on the counter, next to the mix.

"I was tempted to bake a cake for us. But I figured you must have bought this with someone else in mind."

She walked over and picked up the box. "It's

for Max's birthday. Sorry I didn't mention it. You'll be gone before Max can take you on a guilt trip about it."

That's what he'd hoped she would say. What didn't make sense was the baggie.

"Six candles?"

She ran her hand over the contents. "One to grow on."

He squinted. "I don't get it."

Becca bit her bottom lip and looked down at the floor as if she'd find the explanation there.

"Adding an extra candle for good luck in the coming year. All the moms I know do it," she finally offered.

Had his own mother done that for him, and he'd forgotten? He was so young... He pushed down the thought and turned his attention to the casserole. He tore off a piece of foil from a box he'd retrieved and secured it on top of the dish until it was ready to serve.

Becca placed a warm hand on his back.

"Is everything okay?" she asked.

"Yeah. Thinking about my mom. Dad tells me she made our birthday cakes from scratch. And she'd decorate them herself. I doubt she ever knew how much we appreciated everything she did for us."

"She knew. Trust me. I'll spend half the day baking Max's favorite cookies from scratch.

Peanut butter with a chocolate kiss in the middle. He'll grab as many as his hands can hold, even when they're still hot, and run off without saying a word."

"Not very convincing," he said.

She shook her head and continued. "The next morning, even more cookies will have mysteriously disappeared. I'll ask if he took them, but he won't admit it. I tell him that he owes me a kiss on the cheek for every chocolate kiss-filled cookie he ate, and all will be forgiven. No questions asked."

"What happens next?"

"I get all those kisses back, and more."

He choked up. Couldn't help it.

"Sit," he commanded. He wasn't about to let her slip away tonight.

He retrieved a couple of dishes and scooped out a serving for each of them, then sat across from her. She took a huge bite, cheese still connecting the fork to the dish.

"Mmm," she managed to say with her mouth full. "Now, this I remember. But…"

"What?"

She swallowed fully and licked her lips. "Something's missing."

"I know. The black beans."

Becca shook her head. "No. This."

She leaned over the table and gave him an

even sweeter kiss on the lips, then resumed eating as if nothing had happened. He continued as well. He'd shown enough emotion for one night.

Maybe no one else would ever know about this little exchange, but he couldn't face Killer feeling so...*in love.*

"She would be so proud of you and what you've accomplished in your career. I didn't know her, but as a mom myself, I'm certain of it," Becca said.

He suspected she would have. His mother had always been so encouraging of his dad with his career. It was a dynamic he'd hoped to have with Becca. Maybe it was still possible. He'd pursued a career; she'd started a family and made a home. They'd both grown up in the process. Was a second chance out of the question for the two of them?

Not to mention, he was crazy about Max.

Sure, he'd still be gone some, but the money would be insane. He could fly her and Max anywhere. Once he got his title, he'd be in a better position to pick and choose which events he wanted to compete in.

There was plenty of uncertainty in that scenario as well. Like before, he could promise her the world and, in the end, guarantee nothing as far as a timeline. If she wasn't willing to accept everything else he could offer in the meantime, then they'd be back to the same place they were six years ago.

But that didn't mean he was giving up.

CHAPTER FOURTEEN

THE GALLOPING STARTED out as a faint clickety-click, which got louder and closer within seconds. For once, Becca was grateful for the noise. It warned her to quickly tuck the cake mix away in the nearest cabinet, which she would have done last night had she not been so distracted.

Max busted through the door and tore a path through the kitchen and back out again.

A million things were still on her to-do list for his surprise party. Fortunately, telling Cody that he was Max's father before his next competition was no longer anywhere in the realm of possibility.

There was relief in that decision. Not that she had a choice. She'd painted herself into a corner with the whole excuse about the sixth candle when she could have finally spoken the truth.

Max circled back through the parlor and into the kitchen. She whisked him up in her arms as certainly as she'd done the cake mix. Seemed as though he'd grown overnight. He tried to wiggle out of her grip, but she held on, wanting to remember these moments because they'd only happen once this exact way.

Hailey sauntered in, coffee cup in hand. Becca released Max, who promptly left the room.

"Do you think you can take over the breakfast preparation today, or at least for a while?" Becca asked.

Hailey looked back over her shoulder, raised her eyebrows, and pointed to herself. "You're asking me?"

Becca untied her apron and offered it to her. "You don't have to do any actual cooking. Cody will take care of the egg dish. At least, I assume he will."

"Why wouldn't he?" Hailey asked.

"Because he'll be leaving soon"

"He's not leaving early, is he?"

Hailey sounded genuinely disappointed. Becca knew they'd become fast friends and imaginary siblings, but this?

"Not that I'm aware of. I want to make sure he *does* leave, however. He found the cake mix and candles last night. All six of them."

Hailey's eyes widened. She clapped her free hand over her mouth. "What did you say?" she asked, her voice muffled against her palm.

"I said the extra candle was one to grow on."

Hailey wagged a finger at Becca. "You're good. Do you think there's any chance he would cancel his trip and stay for the party?"

"No. Do you?"

"I'm sure he'd like to be there, but no. He's hungrier for a championship than he is for cake and ice cream." Hailey examined the fruit, as if she wasn't sure where to even begin with the preparations.

"Wash the kiwis and remove the skin before you slice them into medallions," Becca said.

"Sounds complicated, but I'm up for the challenge. Question is, are you?"

"What do you mean?"

"You want him to stay, don't you?"

The woman never gave up.

Max circled through again, this time stopping to show off his bucking skills.

"I don't know what I want, except to get through the you-know-what." Becca pointed at Max, who was particularly energetic.

"Max, will you help Hailey with the orange juicer this morning?"

That was something she'd never allowed Max to do out of fear he'd hurt himself. Like riding horses. Maybe Max wasn't the only one who had grown up a little overnight.

Her son looked at her as if he'd misunderstood. Poor little guy was so used to hearing *no*.

Becca nodded. "You heard correctly. You're in charge of the juicer this morning. Remember what I told you? Never put your hands where the oranges should go." She pointed to the jutted dome. "Hailey, help him out, please? Cut the oranges in halves for him and supervise the process. And, if you don't mind, clean up my mess after you finish with the fruit."

If only her assistant could also clean up the colossal disaster Becca had made of her life. Her long-term goal now was to avoid making an even bigger mess of it. The immediate goal, however, was to have Hailey keep Max distracted while she retrieved the rest of the party items from the truck.

Once back in her room with the goods, Becca pulled the first batch of items out from under the bed and proceeded to do an inventory in case she needed to pick up anything else besides the helium balloons.

Mini harmonicas? Check.

Crazy straws for the lemonade? Check.

Birthday card?

"Where did you go?"

It wasn't mixed in with the napkins and plates and table decorations. Must have fallen out. She felt around beneath the bed. Nothing. She ventured back out to the truck and gave it a thorough once-over, feeling beneath the seats and taking everything out of the jump seat.

No luck.

The checker at the store must have failed to put it in the bag. At least that seemed to be the only item missing. Except for a husband to share this whole experience with.

All fifteen of Max's friends had RSVPed. The birthday guests would arrive a little before regular breakfast time, while the B and B guests would be pampered with a room-service buffet that morning, complete with door-to-door beverage service. She'd already lined up some part-timers for that task, with Hailey's assistance.

As far as the rest of the plan went, she would take Max to the barn under the guise of serving orange juice as usual. Instead of guests, his friends would be there, wearing special cowboy party hats and blowing whistles. They'd have snacks and play games inside and outside the barn, then end the festivities with ice cream and cake.

After that, Becca would be able to breathe again. The games would officially be over.

At least, the kind of games that children played.

VERN PEELED BACK the foil and inhaled. "What's this?"

"Leftovers," Cody said.

"You made this too?"

"Yesterday. They're even better the day after, after the tortillas have absorbed all the sauce and the chicken breaks down even more. Trust me."

"Who got in on the beginning?" Vern asked. "The woman you used to be married to? The redhead who runs the B and B, in case you want me to be even more specific?"

Cody studied Vern's expression. "How'd you know?"

"Small town. You could have told me, though. I'm probably one of the few people around here who can keep a secret."

"Then, I guess you won't be able to answer the question I came here to ask."

Vern nodded at the dish. "I see. This isn't a casserole you brought me. It's a bribe."

"I won't even try to lie. You're too smart."

"If you want to know whether she's seeing anyone, I can honestly say I don't think so. At least, not at the moment. Plenty of good men have tried. Rumor has it that one even proposed, but she turned him down. You do know that Destiny Springs has more engagements every year per capita than any other city in these United States?"

Out of all those words Vern had spoken, *proposed* was the only one Cody really paid attention to.

"I didn't know that. Glad she's being sensible and not taking the first offer that comes along."

Was that what'd happened with Max's father? Did she want a family so desperately that she'd said yes to someone who wasn't as committed? Sure, he'd let her down, but at least he'd been honest about wanting to wait to start a family. Wait until he did what he needed to do and could be home more often than not.

And not miss the important firsts.

"Oh, she's not going to settle for just anyone. Nor should she. Especially where Max is concerned. He deserves a good, solid father figure."

"Which leads to the reason for the bribe. I was wondering about Max's father. Not a name or anything. But is he a good person, or even in the picture? I asked you once before, but you ignored me. You forced me to resort to drastic measures."

"Yeah, I remember you asking. And I thought you might still be wondering. I didn't have any information for you then, and I don't have any now. Truth be told, that's one of the best-kept secrets in this little town. He hasn't been around that I've seen or heard of."

"Becca always was an extremely private person. Then she went and got involved with a public one."

"Speaking of which, you still going to Scottsdale?"

"That's the plan."

Vern scooted to the edge of his chair. "Wanna ride Sally? I know you've missed a few days, unless you tried to work the remote yourself again."

Cody shook his head.

"Did something bad happen?" Vern asked.

"I'm afraid so. That's another reason for the casserole. Maybe I should break the news after you've gotten hooked."

"I prefer to get bad news on an empty stomach."

Cody stood and eased the container from Vern's hands. More like pried it out.

"Wait a minute! I'm willing to negotiate." Vern grabbed a fork and made a pathetic attempt to nab a bite.

"I need to show you what happened rather than tell you," he said as he confiscated the fork from Vern. "Follow me."

This time, Cody took the lead, reminding

Vern about the jammed key along the way. Once inside, he handed over the casserole.

"You hold this."

Cody located the jagged end of the cut cord and held it up.

"What happened?" Vern asked.

Now Cody knew how distress looked on Vern's face.

"I had to put old Sally down. More like temporarily incapacitate her."

"But why?"

Cody dropped the cord, pulled the fork out of his pocket and handed it to Vern.

"Max and Perry walked in on me riding. They became much too curious. Perry even located the toggle on the side, sending old Sally kicking. No one got hurt, but I wanted to make sure their curiosity didn't get the best of 'em when no one was looking."

Vern nodded. "I see. No, we wouldn't want that."

"You forgive me?"

Vern waved off the question. "I believe in forgiving anything if the reason for doing so is strong enough."

Becca seemed to have forgiven him for leaving, which couldn't have been easy. Was it enough to give him another chance?

He'd long forgiven her, even though there

wasn't a good reason why he shouldn't. She'd wanted a family with him, a home and a full-time father for their children. She'd wanted him to be around to grow old with, in good health and all in one piece. Difficult to ever consider something like that unforgivable.

After spending time with Max, he understood why Becca had wanted a family so desperately. When it came right down to it, she was better at visualizing than he ever would be.

"Besides, that type of problem can be fixed in the future, if need be," Vern said as he studied the severed cord.

It took Cody a few moments to switch gears back to the previous topic of conversation. "I figured that was the best line to sever."

Vern took a huge bite of the casserole, seemingly lost in thought.

"I'll replace it with a detachable cord and hide it behind lock and key when Sally isn't in use," Vern continued. "Next time you're up this way, you can go for a spin. You are coming back someday, aren't you?"

"If I can fix something that's even more damaged than that electrical cord."

Not to mention more powerful than a working one.

"How about this one?" Rose asked.

Becca stared at the card her mom had chosen but couldn't find the right words.

Maybe she shouldn't have talked the woman into coming to town with her. Either her mom was totally distracted or the headband she'd worn half the day yesterday had been too tight and affected her reasoning.

"A thank-you card?" Becca asked.

"For Monty. For the lovely evening."

Becca eased it out of Rose's grip and put it back in its rightful spot on the spinning rack. "Let's find a birthday card for Max first. Then we can discuss your dating strategy."

"I just thought—"

Becca planted a huge kiss on her mom's cheek. "*My* thought is that he should be getting *you* a thank-you card. But first things first. I don't see any more sentiments like the one I thought I bought. It read *Happy 6th Birthday* and had some purple balloons on the front."

Becca spun the rack slowly while they both skimmed. Rose snatched a card from the bottom rack before it circled around again.

"How about this one?" she asked.

Horses on the front. Black and white, but the balloons were in color. Not a purple one in the bunch, however. Still, it looked promising, especially since Becca had decided to go with a cowboy theme, despite her reservations about encouraging such a lifestyle.

Then again, it was her fault for moving to the Cowboy State in the first place. New England had been her vision. But before he passed, her dad had found this property for her. After that, she couldn't envision living anywhere else.

Rose opened the card, and they read it out loud together. *"I'm not horsing around when I say I hope you have a wonderful birthday!"*

They exchanged glances and shoulder shrugs. Becca held on to it because the choice of kid-oriented birthday cards was limited. Didn't matter what the sentiment read. Max would love it for the horses alone. That was the only thing that mattered when it came right down to it.

"Oh, look! A soda fountain and bar." Rose pointed toward the back of the store. "Let's talk strategy there."

As if Becca had a choice. Rose took her hand and pulled her along as if she were still a little girl. They settled onto some swiveling barstools. A young woman stopped taking inventory of some nearby shelves and slipped behind the counter to wait on them.

"Two root beer ice-cream floats, please," Rose said.

"I didn't realize you were that hungry."

"One is for you. Don't you remember? We used to have these at Avalon Diner in Houston. You were around the same age as Max."

Becca nodded. Yes, she remembered. Those sure were some good times. Before they started moving from property to property. And before the media interfered in their personal lives.

"Do you remember my eleventh birthday?" Becca asked.

They'd never talked about it before. As though, if they didn't speak about the article, it never happened.

"You looked so pretty that day. And happy."

Becca put her arm around her. "I was. They got it so wrong, Mom. You threw the best parties for me. I wouldn't trade my childhood for anyone else's."

"I don't know. I think I'd trade my own for Max's. You're doing an amazing job."

"I'm sure the media would find something wrong with it," Becca added. "Not that I'm going to give them a chance."

The server finished making the floats and placed them in front of Becca and Rose. This was a good spot to transition to a heart-to-heart talk of a different kind.

Becca held up a spoon. "Here's to family."

Rose clinked her spoon with Becca's, then

dived right in. Her father would have approved of her mom dating again, Becca was certain of that. She didn't know Monty well at all, aside from the fact that he was a famous musician. Not just rodeo-famous either, like Cody. Monty was worldwide. He also seemed humble and very much a gentleman.

Otherwise, he was a complete mystery. She didn't want her mom getting her heart broken and having the whole world know the details.

Same way Becca hadn't wanted even the rodeo world to know about her divorce and even less about her pregnancy. It was hard enough going through the breakup privately. Somehow, she was spared the spotlight. The media had chosen to cover his professional wins rather than his personal losses.

"Can I get you anything else?" the server asked.

Becca and Rose both shook their heads.

Rose finally came up for air. "You haven't even taken one bite."

"I'm letting it melt a little, then all those flavors will blend together."

"They'll all get blended in your mouth and tummy anyway, won't they?"

Okay, now Becca really felt like a child.

Rose dabbed at the corners of her mouth and

shook her head. She'd managed to polish off the float in record time.

"I'm ready to talk," she said.

"We don't have to, if you don't want."

Aside from discouraging her mom about the thank-you card, Becca realized she didn't have any good advice to give. Her own messed-up relationship with Cody testified to that. Not to mention she hadn't had a decent relationship with a man since she'd moved here. When she'd tried dating, they either wanted to get hitched after the first date or they were completely undependable.

"No, we need to have this talk." Rose swiveled forty-five degrees to face Becca. "I've been thinking about it almost nonstop."

"Sounds exhausting," Becca quipped.

"I tried to hate him," Rose continued. "I tried to be angry. But how could I be?"

Becca blinked. Her mom needed more strategic planning than first expected. Not that Becca was any kind of expert, but her mom shouldn't be this emotionally invested in any man so soon.

"Maybe you should take things a little slower. Get to know him better. Then decide whether he's worth hating."

"Time is running out. Can't do much in three days."

"He probably needs to check on his house in Jackson Hole. I'm sure he'll visit Destiny Springs again. It's not that far away."

Rose pinched her brows, then laughed. "Not Monty! Your Cody."

"What?" *Ohhh*.

"I hate to break it to you, but the whole introduction to Monty was to win you over again," Becca said. Might as well set the record straight in case her mother had somehow missed that little detail.

"I know. And it worked."

"I'm not so sure I'd admit to being that easily won over, but at least you're being honest."

"Some things are too obvious to deny. But do you know what else worked?"

"Cody's *migas*? I noticed how you went from hating to not hating the thought of eating them."

Rose seemed to mull it over. "That too. But I'm talking about the two of you, when you first got married."

"That's usually when relationships work. In the beginning. Now there's a forty-pound issue that I've yet to deal with. Cody found the cake mix. And the six purple candles."

Rose blinked fast a few times as it sank in. "Did he ask you about them?"

"Yes. I said the extra was 'one to grow on.'"

At that, Rose put her arm around Becca's shoulder. She was tempted to lean into the embrace, but now more than ever she had to be strong. Like she'd had to be strong as a little girl. She never got an extra candle on her cake, like some of her temporary friends in such-and-such city had on theirs.

That might be a tradition for some moms, but the women on her side of the family didn't count birthdays ahead of time. And they didn't celebrate a pregnancy until after their newborn took his or her first breath. Yet another reason why she didn't tell Cody the moment she found out she was pregnant. She had to be sure everything was okay before she even considered upending his world.

"The guilt used to torture me, but now it's killing me. I wouldn't be doing anyone a favor by telling Cody about Max now. He's so close to getting what he's always dreamed of. But after the season comes to an end, so will this secret. It has to," Becca said.

"Losing his focus could endanger his life. Your plan is an unselfish one."

"I never imagined him as a father, but he's so good with Max. And Max is crazy about him."

"I see it too, and that's the real reason I could never hate Cody or be angry with him. Introducing me to Monty was simply the icing on top. Speaking of which…"

Rose dipped her spoon into the whipped cream topping of Becca's untouched float, then licked the spoon clean and set it down.

"I want you to know that even though Cody introduced me to an amazing man, I'll always be on your side, Rebecca. No matter what happens. You're my baby. The one I nearly lost. I'm not losing you now."

Rose's eyes glistened, but no tears followed. Just a loving smile. Becca smiled back, then picked up where her mother had left off with the float. She dipped her spoon deep into the perfectly overmelted dessert and came back with a scoop that had all the ingredients.

She'd set the horse birthday card aside but picked it up and reexamined it. It suited Max perfectly, considering his newfound hobby.

Now she had two cowboys to worry about.

CODY CLOSED HIS eyes and focused.

The chute opens. Killer storms out, spins in tight, bucks forward, kicks back. No air at all in the center of his circles. His body at a forty-five-degree angle with no hooves touching the ground.

The jolts and jerks send shock waves through Cody's body. Shot after shot of pure adrenaline-fueled agility. His every nerve ending is being reprogrammed for perfect form on top of this fifty-point-scoring bull.

If the judges could give the rider even more than fifty, they would.

The eight-second buzzer sounds, and he dismounts, landing square on his feet and walking away, bathed in the roar of the crowd.

He opened his eyes and eased his way back into reality. That had to be the shortest visualization exercise to date.

For nearly two weeks, reality had been a flannel pillowcase on which to rest his head. The softness of it—in such contrast to the bull's coarse fur beneath him, the braided rope across his palm and the unyielding ground he'd land on—had been the battle.

His visualization exercises were suffering. He used to be able to work through every step of the process in his mind. It had little to do with the fact that he didn't have Sally to practice on, although that had helped beyond measure.

He squeezed his eyes shut again. It was too important to not let the softness win.

Since coming to Destiny Springs, he'd collected a whole new set of soft memories that were intent on sending the toughness packing. The feel of Becca's terry apron, the tenderness of her kisses, the smell of her hair. Like rose petals soaked in honey.

Cody hefted himself off the bed, put on his boots and hat and headed downstairs where Hailey was busy arranging a huge bouquet of fresh flowers in the foyer.

"There you are," she said.

He came right out with it. "Can I ask a favor?"

"You can always ask. Doesn't mean I'll say yes."

For once, Cody wasn't in the mood for banter. "Mind if I head over to your place for a while and ride whichever horse of yours is the wildest and craziest?"

Hailey picked up on his tone. "That would be my Morgan horse, No Regrets. Last stall on the left. You won't get anything above a canter, but you're welcome to try and get a gallop out of him. He could use the exercise."

"Thanks. I owe you one."

"Consider it a gift, short-timer."

Even though her place was within walking distance, Cody decided to drive instead. The sooner he did this, the better.

Tacking up the horse was solid, hands-on therapy. Once he got in the saddle, however, the real therapy began. The feel of the hard leather beneath him. The thump of hooves pounding the dirt. The welcome jolts as he eased No Regrets into a canter, urging him to go harder and almost breaking through.

All of it toughened Cody's resolve. Brought back memories of how his mom had rewarded his resolve in their practice arena on the outskirts of Houston. He wouldn't get a solid pat on the back, a fist bump to the shoulder or even a rugged high five for a job well done. Those were reserved for the actual events among the competitors, along with the tough talk and posturing.

Instead, his mom would give him warm, soft hugs. They'd go inside the house where she'd bake chocolate chip cookies to dip in ice-cold milk. When she'd passed, so had the softness.

Until now.

The sun was beginning to set, not only on Hailey's ranch but on his stay in Destiny Springs. He finished riding, groomed No Regrets and put the horse and equipment back in their proper places.

He felt as though he'd retoughened by the time he got back to the Hideaway. No one even noticed him walk past them and across the patio, which was odd but welcome. They were busy enjoying coffee or a cocktail and admiring the sunset. The revolving door of guests usually meant he'd have to switch to showtime gear throughout the day.

His publicist's goal in having him come all this way to meet his biggest little fan and splash it all over social media had fizzled. And the pitch for the fancy book had completely imploded. He'd turned into the overprotective one, standing up to her to nix the angle altogether.

When she'd pressed, he'd sent beauty shots of horses and scenery instead.

She wasn't amused. She even threatened to drop him as a client, so he dropped her first.

Hailey was still doing chores inside. Becca wasn't anywhere around, which was just as well. He didn't want to end this evening on too soft a note.

When Hailey spotted Cody, she dropped the dusting cloth and rushed over.

"I'm so glad you're back. Something happened to Max."

Even the words felt like a bullet to the heart. "What?"

"I'm not sure," she said.

Cody crossed his arms out of frustration. This wasn't the time for games.

"I mean, he's super upset about something but won't say what. Becca is still out with her mom," Hailey continued.

"Where is he?"

"In his room. Last door on the right, next to the master suite."

Cody felt himself launch straight into the gallop that he'd failed to achieve with No Regrets.

His biggest little fan didn't respond to a knock, but Cody swore he heard sobbing. He eased the door open and stuck his head inside.

Max was sitting on the floor, tears streaming down his cheeks. Penny sat next to him, trying to console him by licking his arm.

"Hey, cowboy. Sorry to disturb you. Can we talk?"

Max looked up. He stopped sobbing and wiped at a tear. The little boy was trying to act tough for Cody's sake. The whole scene was heart-shattering.

Cody eased down to the floor and settled in next to him. He leaned against the wall and looked around the room. He had no idea so many shades of purple existed. He even spotted a purple beanbag chair in the corner.

"I didn't want you to see me crying," Max said.

"Nothing wrong with that. Happens to me sometimes. But the reason I came here is because I really need your help with something."

Max's expression changed from upset to curious, and he sat up straighter.

"I was riding No Regrets at Miss Hailey's a while ago, and I couldn't get him to gallop. Since you know so much about horses and all, I thought you might have some suggestions."

Max seemed to think about it. "His real name is Michael. Maybe he'd gallop for you if you call him that."

Cody nodded. "Thanks, I'll give it a try. And I owe you one. Anytime you want to talk about something, I'm all ears." At that, the tears commenced. "What is it, Max?"

"Mommy's gonna be mad at me."

"Why do you think that?"

"Cuz I took something from her room. I was gonna put it back, but Penny tore it up before I could."

"Maybe it can be fixed," Cody said, although the image of his Stetson in tatters suggested otherwise.

Max held out a piece of chewed-up paper. "I found it under her bed. She hides my birthday stuff there, and I wanted to see what she got me."

A birthday card with balloons on the front. Or used to be. At least the words had been spared. *Happy 6th Birthday.* Not even so much as a puncture mark from the puppy's teeth.

Cody's insides compressed into a tight knot the size of a golf ball. He blinked a few times to make sure he was reading it correctly.

"You're five now. You're about to turn six," he said.

Max nodded.

Plus six purple candles. That would mean...

Cody's head fell back hard against the wall. Couldn't help it. It was like he was a lightning rod during a severe electrical storm.

All of a sudden, he couldn't breathe.

CHAPTER FIFTEEN

BECCA DIDN'T WANT to get out of bed until she felt reasonably sure the world had righted itself overnight. Unfortunately, she'd have to venture out of her bedroom to find out.

She played the evening over in her head. After spending the afternoon with her mom, she'd come home to find a son who'd clearly been upset but wouldn't say why, an ex-husband who was tucked away in his room with the Do Not Disturb sign hanging from the doorknob and an assistant property manager who wouldn't look her in the eye.

Nope. Didn't make any better sense in the light of day.

By the time Becca got up and moving, Hailey was in the kitchen, preparing breakfast. Seeing her favorite room in the house in such disarray was more jolting than a full pot of coffee.

"Either you're super hungry or you know something I don't know," Becca said.

Hailey looked up from her task of unwrapping a package of sausage. "Thought you could use some help this morning since you were sleeping in."

"I could use some insight as to what happened to Max yesterday. And don't hold back."

Hailey paused from studying the breakfast instructions.

"I don't know what happened. Max was upset, but he wouldn't tell me why. Whatever Cody said to him helped. I'm sure that when Max wakes up, he'll be his usual adorable self and whatever was wrong will have magically disappeared."

That provided little comfort. Max's eyes had been so red and puffy. But, yes, Cody must have righted whatever had been wrong.

"I didn't see Cody at all last night. He was already closed off in his room by the time Mom and I returned. I don't even know if he got any dinner," Becca said.

"All he told me was that he needed some time alone to do his visualization, with Scottsdale around the corner."

Becca remembered the ritual all too well. The need for privacy and darkness and complete silence. No doubt, having to put out whatever fire—imaginary or otherwise—for Max had drained him.

Even when they were married, he'd switch

from being unusually upbeat to being scary-serious a few days before an event. Although she'd hated that he was leaving, she always wanted nothing more than for him to keep his focus and come back home in one piece, so she never disturbed him during those times.

Cody was obviously sticking with his plan and going to Scottsdale the day after tomorrow, then on to Houston, which was comforting for now.

She would stick to her plan as well, the one she'd labored over since he got here. She would tell him the truth after he got his championship buckle in Vegas. In fact, she'd tell him regardless. No more excuses. Then she could say goodbye to all the guilt, for good.

In fact, she already felt some relief having finally decided on the supposedly right time.

"If you have everything under control, I'll take Penny out for her walk," Becca said.

Hailey saluted. "Yes, ma'am."

Becca went to Max's room and cracked the door. He was sound asleep. So peaceful-looking. Whatever Cody had said to comfort him had obviously done wonders.

Penny knew the drill. She gently uncurled herself from his side without waking him, eased off the bed and ran-hopped to the door.

They took their usual route through the

property. Becca never got tired of looking at it. Although strangers filled the rooms, this was the first place in her life that had ever felt like home. Even more so the past two weeks with Cody around.

She and Penny made the full circle around the property, stopping for a good fifteen minutes to sit and breathe in the silence before returning to the front steps. Every time she walked through that door, the place smelled like home. More specifically, like food.

This time, it smelled like pancakes, which weren't on the menu. What was Hailey up to now?

After quietly letting Penny back into Max's room, she returned to the kitchen. Only, Hailey wasn't the one in front of the stove, spatula in hand.

Cody stood with his back to her, focused on his task. His hair looked more tousled than usual, as if he'd tossed and turned all night. He was barefoot, wearing a white T-shirt and flannel pajama bottoms. Oddly enough, her first thought was how that worked for him in the Flannel Room, when the sheets were made of the same material.

"Someone's up early," she said.

He finished flipping a pancake, turned off the heat and pivoted around to face her. She expected a smile. Maybe a playful reply. What she got was something far different.

He looked so tired. As if he hadn't slept at all. When he folded his arms, the world that had promised to right itself moments earlier wobbled beneath her.

"Where's Hailey?" she asked.

"She went back to her place. I told her you and I needed to talk. I'm leaving for Scottsdale this afternoon."

What was going on? Except, she'd suspected this might happen. Too many distractions here.

"I understand," she said.

"I'm not sure you do," he countered. "I'm not sure I understand either."

It felt as though everything was moving too fast and the floor was shifting beneath her. Had he been crying?

This was kind of the way it happened before they decided to divorce. The emotional distancing.

Except they weren't married now. They'd simply been playing house practically ever since he got to Destiny Springs. But, unlike when they were married, she made no demands. Had no expectations.

If anything, she was trying to encourage him to do whatever he needed to do. Was simply being here too much commitment for him? Too suffocating?

"What's going on, Cody?"

"I need to know the truth about Max's father."

Becca gulped. The question didn't come as a complete surprise. He'd made a few comments but had yet to be so direct.

"He wasn't ready for a family," she said.

Cody avoided eye contact and instead scraped at a spot on the counter with his fingernail.

"Is that what he said?"

"Pretty much."

He looked up. "Does the man even know he has a son?"

Her answer would have been a confident *No* up until this point.

"Not that I'm aware of," she said.

Cody crossed his arms.

She couldn't move. In fact, she could barely breathe.

"Were you unfaithful to me during our marriage, Becca?"

"What? No!"

"I was gone a lot. I know you were unhappy, especially toward the end, and I take the blame. I also know how much you wanted a child. Just tell me the truth."

She stepped toward him, but he shook his head, so she stopped in her tracks.

"I remained faithful to you. Not for one minute did I even *think* about another man."

He looked back at her with a certain intensity.

"Then, that leaves only one possibility, if my calculations are correct. I'll ask this only once. Am I Max's father?"

Becca grabbed the edge of the counter to steady herself.

She started to speak but couldn't find the words. Not that it mattered. He already knew. Somehow.

"Yes," she managed to say.

He bit his lip and looked away. Then he stormed past her.

She followed, catching up once he reached his room. His suitcase was laid open on the bed and mostly packed.

"Cody. Please. Let me try to explain," she said, closing the door behind them.

"I can't do this right now, Becca. I might say something I'll regret."

He grabbed a pair of jeans, went into the bathroom to change, then came back out. All the while, she waited quietly. She wasn't thinking clearly enough to form an explanation. Not one that was justifiable.

He finished packing and zipped the suitcase closed, then sat on the edge of the bed.

She sat on the opposite end, both staring at some fixed point in front of them rather than each other.

They remained in the most heartbreaking silence for what felt like an eternity. She could tell he was holding back tears. She wasn't doing a much better job of it herself.

Finally, he stood and grabbed the handle of his suitcase.

"I need to clear my head. My flight is in a few hours."

Thankfully, his tone wasn't angry. If anything, he sounded as hurt as she felt. Perhaps even more so.

"I wanted to tell you so many times, but days turned into months. And months turned into years," she said, even though she knew he didn't want to hear it. The words sounded weak, even to her.

She also wanted to know how he'd found out, but the point was moot. This was no one's fault but her own.

Becca started to stand, but he shook his head.

"No need to walk me out. I'll be back after Scottsdale and before Houston. I've missed enough of my son's birthdays. I'm not missing this one too."

Cody didn't make eye contact as he passed through the door. But he did have some parting words.

Unimaginable ones.

"By the time I get back, Max will need to know that I'm his dad. If you don't tell him, I will."

CODY SET HIS suitcase down outside Max's bedroom door, careful not to make a sound.

He cracked the door and peeked inside.

Max was all curled up in his purple sheets and blankets. Looking so peaceful beneath an animated universe of stars from an electric globe night-light that splashed the heavens across his ceiling and walls.

Ordinarily, he would have asked Becca's permission to wake up his biggest little fan.

But Max was more than a fan now. Max was his son. A strong sense of ownership and protectiveness shielded Cody from anything Becca would have to say.

Besides, there was no way he'd leave without saying goodbye and letting Max know he'd be back for his so-called surprise birthday.

He placed a hand softly on Max's shoulder. How was one supposed to wake up a child?

He didn't have a clue, but he wanted to learn. Penny, who was curled up next to Max, was now fully awake but respectfully silent. She jumped off the bed, as if she knew Cody's presence there was more important.

Max jerked a little, then slowly opened his eyes. Once he realized who it was, he bolted upright and threw his arms around Cody's neck.

"Hey, cowboy," Cody said.

Becca's apron or the flannel sheets or even the memory of his mother's warm embrace couldn't compare to the softness he felt in this moment.

He wrapped his arms around Max. He wanted to squeeze him as tight as he could but cradled him gently instead. The little boy seemed so fragile.

"Sorry to wake you up."

Max pulled away and rubbed his eyes with both palms.

"That's okey dokey," Max half said, half yawned.

Cody laughed, but only to hide the tears.

"I have some exciting news, cowboy. And I couldn't wait to share it with my best friend."

"Who? Me?"

Cody looked around and spotted a purple stuffed dinosaur at the end of the bed.

He grabbed it and held it up. "No. This guy here."

Max giggled. It was the sweetest sound in the world.

"Of course you, silly."

"Are you coming to my party?" Max asked.

Cody tossed the dinosaur aside and threw up his hands in surrender.

"You spoiled my surprise."

Max stood and started jumping up and down on his bed, falling to his knees at one point but getting right back up.

Cody wrangled him back down to a sitting position.

"I have to leave for a few days, but I'll be there, unless something happens."

Max scrunched his brows. "What's gonna happen?"

I could get injured. Or killed.

"Bad weather could ground my flight."

"You can drive here!"

For fifteen hours? He sure could, and it would be totally worth it.

"If I have to, I will."

"Or we can Zoom!"

Cody had to think about that for a minute. These kids were so much smarter than he was when it came to technology.

"You'll send me an invite?"

Max nodded.

"Then, it's a deal. In the meantime, I have some more exciting news."

Max grabbed the stuffed dinosaur, hugged it tight and squirmed in anticipation.

"I made you a pancake patty. It's in the kitchen. It might be cold by the time you get up, but I'm sure Miss Hailey will warm it up for you."

"You gonna have one too?"

"I will when I get back. I have a plane to catch. And a bull to ride."

"Can I come with you?"

I wish.

"Not this time. You'll have to wait until you turn six. And you'll have to clear it with your mommy."

At that, Max turned serious. "You're not going to tell her, are you?"

Cody didn't even have to ask.

"It's our secret. In fact, if you still have the evidence, I'll get rid of it so that she'll never find it."

Max reached beneath his pillow and handed it over.

Cody promptly folded the chewed-up pieces of paper and shoved them to the bottom of his jeans pocket.

He gave Max a quick kiss on the forehead. The little cowboy didn't even flinch.

"What's the bull's name?" Max asked.

"I don't know. How 'bout you give it one?"

Max gave it some thought. "Alice."

Another female bull. Cody had to laugh. Might as well start being a dad who didn't let his son be teased by other kids for giving bulls a cow's name.

"Isn't Alice a girl's name?" he asked.

Max giggled. "It's a boy's name too. Alice Cooper. Mommy says she loves him."

Funny. He'd never known that about her, aside from the fact that she listened to nearly everything except country music when they'd first met. He'd managed to convert her into a country-western music lover. Apparently, that hadn't stuck.

"Besides, bulls can't be girls," Max added.

Now he really had to bite his lip to keep from laughing.

"Thanks for the info, cowboy. I'll remember that."

Max gave him two thumbs-up, and all of Cody's anxiety melted away.

At least, until he reached the foyer, where Becca and Hailey had partially blocked the front door. That's when something else occurred to him.

He looked at Becca. "Did she know?" He pointed to Hailey.

"Yes. I did," Hailey answered instead.

Another betrayal. They were racking up quickly.

Cody eased his way past them, holding in the hurt. But if there was one thing he could do, it was channel negative feelings for a higher purpose.

In this case, he'd channel them right onto the back of Alice.

CHAPTER SIXTEEN

MAX BOLTED OUT of his bedroom and past Becca and Hailey on his way to the kitchen.

The pair had been like trees in a petrified forest since Cody left. Neither moving an inch nor saying a word.

"I'll take care of his breakfast," Hailey offered.

Becca nodded, but her thoughts stayed rooted in seven terrifying words.

If you don't tell him, I will.

She tried to swallow back the fear.

Cody said he was coming back, but what if he didn't? It would be worse to tell Max the truth and have his little heart shattered if Cody didn't keep his promise.

But it would be even more devastating if Cody told Max first. That would ruin all trust between Max and herself.

How was it even possible to tell Max at all? What words would she use to tell a six-year-old boy news like that? Something like, "Oh, by the way, the man who stayed in our house for two weeks? He's your daddy. Thought I'd mention it."

All she knew was she wasn't going to wait. She wouldn't put it off, like she had with telling Cody. She'd spit it out somehow. Today.

Before breakfast.

Period.

"Good morning, Ms. Haring," one of the guests said as he made his way downstairs.

Becca forced a smile. The reality of work, and of maintaining a happy facade for everyone else's sake was enough to get her moving normally again.

The breakfast had to happen, and it started in the kitchen—the most coveted room in her home. She'd made that room her escape from her past and the heart of her and Max's home.

Now it would forever remind her of the moment she'd avoided, until it refused to be put off any longer.

Hailey was attempting to finish making the pancakes that Cody had started, while Max sat impatiently on a barstool at the counter.

"Cody made me a pancake patty. Hailey's making another," he said when Becca joined them in the kitchen.

Becca shook her head. Her mind had substituted *Cody* for *Daddy*. Although it caught her off guard, it also sounded so right.

"I know! Wasn't that sweet of him?" she said.

Truth be told, she didn't know that was what Cody had been up to.

"He's coming back for my birthday," Max continued.

She wasn't about to confirm or deny something that wasn't in her control.

"Here. Let me do that." Becca eased the spatula from Hailey's hand and finished flipping the pancake her assistant had started with the last of the batter, then placed the one that Cody made in the microwave for a few seconds.

Once she'd assembled a nice, warm stack, she set it in front of Max.

He was ready with the bottle of syrup before the stoneware hit the marble and didn't waste any time drowning the cakes in the liquid energy.

Rose came in as Max stuffed an oversize bite in his mouth. Syrup covered his lips and ran down his chin.

"You're having a pancake party and I wasn't invited?" she asked.

"Cody made a patty for me, but you can have the one Hailey and Mommy made," Max said, his mouth half-full.

He proceeded to unstack the cakes.

Becca would have ordinarily admonished

him to finish chewing and swallow his food before speaking, but her parenting skills were seriously in question.

"Where is Cody, by the way?" Rose asked.

"He left for Scottsdale," Becca and Hailey said in unison, and in an equally sharp tone.

Rose looked from one to the other.

"I thought he was here for a couple more days. Did something happen?"

Max was busy pouring more syrup on Rose's cake. Sure, he was distracted, but Becca knew he would still latch on to anything that was said, so she had to tread lightly.

She nodded and pretended to zip her lips closed and lock them tight.

Rose pinched her brows together and looked to Hailey, who mimicked Becca's attempt at nonverbal disclosure.

"I don't understand," Rose whispered.

"He knows," Becca whispered back.

"Who knows what?" Rose asked.

"Cody. He knows about…" Becca side-nodded toward Max.

"Oh!" Rose's eyes widened. "Are you going to tell Max?"

"Tell me what?" Max asked. Again, with his mouth full.

Yep. He heard every word. Fortunately, the puzzle was missing some crucial pieces.

Becca shifted into full coverup mode. She grabbed an aerosol can of whipped cream from the refrigerator and proceeded to add a smiley face to his portion of the breakfast.

Max took a huge bite right out of the sugary grin, then got a dollop on his finger and licked it clean.

Nothing like a good distraction.

"Good save," Hailey whispered as Becca returned the whipped cream to its place in the refrigerator.

"Tell me what, Mommy?" Max repeated.

So much for that. Becca looked to Hailey, then to Rose. They clearly weren't going to be of any help.

"I wanted it to be a surprise, Max," Becca said.

"Is it about my party? Cuz I already know."

Yeah, she knew he knew. There wasn't a good enough hiding place for all her secrets. In fact, could Max have found and taken the card?

She made a mental note to scour his room. Right after she finished cleaning the Flannel Room.

"What party? I don't know about any such thing. Do either of you?" Becca winked at Hailey and Rose.

"Gosh, no. I don't even know why anyone would be having one," Rose chimed in.

"I heard that parties were outlawed from now on. Just sayin'," Hailey added.

Max giggled. "No, they're not!"

"I suppose we'll find out, won't we?" Becca said. "But that's not what I needed to tell you, anyway. This is much more serious."

Rose and Hailey both got that I-can't-believe-you're-going-tell-him-about-his-daddy-right-now look on their faces.

Becca took a deep breath.

"You're not going to be pouring the orange juice anymore," she said.

Max lost his smile. "Because I broke the glass?"

Before he started crying, she continued. "No, sweetie. You're the best juice-pourer in Destiny Springs. In the entire world, in fact. I'll have to look far and wide to find anyone who can even come close."

Max scooted to the edge of his seat, face and chin dotted with whipped cream and mouth smeared with syrup.

Here goes...

"I'm giving you a promotion, Maximillian Albert Haring. You're about to turn six, and you need a manly job and title. Since Cody isn't here, there's only one person who can fill his boots. You're now the official Rascal's Rodeo Scramble server."

Max jumped off the barstool and started galloping around the room.

If the other guests were sleeping in, they wouldn't be for much longer.

"Inside hooves, please," Becca said.

Her admonishment did nothing to stop the stampede.

If the media stormed her little hideaway, once the news spread about Cody being Max's father, they'd have to deal with their son's cuteness.

For the first time, she knew she could face anything. Perhaps even the spotlight. Not because it would be any easier, but because she'd survived one of the most difficult moments she could have imagined with Cody finding out the truth.

Make that, *anything except what he had told her to do before he returned.*

That was something they should tell him together, she was certain of it. And she would stand by that decision. Which meant the truth would have to wait.

So much for getting it over with.

Story of my life.

CODY LOOKED DOWN into the chute at a very agitated Tornado Tom.

He'd drawn the rankest bull, that was for sure. That meant this win was his, because he had to be the rankest rider at the event.

Old Tom didn't know what he was in for. Cody wasn't being thrown off him or any other bull. Ever again.

Since getting to Scottsdale, his attention had been laser-focused. Not only because he wanted to win. He wanted to get back to Destiny Springs in one piece and claim what was rightfully his.

Cody reached over the chute, grabbed the opposite side, and placed his boot on top of Tornado Tom's back, which prompted some movement. He quickly slid down and pointed his toes forward.

After warming up his rope and setting the handle, he leaned toward the bull's ear.

"Give me everything you've got, Alice."

That earned a strange look from the flank man, but Cody didn't care what anyone thought.

With everything in place, including his own head, he gave the nod.

The chute opened, and he was back on old Sally, with Vern cranking her up to the level that no bull had ever been able to match.

Until this one.

He'd studied the drop on Tornado Tom, and he was ready.

More than ready.

Even so, it felt like the longest eight seconds of his life. As soon as he heard the buzzer, he rolled off, landed on his feet and made a run for it while the bullfighter stepped in.

Exactly like he'd visualized.

He didn't have to look at the score to know who was going to win this one. No question in his mind.

For those eight seconds, it felt as though he'd had everything. Until he scanned the bleachers and realized that without Becca and Max there, he had nothing.

After the win was announced, and after all the events were over and done and the media descended on the participants, he felt more alone than ever.

In fact, he'd never felt this empty after a win. And this was a significant one.

"Barbecue and beer in the tent," someone called out.

Whoever set that up was a genius. It would be his safe haven, where he and the other competitors could cool down and swap stories while the media and fans were relegated to the outskirts.

Unfortunately, it also worked as a media magnet.

"What was going through your mind?" one reporter asked as Cody worked toward the entrance.

Cody put his hands on his hips and shook his head. Never really knew how to answer that question, even though someone posed it every time.

"Staying on for eight and getting to safety in less than three." He gave her his best mischievous grin to make up for lack of substance.

"You ready for Houston?" someone else asked.

"Is Houston ready for me? That's the question you should be asking," he said.

He'd already started thinking about the next event, and even more about how he was going to break the news about Max to his dad. He'd thought about it on the plane. While unpacking in his hotel room. On the way to the arena.

Although he hated to admit it, he was beginning to understand how hard it would have been for Becca to tell him about his son.

Understandable, but inexcusable.

"The little boy you went to visit in Wyoming. The fan. Any pictures you can share? Any plans to see him again?"

None of your business.

Except, he'd made it their business in the first place, hadn't he? At his publicist's direction, he'd been complicit in using Max as a publicity stunt. Or started to. She'd done a teaser—which spread like an ink drop in a bucket of water.

"See him? I suspect I'll have to compete against him someday. Terrific kid. Now, if you'll excuse me."

Cody smiled and dodged the rest of the questions being lobbed at him.

A couple of persistent reporters stayed on his heels but were denied entry at the tent. He turned to collectively address them, anyway.

"Catch up with me in Houston, y'all. I'll answer your questions after I take a victory lap."

"Dream on, Rascal," one of the other riders said as he made his way inside the tent.

"I'm sorry, do I know you?" Cody teased. "Oh, wait! You came in third."

"Second. On purpose. To lull you into a false sense of security before H-Town. Here. Have a cold one. Liquid courage."

"Don't mind if I do," Cody said, taking him up on the offering, even though nonbeer was his go-to.

He took a long swig. The beer went down smooth. Few things tasted that good. Except Becca's kisses.

Whoa! Where had that come from?

"Food. I need food."

The similarity between the layout under the tent and Becca's breakfast spread inside the barn was remarkable, except this one had paper plates and plastic forks, whereas hers had nice china and real silverware.

Using tongs, he fished out the three best-looking ribs from the warmer, then dressed up the dish with charro beans and a heaping serving of potato salad.

The only opening that would give him any air was at a table. The rowdiest one. Mutton busters, in fact.

Or *button mustards*, as Max would call them.

The thought of that night warmed his heart while simultaneously kicking him in the gut.

The last thing he wanted was any reminders of what he'd left behind. Not that he needed to be reminded. He simply needed more time to figure all this out before returning to face another kind of music.

He wandered around back but stayed within the ropes. Only one other person had discovered this little escape. Thankfully, the guy wasn't a reporter.

Cody spaced himself a reasonable distance away from the other bull rider—a newer one who'd gotten thrown in under three seconds. In the background, the band started playing some old-school country song.

This might be as good as it got for a while. Houston would attract even more attention. In Vegas, the spotlight would never be turned off. If he lost, the pressure would be on to try even harder next year. No one walked away once they got that close. If he won, the pressure would be on to do it again. Could he pull off consecutive world championships? Could he eventually beat the record holder?

Or would he do the unthinkable and quit once he reached the top, making him a one-hit wonder?

He looked at the other cowboy and imagined what it must be like to not feel such pressure. Except, the guy was back here for his own reasons. Maybe that's why he'd yet to engage in any conversation and was staring into the sky instead.

Cody wiped his mouth, wadded up and tossed his napkin on top of his paper plate and set it aside. He stood and stretched, which caught the attention of the other rider.

The guy nodded, then resumed his examination of the heavens above.

"Boy howdy, will you look at them stars.

I've never seen such a beautiful night sky. Have you?" he asked.

Cody looked up.

Inky-black background, splashed with bright stars of different sizes and intensities. Like a still version of Max's animated universe on his bedroom ceiling.

"Just one."

"THIS IS AMAZING! Max will be thrilled," Hailey said.

Becca studied the finished product. She'd successfully transformed the barn into stables, complete with fifteen makeshift stalls divided by cardboard strips that Trent had painted the color of wood slats—complete with imperfections—and adorable stick ponies situated in each. One for each partygoer to take home, and one for the party boy to keep.

Taking extra care not to scrape off any icing, Becca removed the cake cover.

A horse's head stared back. It looked...terrified. Its black licorice gumball nostrils appeared to be flared. The black licorice braided harness was a bit off-center but was partially covered with the thin frosting strings of its mane. The whites of its wide-open eyes left little room for its forehead.

With too much already on her plate, Becca

had abandoned her original plan to make the cake herself and had taken a chance on a new local specialty cake-maker instead. Her fault for not providing more than general directions.

Still, no regrets. It was quirky and utterly adorable, if not completely what she'd envisioned.

As a last-minute touch, Becca added a frame around the edge of the rectangular cake plate with some store-bought chocolate icing she had on hand. Now the horse appeared to be looking out of its stall.

She spaced the six purple candles evenly around the edges of the head but left one intentional gap.

"Hailey, when you go back inside to fetch the birthday boy, see if you can find an extra candle in the kitchen. Purple, if we have one, but any color will do."

Time for a new tradition. Or, at least one that was new to her family.

She tucked Max's birthday card beneath the edge of the cake. An extensive unearthing hadn't located the original. She didn't find it anywhere in Max's room, so perhaps he didn't—ahem—*borrow* it after all, because he was the worst at hiding things.

At least there was no chance he could have found the custom-painted, metallic-purple, highly recommended horse-riding helmet, since she'd kept it locked in her truck. He wanted to ride horses. Still. Since she couldn't find a way to talk him out of it, she'd at least keep him as safe as possible.

Hopefully, he wouldn't get the worst kind of surprise. A no-show from Cody.

"This looks so fun!" Mrs. McAdams said as she and her twins entered the barn. She held out a wrapped gift.

"You shouldn't have, but thank you so much," Becca said.

She had specified donations to the Destiny Springs Equine Rescue Group in lieu of gifts, per Hailey's suggestion. In return, they would name a rescue horse after the donor—in this case, Max—which had sounded like a good idea at the time.

If the other guests disregarded the request this year, she'd make a donation directly to the group and get his name on a horse, anyway. Probably what she should have done to begin with.

Max was a child, and birthday gifts were the best part. They also served as gifts to the less fortunate the following year, when she and Max would go through his old toys and decide which to donate to charity.

A few other guests soon trickled in. The

adults mingled, and the children examined the available stick horses, each laying claim to their favorite one and fighting over a couple.

Becca had tried to find a variety of styles—brown-and-white, solid black, white-and-gray—thinking that the effort would pay off. In retrospect, she probably should have made them all the same.

Max ran into the barn, ahead of Hailey.

"Wow!" He did a couple of three-sixties to take it all in.

At least she'd managed to keep the theme of the party a surprise.

The festivities were supposed to have started at ten o'clock. It was edging on ten twenty. Everyone had arrived, except the most important guest of all.

She'd texted Cody at the crack of dawn to make sure he was coming. He texted back, indicating that he was headed to the airport to catch the earliest flight. So far, Max hadn't asked about him. He'd been too caught up in all the attention he was getting from his friends.

Cody had gotten plenty of attention himself in Scottsdale, from what Becca could glean from the event website.

He came in first with a ninety. Not surprising.

What did catch her off guard was how thrilled she was for him.

Not that she ever wanted him to lose. But after seeing her own little boy and his new dream of riding horses, she could picture Cody at that age, having similar dreams. She wanted that little boy to succeed too.

And he had.

"Becca."

She spun around and tried to reconcile her thoughts of Childhood Cody with the man standing in front of her.

"Cody! Cody!" Max ran over with his stick horse in tow, its handle scraping the ground.

"I didn't tell him," Becca said as Max slammed into him, resulting in a smile explosion between the two cowboys.

No matter how Cody felt about her, it hadn't changed anything between him and her son.

Our son.

"How's my cowboy doing?"

"I'm riding my horse. See?" Max showed off his newest acquisition.

"That's a fine one you got there. Say, I need your help with something." Cody started looking all around the room, twisting his neck from one side to the other in an exaggerated fashion.

"I can help," Max insisted.

Cody rubbed his chin and kept looking around.

"I sure hope so. I heard it's someone's special day, so I brought a gift. The thing is I don't see any birthday boys around here."

Max dropped his stick horse and tugged on Cody's arm to get his attention.

"I'm the birthday boy!" he practically screamed.

"I don't know. You look like a young man to me. But since we're buddies and I trust you, I'll take your word for it."

He produced a large brown paper sack that Becca hadn't even realized he was holding. No wrapping paper. No fancy bow. No tissue paper.

No problem.

Max couldn't have been more excited as he plopped on the floor and reached inside the sack as fast as his little hands could manage. He pulled out a purple stuffed horse, with a rodeo logo stitched into its back.

Perry and some of the other boys galloped over.

"Look at what Cody got me!"

Max's friends jockeyed for position and a chance to hold the new toy.

Hailey walked over to check out the excitement, then turned to Cody.

"I hope you're okay with the Flannel Room again," she said.

"That's fine, Hailey."

"How long are you staying?" Becca asked.

Cody scanned the room. "Let's talk outside."

He took the lead and settled on the bench that she'd had installed but which guests barely used.

When she sat beside him, he leaned forward and seemed to study his own hands, which were clasped in front of him.

"I picked up the phone so many times, but I couldn't bring myself to do it," she said.

"I understand how that would be difficult."

She gulped back the tears. He could have been—should have still been—so angry. If the tables were turned, she wasn't so sure she'd understand or ever be able to forgive.

"*Difficult* doesn't begin to describe it," was all she could say.

He leaned back and stretched his arm around the back of the bench. Around her, but not touching. She yearned to lean in to him, but there was a palpable wall between them.

"I guess the question is, where do we go from here?" he asked.

The fact that he had to ask all but confirmed her biggest fear, and one of the reasons why she hadn't been able to bring herself to tell him in the first place. Earth-shaking, life-changing news couldn't even influence his priorities.

The answer was obvious, but only to her.

You should be with your son.

She wasn't going to say that, however. When it came right down to it, she didn't want him to be anywhere he didn't want to be.

"You need to do the right thing. For you."

THE RIGHT THING for all of them was to be completely honest, although Cody wasn't even sure what that looked like anymore. He knew what he felt, but such feelings were so new he didn't completely trust them.

She led the way before he had a chance to say anything.

"The right thing for me is everything I have here. This place isn't just my livelihood. I've built a home, Cody. Max has friends here. He'll be starting grade school soon. Not to mention he's developed a serious attachment to Hailey's horses."

"I'd never want to uproot Max."

"In a way, he will be uprooted once he finds out you're his father. He'll worry about you all the time. He shouldn't have to go to sleep at night and wonder if he's ever going to see his father again. That's why I couldn't bring myself to tell him. It would be giving him the best birthday gift of all, then possibly have it taken away."

He was privately relieved that she hadn't told

him. That was something they should do together.

But when?

If she hadn't been willing to travel occasionally, sleep alone even more and cherish what time they *did* have together before, she wouldn't be willing to now. She had Max to think about.

Make that, *we have him to think about*.

"I don't want him to worry," he said.

"And I'd never want you to plant roots where you didn't want to plant them. I never did."

The scenery was looking too familiar. All similar conversations during their marriage had started this way, with everyone's good intentions taking the lead. The journey always ended at the fork in the road, where she chose one direction and he chose the other.

"I still worry about what you do for a living. Do you have any idea how it felt to not know whether I'd be married or widowed from one second to the next?"

"It's not *that* dangerous. We train. We take all possible precautions."

"Do you love Max? It sure looks like you do. All feelings about what I did aside, do you want what's best for him?"

Cody didn't even think twice. "Of course."

"Would you encourage him to follow in your

footsteps? He idolizes you. Sure, he's more into horses right now, but he'll want to be like you when he finds out."

"I wouldn't encourage him, but I wouldn't discourage him either. If that's what he really wanted."

"Which means you'd be okay with him on the back of one of those beasts. Picture it, Cody."

The thought ripped at his gut. Make that, reached in, tore out his insides and tossed them to the ground like a bull would do to Max's fortysomething-pound body.

"He's a child. I can't envision it with any objectivity," Cody said.

"I can."

Becca looked like she was trying to hold back the tears but was doing a poor job of it.

"I grew up in a household where my mom cheered my dad on. She didn't see the danger, just the reward. I thought you'd be the same, and that wasn't fair to you. Even now, I had this crazy hope that you finally got how important bull riding is to me."

"I do get it, even though it may not seem that way. That's why I won't ask you to stop pursuing your dream. And I won't beg you to stay."

"You shouldn't have to beg any man to stay,

Becca. You deserve better. I mean, look at you. You're smart, sensitive, beautiful."

Talk about being honest.

The boys had all ventured outside on their stick horses. He could have watched them play all day, until he realized that he might not ever have the time to do such a thing. He'd be in Denver or Reno or Prescott. Or some other place that didn't mean anything to him.

Max broke away from the stampede, this time pretending to be on a bucking bronc. He threw himself to the ground and fell pretty hard.

Picture it, Cody.

He didn't have to. He could feel it. All of it, at once. The concussions, contusions, sprains, torn ligaments, broken wrists, shattered ankles, countless shoulder dislocations, two life-flight trips, et cetera, et cetera. And his favorite: nerve damage to his face.

Cody held his breath until Max got up. Of course he would. They were playing.

Unlike real bull riding.

And unlike what he and Becca were doing now.

Max directed his friends to line up behind him and proceeded to take them on a tour of the property, pointing out different things. Although too far away to hear, Cody could imagine what he might be saying.

They drew closer, with Max still talking. This time, he pointed in Cody and Becca's direction.

"And this is the bench Mommy likes. That's her. And that's my best friend," he said, looking directly at Cody with those big copper eyes.

That's when everything clicked, and not only in his head. He felt it in his beat-up bones and, most importantly, in his heart.

"So you're going to Houston tomorrow?" she asked.

Her question was clear. So was his decision.

He was going. But not for the reason she'd think. He couldn't try to explain it either. Not yet. He was still trying to sort out this revelation himself. It would hurt her even more if he couldn't follow through with one of the most difficult things he'd ever have to do: disappoint the man he'd idolized the most in life.

When Cody didn't answer, Becca got up and walked away without saying a word.

He stayed behind. Chasing her would only make it more confusing for both of them.

Max galloped up.

"Wanna go trail riding with us? Perry said you could borrow his horse."

"Maybe later, cowboy. Can you go find Hailey and ask her to come out here?"

Max pulled the reins and galloped in the direction of the barn.

While he waited on Hailey, Cody dialed Vern's house. Thankfully, the old man answered.

"Hey, Vern. Is your grandson around?"

"Parker? You just missed him."

"Would you ask him to give me a call? I want to run something by him. It's a business question. I'll pay him for his time and expertise."

Probably a good thing he hadn't got into some complicated conversation with Parker, because it only took a couple of minutes for Hailey to find him, her arms crossed and brows cinched.

"Yeah? What do you want?"

"We need to talk about something."

"Does it have anything to do with the waterworks I'm trying to mop up inside? What did you say to her? I get that you're angry about Max, but—"

"I'm not angry. I never was. Sit down, please."

Hailey plopped down on the bench next to him.

"I short-sheeted the bed in the Flannel

Room. I'm confessing only so you don't end up wrongly accusing Becca," she said.

"Good. Because now you owe me two favors."

"Is that so? What's the other one?"

"You kept Max a secret from me."

"You never asked."

"I'm pretty sure I did."

"You asked if I knew the father. At the time of the asking, I said I'd met him. Met you, that is. Which makes it not a lie."

"I'm not even going to try to untangle that. I need you to keep a secret for me. Obviously, you're an expert at it."

"Okay. I'll try."

"I need you to do better than that, Hailey."

"Yeah. Okay. I promise."

"I'm going to Houston."

"News flash—that's not a secret. Becca already told me. Hence, the waterworks."

"Let me finish, please."

Hailey made the zip-and-lock motion across her lips. "Thank you. I'm thinking about turning out of the competition. I need to go talk to someone before I make a decision."

She pivoted toward him as she shook her head. "No. You can't. Becca will freak out."

"If I talk to someone?"

Hailey rolled her eyes. "Not that. Dropping out now, when you're so close. Sure, she wished you'd stay, but because you want to. Not out of guilt or obligation. She wouldn't want to be the reason for it."

"She isn't. That's why it's called a secret. Becca isn't to know. Understand?"

"I can't believe you're putting me in this position. You're really going to do this?"

She couldn't stop shaking her head. Now, her arms were crossed tight. Cody looked down at his hands so he wouldn't have to watch it. He felt bad enough already.

"I don't know if I can," he said, although he pretty much did. For a chance at his own happiness.

"If I promise to keep this from Becca, will you promise to call or text me before you make any sudden moves? Give me a chance to talk some sense into you?"

"That's possible."

"You'll need to do better than that, Cody."

Touché.

"Okay. I promise."

"What would you do? Move to Destiny Springs? See if Becca will hire you, full-time?"

Cody laughed. "I won't hold out hope for that to happen. Honestly, I don't know how this will play out."

"Is this some sort of punishment for not telling you about Max? Why are you unloading any of this on me if you don't have a better plan?"

"But I do have one, and it's even riskier than riding a bull. It will also be more rewarding. Whether it's a better idea depends on you. I have a business proposition."

"For me?"

Cody nodded. "I want to bring back a Destiny Springs tradition."

CHAPTER SEVENTEEN

BECCA HAD VOWED that the next time Cody left, it would be the last. That was one vow she didn't plan to break.

Next time, it seemed, had arrived.

Her heart had shattered into too many broken pieces to collect. Forget about ever mending it. After everything Cody knew, he still wanted the only thing he'd ever wanted. Except more of it.

Becca placed her hand on the side of the bed that Cody had slept on and took in a heavy breath before stripping the flannel sheets. Ripping them off quickly, as one would a Band-Aid.

Hailey was taking care of dusting and vacuuming. They'd never tag-teamed before on cleaning a room after a guest left, but this was no ordinary room. And Cody had been no ordinary guest. Becca didn't want to tackle it alone.

The faster she replaced the sheets and any memories associated with this room, the better.

"By the way, I doubt Cody will ever come back, but if he tries to book something, we're full. Understood?" Becca said.

"He booked under a different name last time," Hailey said.

"Then, we start confirming identities."

"Full Homeland Security background check. Got it."

At least Hailey's sense of humor had remained intact. Becca couldn't endure any sympathetic looks or hand squeezes right now. She had her feelings under control, but one word or gesture could burst the dam wide-open again.

He'd left as conveniently as he had arrived. Furthermore, he'd easily dropped his demand that she, or even both of them, tell Max the truth. It was as if he realized he couldn't handle fatherhood after all.

Becca, however, could handle anything—except going through this even one more time.

After removing the myriad throw pillowcases, she knelt to check underneath the bed. Other than a few dust bunnies, it was clean as a whistle.

No such luck with the closet. Sure enough, Cody had forgotten something. His beloved Stetson. Again.

Becca hurled the hat at Hailey as she would a Frisbee, hitting her in the back.

Hailey stopped vacuuming and gave Becca an I-can't-believe-you-just-did-that look.

"Throw it in the dumpster outside, please." Becca turned her attention to the hangers and began spacing them out evenly.

"Seems like a waste. Maybe Max could have it," Hailey suggested.

Becca paused as she closed the closet door.

The obvious answer was *yes*. Give it to Max. But of all the things for Cody to leave behind, he left the one that made her ache for him the most. Seeing it on Max wouldn't work.

"It's way too big. And old. I'll get Max a new one."

And a new father.

Plenty of eligible men flowed through Destiny Springs, and some even made it their home. Now that she was losing the weight of all that guilt, she felt confident in pursuing a relationship.

"Are you sure? What happens when he realizes he left it behind?"

Becca considered it for a moment.

"He left something even more important behind, and he isn't calling about that, is he?"

"Becca, you know I'm on your side, but—"

"I'm sorry. I know it sounds like I'm bitter, but I'm not."

"Clearly."

Becca walked over to the window and opened the curtains that Cody had closed. He always liked to keep the room pitch-black when he did his visualizations.

Once again, she thought about that little boy Cody used to be. The one who dreamed of riding bulls. The one whose father had gifted him with that prized Stetson, a hat that the man had worn during so many wins.

The one who was finally on the cusp of having all his dreams come true.

When that finally sunk in, she felt her heart beginning to heal. He'd mentioned that he was sure she got what it meant to him to ride bulls. She had, but not fully until now.

She got that it meant she had to let go of something that didn't belong to her to begin with. It wasn't that he didn't want to be a family with her and Max. It wasn't personal at all. He wanted what he wanted, and maybe that wasn't something that could be chosen. It was something that chose him.

"You're right. Don't throw it away. That would be wrong on every level. You keep it. Or auction it off or donate it to charity. I can't look at it."

And there it was. The thing that busted the dam.

This time, she willed the tears to stop before they got rolling.

"Speaking of the other thing Cody left behind, where did Rose take Max?" Becca asked.

Hailey seemed to be lost in thought, the way she ran her fingers back and forth over the medallions. "I'm not sure," she said without looking up. "Monty came and picked them both up. Said it was for Max's birthday. Rose mentioned something about a root beer ice-cream float."

Becca picked up the flower vase, tossed the wilting chrysanthemums in the mobile trash can and emptied the remaining water in the bathroom sink. She set the vase down and collected the pile of sheets and pillowcases from the floor.

Hailey unplugged the vacuum and wrapped the cord haphazardly around the thing. It reminded Becca of how Cody had cut the cord on the mechanical bull so that Max and Perry couldn't get hurt playing on it, even though Cody had been using it for practice.

She squeezed her eyes shut. Was everything in this place going to remind her of him?

"You should get dressed up and go dancing. Take your mind off all this. It's still happy hour at Renegade. My treat," Hailey said.

"What about everything we still need to do here?"

Hailey tugged the bedding from Becca's arms and wadded it up in a tight ball. "Let me worry about that. No one is going to die because they don't have a fresh towel by a certain time. And I'm pretty sure I can figure out how to use the washing machine without setting the place on fire."

Becca sighed. "Okay. You're right."

Even Renegade reminded her of Cody, but at least there was a one-hundred-percent chance he wouldn't be there this time.

"Good! You go slip into a pretty outfit and your dancing boots. I'll finish making up this room."

Becca went to her master suite, scoured her closet and pulled out her prettiest dress. Red, which she'd always feared clashed with her hair, so she never had the courage to wear it. But now, courage was all she had left to draw upon.

After freshening her makeup and hair and adding some chandelier earrings, she lassoed some of that courage to look at herself in the mirror. Really look. Not the cursory glances she'd done for the past six years.

"I can work with this," she said, gifting herself with a smile.

A few guests had gathered in the parlor as she passed through. They all turned to look.

"Ms. Haring?" one of them asked.

She paused. "In the flesh."

"You look amazing," he said. "Whoever he is, he's a lucky man."

That made her wonder if she'd really looked that bad the rest of the time. Then decided she wasn't going to beat herself up. Ever again.

"Thank you, Mr. Bassinger. If you need anything for the next couple of hours, let Hailey know."

"Don't you worry about us. Go have fun," another guest added.

"I'll do my best."

"By the way, will Cody be around tonight?" one of them asked.

Funny, but the question didn't hurt. Although she knew it would eventually be asked, she hadn't formulated a response. Yet, the perfect one slipped right out.

"Cody who?" She winked and smiled, as if letting them in on her secret. She had moved on.

Furthermore, her happy hour at Renegade was only the beginning.

That was, if she could even get there. Trent got out of his truck as she was backing out and was trying to flag her down.

Strange of him to show up at this time in the afternoon.

She put the truck in Park and rolled down her window.

"Hope I'm not keeping you from something. Did I get a raise I didn't know about?" He held up his paycheck.

She looked at the figure. No, that was the correct amount.

"Those daily chores you've been doing added up. I meant to tell you how impressed I am with your initiative. I noticed you even tackled several small things I hadn't even written down."

"I'd love to take credit, but the only extra chore I did was the imaginary one. The loose banister. Even though, yeah, I did do a heck of a job." He snickered at his own assessment.

She wasn't laughing. "You mean you didn't fix the leaky kitchen faucet?"

"Nope."

"The hole in the drywall?"

"Must have fixed itself. Imaginary holes have a way of doing that."

"Please say you mended the crack in the threshold at the front door."

"Okay. If it makes you happy, I mended the threshold. But if I did, I don't remember doing it. Come to think of it, I saw that Cody guy walking around with the toolbox. I remember thinking it was weird. I mean, isn't he a guest?"

"Was," she said.

Turned out, he'd been much more than that.

"WHAT ON EARTH are you doing here?"

"Nice to see you, too, Dad," Cody said.

Albert Sayers stood in the doorway and shook his head. "I don't know whether I should send you away or send you to your room."

"While you're making your decision, mind if I come in?"

His dad opened the door and ushered Cody in with a wave of his hand. The place hadn't changed since he'd last seen it. Same velvet drapes with fringed valances and overstuffed furniture arranged for friendly visits rather than television watching.

Softness galore.

His mother had made it that way to cushion the pain when his dad would come home from a rodeo. Barely a hard surface in the whole house.

"Have a seat. I just steeped some tea, unless you need something stronger."

Cody followed his dad into the kitchen and settled into a worn cushioned floral dining chair. His usual chair. The roses had faded and the fabric had thinned from wear on all of them, except for one.

His mom's.

His dad had also become a little more worn, looking a good ten years older than his sixty-five years.

"Why would you think I'd need something stronger?" Cody asked as his dad set the tea-cup in front of him and took a seat.

"Because I told you I'd catch up with you at the venue. You wouldn't be here unless you had something serious to talk about. I taught you better than to get distracted this close to a competition. And, from my calculations, that's about twenty-four hours away. You should be in your hotel room, visualizing."

"You were always the best teacher. I can't say I've been the best student."

"Are you kidding? Your name is gold. I'm so proud of you, son."

Cody sipped from the delicate cup. The hand-painted flowers matched those on the chairs. He'd never noticed that before. How could he have missed it?

The answer was obvious. His mom hadn't been around to point it out. Not that she would have drawn attention to such things. Being in a house full of boys and men, she probably thought it wouldn't remotely be of interest to anyone but her.

If she were here right now, he'd make sure she knew exactly how much it mattered.

Cody mustered the nerve to look at his father. "You may not be so proud when you hear what I'm about to say."

Where to start? That was the question. He hadn't thought it out and needed a few more minutes. Hopefully, his dad's most prized horse was still around.

"Do you still have Goliath?" Cody asked.

"As a matter of fact, I do. Wanna say hello?"

They walked out to the stables, cups in hand. Goliath greeted Cody with an appreciative snort.

"Hey, boy. Good to see you again too."

"Wanna ride him?"

"Not today." *But I know someone who would.*

"Before you go to Vegas, then. I've already paid for my flight and room."

"I hope it's refundable," Cody said.

"I'm not worried. After what you did in Scottsdale, there isn't any bull who can throw you. I noticed your form too. Whatever you've been doing to prepare, keep doing it."

"I saw Becca in Wyoming." Cody came right out with it.

His dad's hand rested on Goliath's withers. "I read that you went somewhere to meet a young fan. Kept waiting to see a picture of you."

"Turned out, the fan was Becca's son. What are the odds?"

His father gave Goliath a solid pat and looked up to the sky as if contemplating.

"Well, isn't that something," he said in a tone that was laced with nostalgia. "I'm happy for her. She always did want children. I hated that y'all didn't have any together."

Cody swallowed hard. "Then, I guess you can stop hating."

He looked directly at his father as the words hit. It took a few moments for his dad to catch on.

"The boy is yours?"

Cody nodded. "His name is Max."

His father reached for the stall door, apparently to steady himself. "Maybe we should sit down for this."

Cody grabbed a couple of nearby folding chairs and set them up in the open air. "Sorry about springing this on you, Dad. I couldn't think of a better way except to come right out with it."

"Don't be sorry. But, yeah, it was quite a spring. So I'm a grandpa? I always wanted to be one. True, I thought it would unfold a little differently. Why didn't she tell you sooner?"

"Because, Dad, she thought your son wasn't ready to hear it. Truth is, she might have been right. I knew she wanted to start having kids early, but I was busy chasing points."

"And she knew you wanted to ride bulls going in."

Cody nodded. "Neither of us were prepared for how fast things were moving, how far I'd go and how many weekends I'd be gone. She didn't sign up for an absentee husband. I get that now."

The two men sat in silence while Goliath neighed in the background. Best sound in the world, next to Max's giggles. Cody looked at the other empty stables and remembered how they used to be at full capacity. His mother had kept him occupied with them while his dad was working the circuit.

"How do *you* feel about all of this, son?"

"I don't really know. Cheated, I suppose. I mean, she didn't even give me a choice."

"Think you'll ever forgive her?"

"I already have. Hard to stay mad at the other half who produced such an amazing little boy. And she's done an excellent job raising him."

"Got a picture you can show Grandpa?"

Cody pulled out his cell phone and found the cutest one of Max and himself at Ribeye Roy's.

"By golly. Looks a little like you. Same mouth, same chin. But favors Becca even more. Two redheads. You're a lucky man!"

Cody wasn't sure how lucky. The two of them were in Destiny Springs, and he was in Houston. But that was going to change. He wanted it to change more than he would have ever imagined.

"He's a handful. And smart like you wouldn't believe."

"Probably got that from our side of the family. For instance, I'm smart enough to know this isn't the only news you came to tell me."

Cody exhaled, more loudly than he intended. This was going to be harder to spit out than the news about Max, and that was saying something. The thought of disappointing his father hurt as much as finding out he'd missed six years of his own son's life. Cody clenched his jaw in an attempt to hold in the tears.

His father continued. "Before you try to tell me what you think is impossible to say, let me tell you a little story. There's something you never knew about your mom. She had a promising rodeo career."

"Actually, I knew that."

"But you probably never knew that it was

more promising than either of us led you boys to believe. She gave it up so that I could chase my dream. And she did so willingly, I might add."

"That's the way it should be." Cody stood to stretch his legs and discreetly wipe the moisture from his eyes.

Albert stood and joined him. Together, they looked out over the property.

"Yes, sir. That was the key," his dad said. "Can't demand someone give up their dream. If you do, and they give up and give in, it'll never work out."

"But you didn't have a choice. You didn't willingly give up yours to raise us. You had to."

"That's where this whole *willing* thing gets a little tricky. When your mom died, I was in the same place you are now. So close to a title I could practically reach out and grab the buckle. Your grandparents offered to step in and help raise the three of you when I traveled, which was pretty much every weekend. Like you do. Matter of fact, they insisted."

Cody shook his head. "I'm confused. That didn't happen. You dropped out."

"Probably for the same reason you're planning to drop out now." His dad looked at him. "Beat you to the punch, didn't I?"

Cody squeezed his eyes closed. The hard truth had come out, and his dad had laid out a soft cushion for them both to land on.

"Yes, sir. But why do you think it's for the same reason? I haven't told you mine."

"Because I couldn't get off those bulls fast enough after your mom was gone. In fact, I always hated leaving for any amount of time when she was still alive. Not that I didn't want to ride. I just hated missing the important moments."

"The firsts," Cody said.

His dad nodded.

"You did seem happy, being at home," Cody added.

"Nothing compared to being there for you boys. Y'all were as rambunctious as kids can get, and I loved every minute of it. The same way I suspect you're gonna love every minute you spend with Max from now on. And those minutes? You can never get the missed ones back."

"Becca doesn't know yet. I wanted to tell you first. I also wanted to make sure I could go through with it."

"Pfft. Baloney."

Cody cocked his head. "Did you say what I think you just said?"

"I did. You can get anything you set your mind to. You've proven that."

"Almost proven. And I'd be giving that up. What should I do?"

"Go to your room. Practice your visualization exercises like I taught you. Except this time, visualize what you *really* want your life to look like."

CHAPTER EIGHTEEN

"WELL, IF IT isn't the celery lady," the bartender said the minute Becca sat down at the bar in Renegade.

Oh yeah. That.

Not exactly the way she'd intended to start her evening, but she'd play along.

"In the flesh!" she said.

The bartender wiped down the bar in front of her while shaking his head.

"Yep. The celery-stick request was a first. In fact, it was a night of firsts. No one has ever ordered a zero-alcohol beer before. I'm glad that's what he was drinkin', with the way he bolted out of here like a madman."

Zero alcohol? "When did he leave?" Becca asked.

"Right after you. Left a big tip but took the celery with him."

Becca tried to process this new script. She'd jumped to more than one wrong conclusion. Cody hadn't been drunk that night, and he hadn't stayed out late. She straightened against the tug-of-war ensuing between her head and heart, ultimately concluding it was all in the past now. She needed to disinvite those memories.

Tonight, she should make it all about her and her feet. On the dance floor.

She turned to the gentleman sitting next to her. "Would you like to two-step?"

"Absolutely." He set down his drink and escorted her to the dance floor.

This was more like it. Becca, getting back her groove at Renegade.

The cowboy was being quite forgiving for all the times she jammed his toes. She looked around for the dance instructor she'd met last time she was there, hoping they could butcher the dance floor together. No sign of him.

When the song ended and another began, her current partner continued leading.

Brave man.

They'd barely made it around once when Hailey ran onto the dance floor and tapped the guy on the shoulder, bringing their two-step to a grinding halt.

"What are you doing here? Is Max okay?" Becca asked.

"He's still safe and sound with Rose. May I cut in?" she asked.

The man looked to Becca for permission.

"Sure. This is super weird of you, but knock yourself out," she said.

This whole surprise appearance made her feel off-kilter anyway. Hadn't Hailey promised to take care of things at home? Meanwhile, the man broke his connection with her and positioned his arms to receive Hailey.

She stepped back. "Not with you. With *her.*"

The look of shock on the man's face was priceless, especially when Becca agreed. Though her own expression must look equally confused. Hailey placed her right hand around Becca's waist, and they joined their free hands, with Hailey taking the lead.

"You do realize that you're cramping my style," Becca said.

Tonight, however, was all about breaking the rules. Two-stepping with her best friend certainly qualified as one.

"Not exactly my thing either. But extreme situations demand extreme measures. Besides, I could tell you weren't into that guy."

"I'm afraid to ask. What extreme situation?"

"What you lack in two-step skills you make up for in good instincts," Hailey said.

"Thanks. By the way, you're not a bad dancer."

"Focus, Becs. I got a text from Cody. I tried

to get ahold of you, but you've obviously been busy."

"That was kind of the point of coming here, wasn't it?"

The possible reasons for the text hit her, and she felt her enthusiasm for being out on the town implode. Was he hurt? The competition in Houston hadn't started. At least, she didn't think it had.

"Is he okay?"

"Physically, yes. But I can't testify to his mental state."

"If he's upset about leaving his hat behind, tell him we'll FedEx it to him."

"No. He's turning out from the competition. Says he's going to talk to someone first and give the rodeo folks a notification before the introductions but no sooner. Doesn't want a lot of questions."

Becca stopped cold in the middle of the dance floor, causing a massive pileup and a few choice words directed her way.

"Why?" she asked.

Hands still entwined, Hailey led Becca off the dance floor.

"I suspect it has to do with something he asked me about at Max's party, but I promised to keep that a secret too."

"Too? You mean you knew he was going to do this?"

"I knew he was considering it. He made me swear not to tell you, but this is too important. Besides, he promised to give me a chance to talk him out of it before making a final decision, but the rascal won't answer my texts or calls. From the tone of his text, it sounds like he's made up his mind."

"Not if I have anything to say about it." Becca returned to the table where she'd left her purse and coat.

Was he planning to withdraw because of her? Because of Max? If either were the case, that was the last thing he should do.

Furthermore, he'd earned it, without her full support, when she could have—should have— met him halfway all along. Not because she wasn't scared for him. Not because she wasn't hurt that he chose the rodeo over her and Max. But because she still loved him. For who he was, not who she thought she wanted him to be.

"Can you handle breakfast tomorrow? Maybe the next day too?" Becca asked.

"You know the answer to that. But we always have the packaged blueberry muffins to fall back on if I burn down the kitchen. You're not going where I think you are, are you?"

Becca tucked her bag under her arm, retrieved her coat from the back of the chair and haphazardly draped it over her shoulders. "If I can pull it off, I am. Don't forget the orange juice, because Max won't be there to do it."

"I thought you promoted him to Rascal's Rodeo Scramble server."

Hailey was right. "Semantics."

"You should call Cody instead. Seems a little easier and might work as well. Not to mention, it would be a lot faster."

Becca shook her head. "This is an important event. I'm not going to let him throw it away. If I succeed, there's something he'll need that can't be handled over the phone."

"I totally agree. He needs you and Max to be there in the stands. Cheering him on."

"No. Something even more important."

His lucky Stetson.

Becca tiptoed down the hall, carrying her heavy suitcase rather than rolling it across the hardwood. Didn't want to awaken any of the guests upstairs.

With the help of a night-light, she managed to reach the parlor without banging into a wall, but the silhouette of a figure on the sofa knocked the breath right out of her.

Hopefully, her audible gasp wasn't as loud as it felt.

Rose turned on the lamp. "I'm sorry, sweetheart. I didn't mean to scare you."

Becca put her hand to her chest. "That's okay. I was thinking I could use a cup of coffee to wake me up. That is no longer necessary. What are you doing up?"

Apparently, her mom wasn't planning to roam any farther than the parlor. Otherwise, she'd be wearing something other than an oversize bathrobe with the Hideaway logo and some fuzzy slippers.

"I wasn't going to miss seeing you and Max before you left."

"That's sweet of you, but we'll be back before you're scheduled to return to Bar Harbor."

"Actually, I may spend a couple of days in Jackson Hole and leave from there. Monty invited me. He's setting me up in a room at the Snake River Lodge."

"Fancy. It probably won't have spandex pillowcases and an in-room gym. Think you can survive?"

"I'll manage. I'm more worried about you."

Becca set the suitcase down, realizing the weight of it, which was still nothing compared to the weight of her decision to do this.

"I'll be fine, but I'm concerned about Max.

I'm dragging him all the way to Houston, and despite my best efforts, I might not even get to see Cody. Much less find him in time."

"Why not call him?"

"Because I know how he is. I won't be able to influence him. Once he gets something in his head, he follows through."

"You think you can influence his decision in person?"

"No. But I'm betting Max can, and I can't risk attempting it over the phone. Seeing him turns Cody to mush. Plus, Max has never been to a real rodeo, thanks to me."

"Now he's getting to go to one of the biggest ones on earth." Rose silently clapped her hands.

Yep, the woman was still on Team Cody. Although, to be fair, she seemed to be cheering for all sides.

"If I find a reseller, we'll be there. Otherwise, all Max will get to see is the parking lot. It's sold out, and I didn't have any luck online. Even if I get inside, I won't know where to start looking. I was thinking I'd have him paged."

Even thinking about it was making Becca tired. She gave in to her fatigue and sat next to her mom, if only for a few minutes.

"This is an easy one, Rebecca."

"Maybe so, but I'm too exhausted to figure

it out. And more than a little scared that I can't pull this off."

"Not the way you're planning to go about it, you won't."

"Gee, thanks for the vote of confidence."

She looked at her mom. Even without a stitch of makeup and with her bedhead hair, she was still a great beauty. She was also a straight shooter, and her assessment of Becca's plan was spot-on.

"I'm only saying that there's an easier way. Get it? 'Easier Way'? It's one of Monty's songs," her mom said.

"If the solution is in the lyrics, I'll have to google them, because I'm not familiar with it. I'm more rock and roll than country, despite what some of my life choices might imply. Not to mention, my brain is busy juggling a million other details and dropping most of them."

Rose placed her hand on Becca's knee. The warmth of it was comforting, even though the woman wasn't otherwise being of much help.

"Monty has played at rodeos longer than you've been alive. He has connections. *That's* your ticket," Rose said.

Becca let her head fall back on the sofa cushion. "You really think he'd be willing to help?"

"I'm afraid he'd insist if I told him what's going on. He's that kind of man."

"Then, tell him everything. Soon enough, the rest of the world will know, anyway."

Rose clapped her hands again without making a sound, then clasped her fingers tight as if in prayer. "Consider it done. He's picking me up for breakfast. By the time you and Max land in Houston, I'll have some instructions for you."

Becca stood, feeling more optimistic now that at least one of her obstacles had been removed.

"I guess it's time," she said. "Will you wait for us here?"

Rose nodded.

Becca tiptoed back down the hall to Max's room. She tapped lightly on the door before opening it. He didn't stir. She sat on the edge of the bed, placed her hand on his arm and gently shook him awake.

He opened his eyes and smiled.

"Hey, sweetie. Mommy has a big surprise for you."

Max sat up, fully awake.

"Another party?"

"No. This is a zillion times better."

CHAPTER NINETEEN

CODY TOOK ONE last stroll through the staging area en route to the locker rooms. This would be the last time his boots walked these grounds. At least, as a competitor. Funny thing was, he couldn't be happier about it.

Then again, perhaps *happy* didn't do the moment justice.

This—*this*—would always be his. All his wins. All his experiences. None of it could ever be taken away. Adding one more wouldn't make that part of his life any more precious or meaningful. But subtracting the biggest prize of all definitely would.

He shook his head and smiled when he considered that this was his first time walking around these grounds as a dad. Or, at least, knowing he was one.

"Are you lost, Rascal? Because, if you are, I can point you in the right direction." The other bull rider pointed to a big fat Exit sign.

"Very funny. I just hope you remember to

lean forward and hold on to the rope with both hands this time," he teased.

Bull riders. Such a supportive group of guys. He, for one, couldn't wait to be cheering all of them on from the sidelines.

The guy laughed, shook his head and double-checked the tape on his ankle. Cody looked at the clock. He wanted to wait until the last minute to act on the biggest decision of his life.

Strangely enough, it was also one of the easiest.

An empty bench beckoned. He eased onto it, closed his eyes and allowed all the chatter and posturing and background noise to fade to a soft murmur. Once that happened, his visualization process shifted into motion. Just like his father had taught him. Only this time, he wasn't setting the rope. His hips and legs weren't at one with the beast. This time, he was leaving everything to chance.

Destiny Springs. Becca. Max. He could totally visualize it.

"Cody?" A woman's voice seemed to slice through the background noise.

Becca. His visualizations had never seemed this real before. He squeezed his eyes shut even tighter and searched for her voice again.

"Cody, we need to talk."

Whoa! He opened his eyes. Becca and Max

were a few feet in front of him. He blinked several times, then stood.

"What are y'all doing here?"

Becca looked down to Max, who couldn't stop grinning and wiggling. He finally broke loose from her hand and body-slammed Cody as he'd done that first day.

"Max wanted to see you compete. How could I say no?"

"Becca, I—"

"Hailey told me. Please reconsider. This is too important."

"I could get hurt. I want to be around," he whispered in hopes that Max wouldn't hear.

"We'll be hurt if you don't follow through. I'm sorry it took me so long to realize it. Besides, nothing bad can happen if you have this." She pulled the Stetson from behind her back and handed it to him.

He rubbed his fingers over the medallions, like his father had done right before gifting it to him. That was the day the man had hung up his spurs for good.

"Max, do you mind taking care of this for me for a while? They make us wear helmets now. But it's sure to be lucky if my best friend is in charge of it." Cody put the hat on top of Max's head and adjusted it so he could see.

"Who's the bull you're riding?" Max asked.

"His name is Killer," he said.

"Does he want to hurt you?" Max asked.

This time, Cody detected a bit of fear, which was something Max had never shown before. "I'm not gonna give him the chance." In fact, no one was getting hurt today. Or ever again. Cody was going to make sure of it.

"Then, you're withdrawing," Becca said.

He knew that look of disappointment too well. Only this time, she was disappointed that he might not ride. "You two better go find your seats. You don't want to miss the introductions." He knelt down to Max's level. "I think Killer needs a better name. Then maybe he won't be so mad about me being on his back. How about you pick out one?"

Max gave it some thought. "Patty!"

"As in...Patrick?" Cody asked.

"No. Pancake Patty! Like the one you made me when you left."

Cody couldn't help but laugh out loud. "Patty it is," he said.

Max offered up his cutest smile to date. Cody straightened and looked at Becca. The disappointment within her expression had faded, replaced by what he could only define as cautious optimism.

He reached over and pulled her in, fully embracing her. He grabbed a handful of her hair and breathed her in, even though he should avoid such softness right before a ride.

"It'll be perfect," he whispered. "What else did Hailey tell you? I'm pretty sure she's the reason you found out. I'll have to remember to thank her for spilling that particular secret."

"She did mention that there was something else but wouldn't say. Why? What is it?"

He took a few steps back and offered up that mischievous grin. The one she loved to hate. She crossed her arms, shook her head and smiled.

"You're going make me wait, aren't you?" she said.

He turned on his heels and headed to the staging area.

She'd find out soon enough.

CODY HADN'T BEEN EXAGGERATING. It took forever for Becca and Max to find their seats. Of course, they had to stop for nachos and popcorn and lemonade along the way. They missed the introductions, but no chance they'd miss the main event.

She was excited for Max but terrified for Cody. What had she done? Was she crazy, talking him out of withdrawing?

While Max scooped up as much cheese as possible on each chip and watched the activity in the arena as they set up the next bull rider, Becca took the opportunity to call Hailey.

"Did you do it?" Hailey launched in without so much as a hello.

"Yes. I found him. Max and I are in our seats. I think Cody's up next. Are you going to tell me the other secret, or do I have to extract it from his lifeless body?"

Oops! She probably shouldn't even joke about that around Max. Fortunately, he was busy licking cheese off his fingers.

"I'm saying nothing. I've interfered enough, although I'm glad I did. Trust him," Hailey said.

"How can you be so sure?"

"We have a special bond. I can't explain it. Plus, he texted me fifteen minutes ago and threatened me if I breathed a word about the other secret. Have a little faith, okay?"

"I don't have a choice. He's on now." Becca turned off the phone without properly ending the conversation.

This was it. He was in the chute. On top of what looked like a very large and restless beast.

"There's Cody. Can you see him?" Becca said to Max.

Max stood up, then started jumping up and

down. She turned to the people sitting behind them.

"Let me know if he's bothering you."

They waved it off, so she turned her attention back to the arena. And held her breath. The chute was about to open.

This time, her eyes would stay open as well.

"SHOW ME WHAT you've got, Patty."

Killer didn't seem too fond of the name, the way he turned restless in the chute. Fortunately, Cody was already on his back. Otherwise, his leg would have been crushed going in.

He breathed in through his nose. Took in everything, including the pure wrath he felt beneath him. Nothing soft about this one or what he was about to do. With braided rope in hand, Cody gave the nod, and the chute opened.

He rode the jump into the turn. The ground blurred below, but his hips stayed up under him. The seconds ticked in his head as he kept his back straight. He anticipated each turn, each kick, as Killer got hotter and hotter.

Three seconds in, five remaining. He sensed it coming up: a safe place to dismount. Time to either bail or stay on and ride it out. Not that it mattered. The outcome was predetermined.

He promised himself nobody was going to get hurt, and he meant it.

Four...

Cody closed his eyes. He never closed them, except to visualize. This time, all he saw were those crazy animated stars on Max's bedroom ceiling.

Three...

He loosened his grip, and allowed himself to flip off the back, landing feet first, briefly falling backward to the ground but just as quickly getting up and making a run for safety as the bullfighters stepped in. Once safe, he waved at the disappointed crowd, all of whom were likely unaware of what really happened.

"Tough break, man. Looked like you had it in the bag," one of the guys said.

"Trust me, I do," he responded, as he dusted himself off and headed for the back.

She'd be there soon. Make that *they would be there*.

His former self had willfully rolled off a championship-guaranteed bull and walked away.

Scores from the judges: fifty for the bull, zero for the rider.

The score from himself? One zillion...and counting.

CHAPTER TWENTY

CODY HAD VISUALIZED holding a world-championship buckle so many times over the years, he could practically feel the flash-cut berry edge, differentiate between the three types of gold and make out the painstakingly hand-engraved scene and words.

In all that time, he would never have imagined holding something infinitely better. Not to mention much softer and squirmier.

The moment Max spotted Cody, he broke away from his mommy and jumped into Cody's arms with more energy and intent than any bull.

"Hope you're not too disappointed in me, cowboy," he said.

Max pulled back to where their faces were a foot apart. Not a lick of disappointment in those copper eyes. All he saw was Becca and himself in every feature.

"Why? You won, didn't you?" Max asked.

Cody didn't even have to fudge the truth this

time. "As a matter of fact, I did. I won the best prize I could ever hope for."

You.

Becca stood some distance away, looking softer and more beautiful than ever. Her boots were pure country, and her faded jeans hung low on her hips but were held up by a thick brown leather belt. Her long-sleeve, white-and-gray rock concert T-shirt was dotted with something that looked like cheese stains.

He set Max down, walked over and embraced her without reservation.

"Why did you do it?" she whispered.

"Do what?"

"I can visualize too, you know. I may not have actually watched you ride a bull before, but I've heard you talk about it."

"You mean you were listening all that time?"

She softly laughed. "Every word. Even the ones I didn't want to hear. This time, I watched every move. You let go."

Of course, she would know what letting go looked like. He'd let go of her six years ago.

"It occurred to me that a world-championship title pales in comparison to that of *Daddy*. Y'all can get me a different kind of belt buckle for Father's Day. Just a suggestion."

"Is it too late for me to tell you that I want you to have both?"

Cody swallowed. Hard. "I'm afraid it is, because I want to be around and healthy enough to wrangle with our little cowboy. And strong enough to never again let go of what I want most."

She tried to pull away, but he held tight.

"You're going to have to let go of *me* at some point. Temporarily, at least," she said.

"Not until you say *yes*."

"What's the question?"

He pulled away enough to look into her eyes. What he saw, besides the warmth and richness, was his future. That gave Max the opening he needed to squeeze between them.

"Well?" she asked.

Her smile told him that she knew what he really wanted to ask. But they needed to get some business out of the way first. He bit his lip and counted to eight. Her breathing became heavier every second that passed.

"I need a place for the trail riders to stay, and I was thinking about the B and B," he finally said.

Becca closed her eyes and shook her head. "Not the question I was expecting. What trail riders?"

"You mean, Hailey didn't spill the secret while I was out there riding Patty? I'm investing in her horses and stables. Parker is helping us with the numbers. Together, we're going to revive a Destiny Springs tradition."

"We get to ride horses!" Max shouted from below.

"I'm the last to know about this?" Becca asked.

"Being the last to know doesn't have to be a deal-breaker. I speak from experience," he said.

She seemed to be giving it some serious thought.

"I'm not so sure I can accommodate more guests. I need a cook and a handyman to fill in the gaps when Trent isn't available. Do you know of anyone who could fill those boots?"

"I have one person in mind. He's an out-of-work bull rider, if that isn't too much of a liability."

"As long as he's good with kids."

Cody looked down at Max. "He tries to be."

On a whim, he kissed Becca on the cheek, but she had other plans. She wrapped both hands around the back of his neck and pulled him fully in to where their lips were less than an inch apart.

"I told you Mommy likes you," Max said.

Becca pulled away as he was going for it. "Max told you that?"

He shrugged.

"Well, he got it half-right," she said.

"Oh, really? How so?"

"I do like you. But more than that, I love you. I never stopped."

Cody's scarred, worn-out, banged-up knees went weak. Good thing she didn't say those words before he'd gotten on that bull tonight, because they'd just turned him to mush.

He rested his forehead against hers and whispered, "I never stopped loving you either."

Becca rewarded him with a tender kiss, which made Max giggle.

"There are a few other confessions we'll have to deal with." He looked down at their son, who seemed oblivious that their discussion was about him.

"You can do it, if you want," Becca said. "I'll support whatever version you decide."

Now wasn't the right time to tell Max the truth. When would it be?

The struggle was real. But it was a struggle he was more than eager to take on.

Eventually.

"THERE Y'ALL ARE!"

Cody's father ambled into the back area, personally escorted by a security guard. No surprise. Eight-Second Al would always get the royal treatment.

"Dad? What are you doing here? I thought you decided not to come."

Becca and Cody broke apart at the same time, releasing Max from his self-inflicted imprisonment.

"What? And miss seeing my son make the best decision of his life? It's so good to see you again, Becca."

"Likewise, Albert."

The man embraced her as though six years hadn't passed between them, then whispered in her ear. "Humor me. Call me Dad. I'm hoping to hear it again, and a lot, if you know what I mean." At that, he pulled away and looked around. "Now, where is this young man I've heard so much about?"

Cody pulled Max to his side. "Dad, this is Max."

"This can't be him! You told me he just turned six. This is practically a grown-up," he said to Cody.

"I am six," Max interjected. He held up his fingers and counted on them. "One, two, three, four, five, six."

Mr. Sayers put out his hand, and Max shook it. "Nice to meet you, young man. I've heard amazing things about you."

Becca leaned in and whispered, "We haven't told him yet."

Mr. Sayers winked in acknowledgment. "I understand you want to ride bulls. But if you ask me, horses are the way to go," he said to Max.

"Mommy doesn't like me to ride horses either, but she lets me now."

Becca's heart sank. Was she that awful, discouraging all the men in her life from pursuing their dreams?

"I bet she'd be okay if we go try to find a few to look at, though. Maybe even pet," he said, taking Max's hand. "You two can find something to talk about while we're gone, I trust?"

Becca could think of lots to talk about, although they didn't have to talk at all for her to be happy.

After the pair left to wander, it was down to the two of them. Like it had been when they were first together.

"Sorry about Dad. He can be a little...insistent. Like me. So I'm going to state the obvious. You never answered my question."

"About whether I could host your trail-ride guests? I'm pretty sure I did."

He closed the distance between them and embraced her.

"Not that question. The one you know I'm about to ask."

Becca swallowed back the tidal wave of emotion.

Houston. Nine years ago. He'd pressed her to say *yes* before he'd even popped the question. Was history repeating itself? The better question was, could they make it right this time around?

No doubt in her mind that it was worth it to try.

More than worth it.

EPILOGUE

Three months later

"DADDY! DADDY! GUESS whom I am!"

Cody had barely swallowed the first bite of his chocolate bull's-head groom's cake when Max served up the sweetest greeting a cowboy could ever hear.

His beautiful bride was watching from afar. Smiling. How could one man be so lucky?

Strange to think that their arguments used to be about when he would quit. From now on, it looked as though they'd be having loving discussions about whether he'd ever ride again.

Truth be told, there was only one bull he intended to tackle before hanging up his spurs for good. Sally on espresso. He'd vowed before not to leave Destiny Springs without lasting eight seconds on her. Now that he was back to stay, he intended to keep his vow, along with the one he'd just made with Becca.

He gifted her a wink. She'd already filled

him in on Max's little game and gave Cody tips on how to respond.

"Hmm," he said, turning his attention back to his son.

He squinted his eyes, rubbed his chin for effect and took his sweet time.

Oversize Stetson, Fender acoustic guitar...

"I know! You're Alice Cooper!"

He had to bite his lip to keep from laughing at the look of sheer frustration on Max's adorable face and the exasperated huff that followed. In his periphery, he noticed Monty searching high and low for something. Make that *a couple of somethings* around the stage and makeshift dance floor that had been set up on the Hideaway's big, open back lawn. Rose was by his side, assisting, and the two of them kept laughing and smiling through it all.

"No! I'm Gummery Legend," Max insisted.

Cody raised his brows and nodded. "Ah, yes! I see it now."

He saw it, all right. Clear as day. Max had been the one who'd stolen his hat that first morning. He'd lay money on it.

That wasn't the only thing Max had stolen. Cody placed his hand over his heart, only to find it was exactly where it should be after all. Right here, in Destiny Springs.

"I'm not completely convinced," Cody

added. "The real Gummery Legend would give his hat and guitar to that man over there who seems to have mysteriously lost his." He pointed toward Monty and his mother-in-law.

Max giggled, then promptly ran over to Monty and Rose. Instead of being miffed, they seemed completely charmed by the little rascal.

Becca walked toward him, still in her off-the-shoulder satin wedding dress and matching white cowgirl boots. Although she'd worn a veil during the brief ceremony, he insisted that had to go the moment after he kissed the bride. He didn't want anything obstructing her beauty. It almost looked as though she were moving in slow motion, with the way some wavy tendrils blew across her face with each step. Even the soft, extended kiss she planted on his lips felt like a dream he hoped to never awaken from.

"You never told me that Max was the one who took my hat that day," he said.

"You never asked."

Why did he keep getting caught up in those words? Hailey had used them as a defense as well.

Hailey, his sister from another mister, seemed to be taking her maid of honor dress in stride, with its full skirt and sweetheart neckline. So different from her usual flannel shirts and bulky sweaters and ripped jeans. The dress suited her beautifully, nonetheless.

Becca had insisted on purple—Max's favorite color—and Cody was in full support of it for that reason. He'd been a good sport about wearing a purple shirt beneath his black jacket, once Becca gave in to his choice of pants and shoes. Or, rather, jeans and boots.

Negotiation was their new house rule. Second only to good-morning hugs for everyone. Anything to see Becca and Max smile.

The maid of honor was wearing a smile too. Cody liked to think he had something to do with putting it there. The process of breathing life back into Sunrise Stables had officially begun. Last month, Hailey had pulled the old sign out of storage. Cody had polished it up and rehung it at the entrance. He'd hired some experts to come in and decide which horses were trail-ride ready and which needed some training.

As far as the numbers end of it went, the obvious choice had been Parker. The fact that the city slicker accepted the job to handle the books and make recommendations to revive the business had nothing to do with the fact that he had a crush on Hailey and she had a crush on him. Nothing at all.

Yeah, right. Just like it had nothing to do with Cody asking him in the first place. He shook his head and felt that mischievous grin spread across his face. About that time, Hailey looked over. She rolled her eyes, then mouthed *Thank you* when Parker wasn't looking. Cody gave her his best cowboy nod.

Becca returned to mingling with the wedding guests, leaving him standing alone. No matter. He got to be with her for the rest of their lives. It would be selfish for him to not share her now.

At least he wasn't having to share her with the media. Not yet, at least. They'd sniffed around after hearing that he had no plans to compete anymore. But he'd throw them off his and Becca's and Max's trail by using his rascal charms, offering generic one-liners, and steering the conversation to other riders. There were several to get excited about—a twenty-two-year-old kid, in particular. Rookie of the Year last year, world-champion contender this year. *That* was the real story they should be chasing. Cody couldn't be prouder, even though he barely knew the guy.

If the media ever circled back around, they'd have trouble getting much of anything out of all the secret-keepers in this little town. Not to mention Becca, Max and he would be standing hand in hand in hand. Rumors couldn't tear them apart. And the truth was what brought them all back together in the first place.

Just as he was feeling as though nothing could shake him, Penny clipped the side of his leg while fleeing from the little flower girl. Apparently, the pup had taken a page out of Max's playbook. She'd once again confiscated someone else's property and declared it a toy. This time, it was the rose-petal basket. The weave of it was about to be unwoven, and the remaining petals were destined to be scattered across the lawn.

Vern filled the void that Becca had left behind. Two huge pieces of cake—of both the bride's and the groom's—balanced on his plate.

"They say you don't marry the person you can live with, you marry the person you can't live without," Vern offered between bites.

Cody wanted to say that *they* didn't know what they were talking about, because he was going to live just fine with Becca. And Max.

Vern always added a wise, contemporary amendment to his sayings, so Cody waited.

And waited.

"And...?" he asked.

Vern shrugged. "Nothing."

The man took another bite and looked straight ahead at the empty makeshift stage that had been set up for toasts and speeches and dancing. The DJ who Becca hired had yet to arrive. The guy obviously got Cody's eleventh-hour message that the gig was canceled but he would get paid nonetheless. Even though Cody had been planning the substitute and special surprise for weeks, he didn't want Becca finding out. She'd been double- and triple-checking everything, as she was prone to do.

The groom's cake had been Becca's fun gift to him and her way of saying she didn't want to change him. If he ever wanted to ride bulls again, she would support him. His fun gift was to let her know he didn't want her to change either, and what better way to do that than through a song?

Monty lifted the guitar strap over his head and stepped onto the stage. He strummed a few notes and twisted a couple of tuner pegs. All of a sudden, Becca was at Cody's side.

"What's he doing? Where's the DJ?" she asked.

"The groom asked me to play this tune as a gift to his beautiful bride," Monty announced. "He wants to call it their song, but the real title is 'You and Me.' Will the lovely couple please step forward for the first dance? Everyone else is welcome to join in after a couple of bars."

Cody took Becca's hand and led her to the front.

"What's going on?" she asked.

Monty played a few notes, which Cody didn't recognize but Becca obviously did. That was the whole point.

"You asked him to play Alice Cooper?"

Cody nodded. "Max tells me you love him. I'll try not to be too jealous."

"There's only one man I love, and he's the sweetest to make our song a soft-rock ballad. Not your thing, I know—"

"*You're* my thing," he interrupted. "You and Max. And everything that comes with it."

She didn't say a word. Didn't have to. That beautiful smile said it all.

"I'm curious about one thing, though," he said. "What song were you dancing to when I first saw you again in the kitchen? When you thought no one was watching?" Becca lowered her chin. Was she blushing?

She looked up again. "You know, I don't remember. In thinking back, all I can hear in my head is your voice."

They swayed to the lyrics of the ballad. After the tune was done, they slow-danced to several country songs that followed—some of them Monty's, some by other musicians— while everyone else two-stepped around them.

They broke away only once, when his dad insisted on cutting in. At which time, Cody asked Rose for the honor of a dance. Yet, he and Becca melded back together as if they'd never been separated. They stayed that way as Monty serenaded the sunset.

The crowd thinned as the evening stars began to thicken. Becca lazily raised her head from his shoulder, as if awaking from a deep slumber.

"What are you smiling about?" she asked.

He wanted to say *Everything*, which would be true. However, one thought in particular kept tugging at the corners of his mouth.

"My new name," he said.

Becca cocked her head.

"Daddy," he clarified. "Thank you for being the one to tell him."

"I fumbled a little. But I couldn't have done it at all without you by my side. I think he took it extremely well. In fact, I've never seen him that excited about anything."

"The feeling is mutual," Cody said as he leaned in to kiss the mother of his son. As he did, he sensed a little tension and pulled away.

"Everything okay, Mrs. Sayers?"

"Just thinking that maybe you could take the lead in the next heart-to-heart. Max told me he likes Elizabeth Anne," she said.

"Our flower girl?"

"Yep. Problem is, rumor has it Elizabeth Anne likes Max's best friend."

"Well, that's an easy one. I'm already spoken for," he said, attempting his most mischievous grin.

Becca rolled her eyes. "Not you. Perry! Still, I'm not sure how we'll ever explain these kinds of things to our precious little boy. The thought of anyone ever hurting him—"

Cody pulled her back in, even closer, and held her tight.

He didn't have the answer either. All he knew was that they'd figure it out. Together. There might not even be such a thing as a perfect explanation for matters of the heart, yet everything would work out perfectly.

It already had.

* * * * *

Get 4 FREE REWARDS!

We'll send you 2 FREE Books plus 2 FREE Mystery Gifts.

FREE
Value Over
$20

Both the **Love Inspired®** and **Love Inspired® Suspense** series feature compelling novels filled with inspirational romance, faith, forgiveness, and hope.

YES! Please send me 2 FREE novels from the Love Inspired or Love Inspired Suspense series and my 2 FREE gifts (gifts are worth about $10 retail). After receiving them, if I don't wish to receive any more books, I can return the shipping statement marked "cancel." If I don't cancel, I will receive 6 brand-new Love Inspired Larger-Print books or Love Inspired Suspense Larger-Print books every month and be billed just $5.99 each in the U.S. or $6.24 each in Canada. That is a savings of at least 17% off the cover price. It's quite a bargain! Shipping and handling is just 50¢ per book in the U.S. and $1.25 per book in Canada.* I understand that accepting the 2 free books and gifts places me under no obligation to buy anything. I can always return a shipment and cancel at any time. The free books and gifts are mine to keep no matter what I decide.

Choose one: ☐ **Love Inspired**
Larger-Print
(122/322 IDN GNWC)

☐ **Love Inspired Suspense**
Larger-Print
(107/307 IDN GNWN)

Name (please print)

Address   Apt. #

City   State/Province   Zip/Postal Code

Email: Please check this box ☐ if you would like to receive newsletters and promotional emails from Harlequin Enterprises ULC and its affiliates. You can unsubscribe anytime.

Mail to the Harlequin Reader Service:
IN U.S.A.: P.O. Box 1341, Buffalo, NY 14240-8531
IN CANADA: P.O. Box 603, Fort Erie, Ontario L2A 5X3

Want to try 2 free books from another series! Call 1-800-873-8635 or visit www.ReaderService.com.

LIRLIS22

COUNTRY LEGACY COLLECTION

19 FREE BOOKS IN ALL!

Cowboys, adventure and romance await you in this new collection! Enjoy superb reading all year long with books by bestselling authors like Diana Palmer, Sasha Summers and Marie Ferrarella!

Get 4 FREE REWARDS!

We'll send you 2 FREE Books plus 2 FREE Mystery Gifts.

FREE Value Over **$20**

Both the **Romance** and **Suspense** collections feature compelling novels written by many of today's bestselling authors.

COMING NEXT MONTH FROM
HARLEQUIN
HEARTWARMING

#435 A WYOMING SECRET PROPOSAL
The Blackwells of Eagle Springs • by Amy Vastine
After an accidental Vegas wedding, Wyatt Blackwell and
Harper Hayes end up in Eagle Springs. He's trying to save his
family's ranch. She's trying to save her online image by playing
happy family. Will they end up saving each other?

#436 A COWBOY THANKSGIVING
The Mountain Monroes • by Melinda Curtis
Orphan Maxine Holloway and her daughter are spending
Thanksgiving with the Monroes—who seem entirely too warm
and boisterous. And there's something about Bo Monroe. He is
Max's complete opposite, but could he be her perfect match?

#437 HIS SMALL TOWN DREAM
The Golden Matchmakers Club • by Tara Randel
Businessman Adam Wright went from Wall Street to wilderness
expeditions after his broken engagement. Marketing exec
Carrie Mitchell is just passing through, chasing the corporate
dreams Adam left behind. Will an unexpected connection make
her want to stay?

#438 HER MARINE HERO
Polk Island • by Jacquelin Thomas
Fashion designer Renee Rothchild has one rule—don't date
military men. Too bad she's falling for Marine Greg Bowman.
With his discharge coming, she's ready to give love a second
chance after a broken engagement. Until unexpected news
changes everything.

HWCNM0722

Visit
ReaderService.com
Today!

As a valued member of the Harlequin Reader Service, you'll find these benefits and more at ReaderService.com:

- Try 2 free books from any series
- Access risk-free special offers
- View your account history & manage payments
- Browse the latest Bonus Bucks catalog

Don't miss out!

If you want to stay up-to-date on the latest at the Harlequin Reader Service and enjoy more content, make sure you've signed up for our monthly News & Notes email newsletter. Sign up online at ReaderService.com or by calling Customer Service at 1-800-873-8635.

RS20